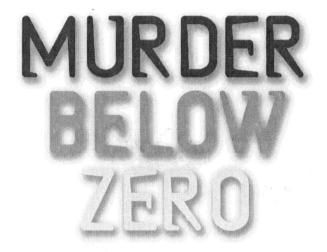

MURDER BELOW ZERO

To Virginia —

You missed a great
50th Reunion.

Best regards
Ron Lovell

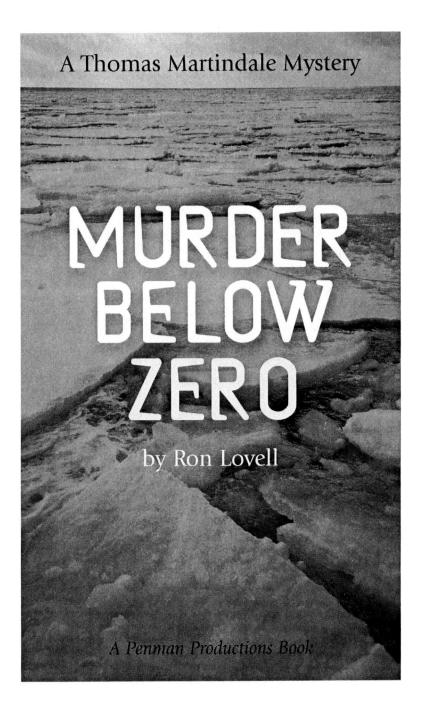

A Thomas Martindale Mystery

MURDER BELOW ZERO

by Ron Lovell

A Penman Productions Book

Penman Productions, Gleneden Beach, Oregon
Copyright © 2005 by Ronald P. Lovell

Printed in the United States of America
Library of Congress Control Number: 2005902783
ISBN: 0-9767978-0-1

Cover and book designer: Liz Kingslien
Editor: Pamela Lamb
Cover photo: Ivan Rothman
Author photo: Alice Richmond

The ice was here, the ice was there,
The ice was all around,
It cracked and growled, and roared and howled,
Like noises in a swound.

— Samuel Taylor Coleridge,
The Ancient Mariner, Part II

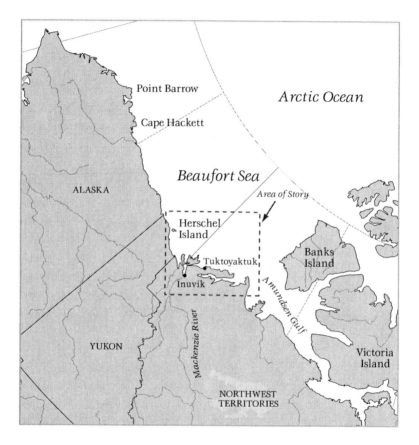

Point Barrow

Cape Hackett

Arctic Ocean

Beaufort Sea

ALASKA

Area of Story

Herschel
Island

Tuktoyaktuk

Inuvik

Banks
Island

Amundsen Gulf

Mackenzie River

YUKON

Victoria
Island

NORTHWEST
TERRITORIES

One

The Eskimo man had been drinking all night and now it was morning. By rights, he should have been passed out a long time ago, but he was still talking a little too loudly for the comfort of those sitting near him in the waiting room of the airport in Edmonton, Canada.

I had first heard him on the flight from Denver the night before, demanding drinks after everyone else was ready to settle down for some sleep. He had become somewhat abusive when the stewardess cut him off and only got quiet after the first officer came back and talked to him. After that, he must have fallen asleep because I didn't hear anything more for the rest of the trip.

About sixty passengers had gotten off the plane at the ungodly hour of 2 a.m. and all but ten had disappeared into the early morning darkness. I had decided it was easier to kill time walking around the terminal than driving to town to sleep a few hours in a hotel. I spent the first hour after our arrival walking the labyrinthine corridors of the terminal building while I waited for my early morning flight to the Arctic.

By the time I got back to where I left my bags in the care of an elderly couple who looked like missionaries, the man had succeeded in running off everyone in his immediate vicinity. He was slumped in a chair, his long legs splayed in front of him, his head alternately upright, then jerking abruptly so that his long black hair dangled over the back of the chair.

"Hey buddy," he yelled as I came into his line of sight. "Wanna have a li'l drinky?" He held up a silver-colored flask and turned it over. When nothing came out, he peered up into the small opening, a quizzical look on his face. "Where'd you go?"

He looked at me like a child who had lost his favorite toy.

"I'm kinda tapped out, I guess. I shoulda looked before I invited you. Could you get me a refill?"

His eyelids drooped as the words slurred out of his mouth. A thick tongue made what he said nearly unintelligible.

"I don't think I can help you," I said, sitting down just out of his reach. The man took offense and got to his feet unsteadily.

"You too good to help me?" he yelled, suddenly lunging at me and taking a swing at my chin.

"Just a minute, pal," I said, putting up both hands to fend off his punch. Just then, two uniformed policemen came out of nowhere and grabbed the man by both arms. His legs buckled quickly but the policemen kept going, forcing the man down on his stomach while they kept his arms behind him. They were from the Royal Canadian Mounted Police, otherwise known as the RCMP.

"Yeoohaah!" He started screaming from the pain.

"He wasn't hurting me," I said, trying to get them to ease their grip. I reached for the arm of the nearest officer. He pulled away from me.

"Stay out of this, sir," he said. "This isn't your fight!"

"Yeoohaah!" the Eskimo man chimed in as if on cue. "You're breaking my fuckin' arms!"

At that, the officer, kneeling next to the man twisted even tighter and put his knee on the man's neck.

"You're going to choke him," I yelled, grabbing at the officer's shoulders. In a matter of seconds, I found myself yanked backwards.

"I don't want to put you in restraints, sir," said the first officer. "Please back away."

By then, a sizable crowd had encircled the four of us, as other passengers booked for the flight arrived. I was grateful for the witnesses and decided to draw them in as allies.

"This man wasn't hurting anyone when these officers jumped on him," I said, with no small amount of exaggeration. "He's a native and I guess they think they can push him around anytime they feel like it."

"Leave him alone!" someone in the back of the crowd shouted.

"Justice for all native Inuits! They were here first!" yelled another.

The number quickly swelled to fifty or more and the officer not restraining the man bent down and whispered in the ear of his partner. That officer then abruptly brought the Eskimo man to his feet and clamped a pair of handcuffs on his wrists. The other officer stepped towards me, grabbing both of my arms and pulling them behind my back. I was about to get cuffed myself.

"What is the meaning of this?" said a loud voice from the edge of the crowd. "This man is an American! You can't do this to him!"

The people parted to allow a small man with a red beard to step to the front. My soon-to-be boss Clifford Jameson had arrived. With an elaborate flourish, he pulled out official looking credentials and flashed them at the officer holding me.

"Sergeant," he glanced at his nametag. "Barnett, is it? I certainly hope the RCMP has an adequate explanation for forcibly detaining an eminent American writer who is joining me on an important Arctic research expedition—a research expedition, may I say, that is sanctioned by your government. Who is your superior and how can I reach him?"

Jameson's words startled the officer. He dropped both my arms and put away the handcuffs immediately.

"That's better," said Jameson. "Now you are acting rationally." He stepped up to me. "Are you all right, Tom?"

"Yes, sir, I am," I replied, rubbing my wrists in a theatrical manner even though they were far from being injured. All of us—me, Jameson, and most of the crowd—now turned our attention to the other officer. He didn't move, but stood behind the Eskimo who seemed to have sobered up. Every once in a while, the officer—his nametag read St. Pierre—pulled on the handcuffs as if to reassert his power.

"This man is one of my staff members too. His name is Ben Aniak and he's an American citizen. I will take full responsibility for both of them. Their work is vital to the research project, a project I might add, funded in part by your government."

Barnett walked over to St. Pierre and the two conferred in low tones. After several more yanks on the cuffs, St. Pierre unlocked them, giving Aniak a shove in the process. That enraged the Eskimo, who wheeled around and seemed about to strike the officer.

"Tom Martindale," I said, grabbing Aniak's hands and forcing him to shake. It'll be great to work with you." He looked momentarily confused, then returned the handshake.

"Yeah, sure. Nice to meet you."

"Tom. Tom Martindale."

"I trust you can keep your staff members in line, Dr. Jameson," said Barnett, as he handed back the credentials. "We won't let this kind of thing slide next time."

"You can be certain of that," said Jameson, pulling both Aniak and me away from the departing policemen. "Get your things and we'll move as far away as we can from these thugs," he whispered. We followed meekly, the Eskimo staggering slightly as he attempted to lift a large duffel bag over his shoulder. I helped him along while dragging my own baggage behind me. Jameson was leading us to a corner of the waiting room where a large group of project staff members were gathering as their various flights arrived from elsewhere.

"I don't like to expend personal capital like that," hissed Jameson to me as we neared the larger group. "I don't like to be embarrassed in public by someone who should know better. You may have forgotten that *I* determine who works on this project. You won't be with us very long if this kind of thing continues!"

Before I could reply, the diminutive scientist entered the enclosure of leather chairs and benches and greeted people waiting there. Aniak knew a few of the people and was shaking hands with them. I was left standing alone like a schoolboy the teacher was blaming for starting a fight he really had no part of.

"Is that Tom Martindale?"

The woman's voice was very familiar. Susan Foster stepped forward and smiled a smile I knew all too well.

"I saw your name on the staff roster and I couldn't believe we'd be working together again," she said as she hugged me and gave me one of those kisses that never quite connect with your face. My return embrace was as tentative as her air kisses. We were, after all, former lovers who had parted years before under less than amiable circumstances. Even fifteen years couldn't ease the pain of our breakup over something I'd just as soon the world—and the members of this research expedition—never find out.

"Sue. This *is* a surprise."

"You look exactly the same, Tom."

"Quite a bit more gray around the edges, I'm afraid. You look good too, Susan."

We were checking out each other like gawky teenagers at a dance. Actually, Sue had aged. She was no longer as slim as when we were together, but who was I to tell the truth?

"You remember Scott, don't you, Tom?"

She stepped aside to reveal a tall blond man I also knew. Scott Szabo was a former student whose relationship with Susan had contributed to our estrangement. Even though many years had passed, just the sight of them together brought it all back.

"Hello, professor. Nice seeing you again."

"Same here, Scott. This is really a surprise, I mean seeing the two of you again."

The three of us walked over to some chairs and sat down. I was already feeling uncomfortable with the situation.

"Saw your name." We both started to say the same thing, then stopped.

"You first," I said, with a laugh.

"Cliff Jameson showed me the staff roster on the flight up from L.A. I was pleased that you'd signed on. Arctic information officer and historian?"

I nodded.

"Right up your alley."

"You're doing marine biology as chief scientist?"

"Don't I wish," she said, a disappointing look flickering momentarily in her eyes. I'll be codifying the research results of the other scientists."

"Something any technician could do," scoffed Szabo disdainfully. "In fact, I'm one of those scientists whose work she'll be codifying, right, Suzie Q?"

"Don't call me that! I hate that name!"

Szabo didn't reply, but looked pleased with himself as he gazed across the waiting room.

"Where's Derek? I need to see him."

He got up and walked over quickly to a man who could have been his twin: tall, thin, handsome, but with brown hair. They embraced and sat down on a bench away from everyone else. They were soon whispering to one another, the talk occasionally interrupted by uproarious laughter. Susan's face was now a mask of sadness.

"What's going on here, Sue? You and Scott," I brought my hands together "a couple?"

"I know you've never approved of him or me being with him. I just can't help it."

"Yeah, I admit he pissed me off then and he pisses me off now. Seeing him brings back memories I'd just . . . That's not it, though. Look at how he's treating you like you don't exist. Who's that other guy, anyway?"

"Derek Peters. A friend of Scott's from the university. They work together a lot."

"It looks like more than work, Sue. I told you before that Scott swings both ways. He even made a move on me! Why do you stay with him?"

"Tom! Stop! I don't want to hear this!" She got up and started to move away.

"Susan. Sit down! I won't say anything more about this. I promise. Let's just talk about something else. Like who are these other people?"

She resumed her seat and relaxed a bit, although she glanced occasionally at Scott and Derek, still very much enthralled with one another.

"Besides Jameson, Scott, Derek, Ben, and you and me, we have Jane Baugh, that no-nonsense looking woman of fifty or so over there. She's a marine biologist. Alan Hopkins, that bearded crazy-looking guy standing next to Ben. He's a geologist who specializes in ice. That's Paul Bickford over there."

"He looks like he's been in the Army or Marine Corps, with the short hair and lean and mean look."

"I'm not really sure what he will be doing. Cliff was pretty vague. Some kind of government liaison, I think."

"Who's that thin guy with the ponytail?"

"That's Danny Salcido, a technician who's good at communications. He's talking to Carmen Ames. She's Jameson's secretary."

"What a looker," I said, "next to yourself, of course." The young, curly haired woman was smiling and nodding at Salcido and Jameson, who had joined them.

"Tom, you haven't told me about your job on this trip," she said, putting our earlier disagreement aside.

"I'm the PR guy and historian. I'm on a one-term leave from my journalism teaching duties at Oregon University because I just couldn't let this chance pass me by. I mean the Arctic, whales, big-time science. I'm also doing some research of my own. Have you ever heard of the ice disaster of 1897?"

"No, I haven't."

"In the late summer of that year, the ice pack formed earlier than usual. It trapped a lot of whaling ships along the northern Alaska coast. We'll be working that same area. I've got an old diary from that time I want to annotate with my own observations. Maybe I'll make a book or an article out of it."

"Sounds fascinating, Tom."

I wasn't sure if she really meant it. Were her eyes glazing over? Did she stifle a yawn? Well, hell, she asked the question.

"What about you?"

"After I left the university, I drifted around a lot, became kind of an academic vagabond, really—a year of lecturing here, a limited research grant there. A living, but nothing long-lasting. It's pretty hard to get your reputation back when you've been jailed on a murder charge."

"But you were cleared years ago! It was bogus from the start anyway!"

Susan had been charged and jailed for the murder of Howard Phelps, her mentor at the Marine Center. She was released after I figured out who the real killer was. Oddly enough, my help had driven us apart.

"You know it and I know it. But the way academics are, it held me back anyway."

"Yeah, don't I just. Many of them are jealous and gossipy—always ready to retaliate and ruin someone's chances."

"Of course I didn't help myself very much," she said sadly. "I mean getting arrested for murder isn't exactly a valid resume item. I'm sick of thinking about it!"

"So how did you get hooked up with Scott?" I asked, to change the subject. "Not the relationship part, the career part."

"He helped me get on Cliff Jameson's staff at UC San Diego. You remember he was from California and went back there after he got his Ph.D. from Oregon University. We'd still been seeing each other every few months over the years. He's a marine biologist on the staff there and got me an interview for an opening too. I clicked with Cliff and he hired me right away. That was two years ago. I collect data and analyze it for other scientists. I've been helping Scott get published. He's making quite a name for himself."

"I'll bet he is, but you're doing most of the work!" I whispered, as we both watched Szabo and his buddy Derek walking toward us.

"You two make a cozy-looking couple, now don't you?" Szabo said. "Trying to get some of the old magic back?" He had a funny look on his face as if he was trying to decide whether to say something. "I guess that isn't really possible, with your little, er, a problem, eh, Tom?"

I looked at Susan but she looked away, her face suddenly turning red. "I'm sorry," she said. "I shouldn't have told him."

I ignored her.

"Look, Scott. I'm not sure why you're trying to pick a fight with me, but I'm not going to take the bait. We're going to be spending a lot of time together this summer, so let's make it bearable."

Szabo looked surprised that I didn't respond angrily. He shrugged and then walked with Peters to seats across the waiting area.

"I guess you must have trusted him a lot to tell him about us," I said to her, looking straight ahead. "As you can see, that trust was misplaced. I had Scott pegged years ago. I decided then that he was the kind of person who used people to get what he wanted. He hasn't changed. He's using you and it looks like he's about to cut you loose. I'm sorry about that but it's gone beyond the point where I can do anything about it. I wish you good luck but I'm not going to be dragged into your situation. It's your mess! This is going to be tough enough for me without . . ."

"Without getting involved with me again," she said, tears rolling down her face. "I know you think I'm foolish. I guess I am."

I got up and held up my hands, as if to fend off whatever she was going to say. Cruel though I was acting, I'd heard this kind of thing from her before and didn't want to go through it again.

"Will you watch my bags? I'm going for a walk around the terminal. I think there's still time before our plane leaves."

I needed time to think, and a leisurely stroll along the maze of hallways spreading out from the center of the terminal would give me that. It was still early, so the airport was just coming alive. People were unlocking the front doors or rolling up the metal grillwork of the various shops on the main concourse. In restaurants, waitresses were taking orders from the few diners sitting at tables while chefs in tall white hats worked over steaming stoves in the kitchens at the rear.

What I call my problem may not be very interesting to anyone who doesn't know me. Most of the time I don't think about it. But Scott Szabo's taunt brought it all back and caused it to churn around in my mind.

Years before in my reporting days, I was shot in the groin while covering a prison riot. The wound healed quickly but it left me with problems I'd just as soon people didn't know about.

Another friend, Angela Pride, a woman who knows how to keep her mouth shut because she's a police officer, says that I compensate for this failing by taking too many chances and putting myself in danger unnecessarily.

I returned to the gate area in a half hour in time to see people surround our leader, Clifford Jameson. He was holding a clipboard and checking names off a list. After they had talked to him, members of the expedition were packing up their gear and walking into the jet way and onto the plane.

"Martindale. There you are," he said cheerfully. "I thought I'd have to send a search party after you. I'll check you off."

I hoisted the one large duffel bag onto my shoulder and picked up another smaller bag that was serving as my briefcase. Everything was canvas on this trip. I had enough trouble packing clothing for the two-month expedition than to be worn down by any added weight from the luggage itself. With the ship so well equipped, I even left my laptop computer at home.

✧ ✧ ✧

The regularly scheduled Pacific Western flight from Edmonton to Inuvik would take over 6 hours. After that, the party would switch to two smaller planes for the additional 2 hours to Tuktoyaktuk, the small town on Kugmallit Bay from where our research ship would be sailing.

The aircraft was a medium-sized one, an MD-80, I think. It was vacant enough this morning so that we could spread out in the cabin and travel in comfort that is rare in these days of big crowds and limited space. I hadn't seen Susan or Scott since our encounter in the terminal and didn't look for them now. I selected a window seat over the left wing and stowed my bags in the overhead bin.

I dozed for a while, then felt someone sitting down next to me.

"Professor, I wanted to apologize for all that stuff in the terminal. I was being a real dumb shit."

Ben Aniak was sober, but his bloodshot eyes were a reminder of his hard night before.

"That's okay. Is it Ben?"

"Yeah. Ben Aniak."

We shook hands as I pulled my seat back up.

"I don't always act my best when I've had too much to drink," he said, shaking his head sadly. "You know the old story about Indians not being able to drink. Alcohol's like poison to us. I try to keep from drinking, but I don't always succeed."

"How did you hook up with Jameson?"

"I spent a year in college in San Diego and took a class from him. That was before I dropped out to spend my time surfing."

"Surfing?"

"Yeah, a surfing Eskimo. Isn't that a crackup?" He laughed at the irony of the image.

"So what brought you back to the Arctic? There aren't any waves to ride up here."

"You got *that* right. Believe it or not, I missed all the cold and desolation. Dr. Jameson hired me to coordinate with the native nations up here. I speak the languages and know the cultural taboos. I mean, I was raised around all this stuff. It's a big break for me and I hope I don't screw it up."

"Is that why you drink?"

His eyes flashed. "What's that supposed to mean?"

"Now don't get sensitive on me," I said. "You just told me about that kind of battle. I just meant that this has created pressure because you've got so much to live up to."

"There's no doubt about that, man. I feel it." He turned away and looked toward the window to the opposite side of the plane, where sunlit clouds rolled by.

"Look, Ben. I don't know you and you don't know me, but I'll give you some advice anyway. Quit worrying about what other people think."

I wanted to say more like quit carrying around the burden of native people everywhere on your shoulders and thinking only you can save them. But that would have made me sound pretty preachy. I looked out the window on my side of the plane. Far below, patches of soggy tundra were visible occasionally through the puffy clouds. "End of lecture."

"Thanks a lot, man. You seem like a real nice guy. I hope we get to work together." He looked around conspiratorially and lowered his voice. "I'd watch my backside if I was you."

"What do you mean?"

"That blond fruitcake and his fairy pal."

"Scott and Derek?"

"Yeah. I saw you talking with 'em in the terminal along with that gal with the big hips."

Susan was so sensitive about her vanishing looks, she would have collapsed in tears at that remark.

"I heard 'em discussing ways to get even with you. I kept my eyes closed so they thought I was still drunk. I was kind of out of it, but I know what I heard."

"Which was what?" I asked with an edge to my voice. "Don't drag this out. Tell me!"

"The Scott guy, the blond. He said you'd screwed him over in the past and he's been itching to get even with you ever since. He said he'd have plenty of chances on this trip. He said something like, 'Let me count the ways,' or some similar shit."

Aniak got up and started to walk away. I grabbed his arm.

"What else? Did he say what he would do? Or when?"

"I've said enough. That's all I know. Just watch yourself, that's all. We're going into country that is dangerous on the best days. If someone wants to do you harm, let's just say they'll have plenty of opportunity."

He walked down the aisle.

"Ben. Ben," I said in as loud a whisper as I could make and still avoid attracting attention, but Aniak kept walking and did not turn around.

✧ ✧ ✧

Two

The first thing I saw after we landed in Tuktoyaktuk, Northwest Territories, was a young native woman leaning against the terminal building, smoking a cigarette. She didn't have to say anything to make me smile. Her T-shirt said it all: "Tuktoyaktuk is not the end of the world, but you can see it from here." The little kid standing next to her was wearing a sweatshirt that read "Tuk U."

Our party had transferred from the jet at Inuvik into two smaller prop planes for the flight up the Mackenzie River Delta into this bleak town on the northernmost tip of the North American landmass. The views were breathtaking with shimmering water interspersed with patches of green tundra, but the town was a dump. Cheap, manufactured buildings sat at tilted angles, the result of constant heaving as the earth froze and melted intermittently throughout the year. As we neared the ground, I could see individual structures more clearly. Even though many of them were new, few had been well cared for. Yards were strewn with rusting refrigerators and junk cars. And, despite the prevalence of snowmobiles, a line of tethered dogs milled around in front of each dwelling, howling and barking constantly.

I had steered clear of everyone else, except Paul Bickford. I was curious about him so as soon as we were on the tarmac, I walked over to him and introduced myself.

"Tom Martindale. I'm the PR guy."

"Paul Bickford. My role is undefined so far."

We shook hands and he seemed friendly enough, but someone not interested in small talk. Jameson's shout ended any chance for us to say more.

"Find your own luggage and carry it to the vans," he said, gesturing toward three large vehicles parked near the terminal building. "We're going right to the ship."

He kept consulting his clipboard and counting heads, as if one of us had somehow escaped by falling out the window of the plane.

"Let's snap it up, people." His voice took on the tone of a harried tour guide afraid of losing one of his clients in a hostile locale. In many respects, I guess he was exactly that. We dutifully picked up our bags and carried them to the vans, pitching them in the rear section.

"It isn't a long trip, so snuggle up so we can make it in one pass."

I got in and sat in the rear seat, Susan on one side of me and Derek Peters on the other. She looked more haggard than before. He checked me out and smiled, displaying perfect teeth to match his perfect face. He didn't look like someone who wished me bad luck. If anything, he acted a bit sheepish to have been a part of Scott's earlier outburst.

"So what do you do, Derek?" I asked.

"I'm not really sure. Scott set this up for us, so we could be together. I'm his assistant, I guess."

Since when does a junior researcher rate an assistant? And was he so clueless that he didn't know that Scott and Susan had been a couple? She sat on the other side of me in silence, not joining the conversation but looking more miserable by the minute.

"You have an extensive background in marine biology?" I said, thinking I knew the answer already.

"I'm working on my B.A. in psych," Derek answered eagerly. "Scott said he'd teach me everything I need to do the job."

"I'll bet he will," I said, still baffled about Scott Szabo's ability to get a job for his friend when positions on research expeditions were scarce.

The vans drove along a road that paralleled the airstrip, before entering a narrower lane that ended at a small dock on Kugmallit Bay. On the way we passed the complex of the Canadian subsidiary of the huge petroleum company that had caused the largest oil spill in history. Its employees had explored the Beaufort Sea for thirty years, working from off-shore drilling platforms. They lived in a sprawling assemblage of manufactured buildings perched on cement pilings resting on the shifting tundra.

I felt uncomfortable sitting next to Sue in the 10-minute ride to the dock. We just didn't seem to have much to say to one another anymore. We got out of the vans and started lifting our bags out of the rear compartment. I tried to help Sue with her bags but she waved me off. We walked in silence the short distance to the dock where a small ferry waited to take us out to the ship anchored just off shore.

Jameson reappeared with his clipboard and began reading the names of those he selected to go first.

"Foster, Szabo, Martindale, Aniak," he shouted.

I stepped easily into the boat, then lifted my bags in place near my feet. Back on the path, Ben Aniak was having trouble with his luggage: two duffels and a cardboard box marked "microscope." As he got onto the ferry, he stumbled and lost a grip on the box, which tumbled end over end toward me. I stopped it with my foot, then heard the distinctive sound of breaking glass. Aniak looked horrified, his face reddening as I bent down to examine the damaged box.

"Ben, your microscope's broken. Maybe we'd better take it out and check it for damage. What do you think?"

"That's okay, I'll get it." He raced to my side and picked up the box, abandoning the other bags on the dock. As he lifted the carton, I smelled the distinctive odor of whiskey and saw a stain rapidly spreading along the cardboard bottom.

Our home for the next two weeks loomed just beyond the entrance to the bay, its sleek shape rising and falling on the constantly moving waters of the Beaufort Sea.

The United States Coast Guard Cutter *Polar Sea* is billed as the world's most powerful nonnuclear icebreaker. Commissioned in the 1970s, this 399-foot-long, 13,000-ton ship can carry as many as 190 people. I read these facts in a brochure as we plied the waves and left the bay for the open sea. I wanted to find out more about where I would be living and working.

The *Polar Sea* and its sister ship, *Polar Star,* are the largest cutters the Coast Guard operates. Several features make these vessels ideal for open water icebreaking: reinforced hulls, special bows, and a system that allows rapid shifting of ballast to increase the effectiveness of the ice breaking. They serve both the Arctic and Antarctic as the base of operations for scientific research projects and as a way to resupply remote stations.

The ship would be doing both for us. It was a place for us to live and work as we conducted various ice experiments. Although no one had mentioned it, I suspected that the data collected on the voyage might help determine how free of ice the Arctic was. That information would then have implications for national security.

Later, the ship would carry us to Herschel Island, which had been the winter refuge for whaling ships and their crews 100 years ago. We would be spending several weeks on the island studying the ice pack as it crept slowly southward in the early fall.

Crew members stood by to help us off the boat and up the dangling stairway to the deck.

"This way please, sir," said an officer wearing lieutenant's bars and holding a clipboard. "Name, please."

"Martindale. Thomas Martindale."

"I don't see it. Oh, there it is," he smiled, putting a checkmark on the page. His nametag read *Madison*. "The ensign will show you below."

I turned to see the smiling face of a young man who looked like he belonged in my freshman news writing class. His name was Zinko, according to his nametag.

"Have we died and gone to heaven or not," said Scott Szabo to Peters as they stepped onto the deck just behind me. "I mean all these hot guys."

They smiled a bit too much as they gave the lieutenant their names.

"How old are you, sailor?" Szabo asked the shy ensign who probably got the drift about where this was heading, but said nothing.

"Old enough to be wary of you," I said.

Szabo laughed heartily but Peters looked embarrassed.

"Let's just cool it for now, Scott," he whispered.

Behind us, the others were stepping onto the deck and giving Madison their names.

"If you gentlemen will follow me, I will take you to your quarters," said Ensign Zinko, who recovered his composure and led us to what he said was the second deck. We went down one set of stairs and gathered around him in the hallway.

"Your specific berthing assignments have been made by Dr. Jameson," he announced in a voice slightly elevated so all could hear him. "You will sleep two to a stateroom. Each stateroom has its own head. That's what we call a bathroom. Mr. Dunn has asked me to remind you that in the close-quarters environment of the ship."

"I like the sound of that," muttered Szabo.

Zinko blushed again and continued, "In these close quarters, cleanliness and personal hygiene are high priority. It is important that you maintain your berthing areas. We provide you with blankets and linen. There is approximately 24 cubic feet of locker space for each of you to store your valuables. You were told to bring padlocks to secure the lockers." He looked around in anticipation and several men dangled locks from their fingers. "Good deal! Did you bring hangers for your clothing?"

Most of us nodded and he pressed on.

"If you choose to eat in the wardroom . . ."

"Do we have a choice?" said Szabo, clearly enjoying every opportunity to rattle the young ensign.

Clifford Jameson had had enough. "I suggest you save your smart remarks for your friend and not waste our time here," he said as he moved next to Szabo and Peters. Now it was Szabo's turn to blush.

"Sorry, boss. I was . . ."

"You were just being an asshole," said Jameson, cutting him off. "Go on, ensign. Sorry for the interruption."

"Thank you, sir. I was saying about eating. If you eat with us, you must sign up on the clipboard every morning before 1000 for lunch and 1500 for dinner. This allows the cooks to prepare and account for each meal. Meals will be served at scheduled times, but we will be flexible according to your science schedule. If your meals are paid for in advance, you may use the crew's mess deck as well. If you are in a hurry to get back to work, I highly recommend the chow line on the crew's mess deck. You don't need to sign up in advance. In addition to regular meal times, the chow line serves midnight rations at 2300 each and every evening. These are usually leftovers or sandwich fixings. The cost for meals is $6 per day, including breakfast, lunch and dinner. Unless it's part of your lodging package, you pay that when you leave the ship, by check if possible. May I say, ladies and gentlemen, that the food is very good on Coast Guard ships. I think you will enjoy it."

He walked us along the hallway to an intersecting corridor. "I believe you will be making the cabin assignments, sir?" He looked at Jameson, who stepped forward, his ever-present clipboard at the ready. Everyone gathered around him.

"Cliff, you'll have a cabin by yourself." The tall man nodded and picked up his gear.

"Let's have Scott and Tom together," he said without looking up.

"I don't think that's such a good idea," I replied.

"Derek and Danny," he continued, paying no attention to me.

"I don't want to have anything to do with that fag," the ponytailed Salcido shouted. "Anybody but him!"

Peters turned red but didn't say anything. Szabo moved toward him, as if to offer some protection. As always sticking to the script, Jameson ignored everyone. "Carmen, you'll be bunking with Susan." Both Susan and the bubbly secretary nodded and smiled at one another. "No argument? That is a first!"

He turned and looked at the remaining people, then his clipboard. "Ben and Alan." The Eskimo and the geologist didn't seem bothered by the room assignment and said nothing. "That leaves Jane and yours truly. We aren't going to share a room, so don't get your hopes up. We'll be in the two smaller cabins. We're both workaholics so that should suit both our schedules."

"We're both old too," said Jane with a straight face. "We don't want to subject all you young people to witness the aging process in action." She laughed heartily and everyone joined her, even Jameson.

"I think that does it," he said, indicating with his brusque manner that the cabin assignments were final. Everyone began to pick up baggage and form a line in front of Ensign Zinko who started passing out keys. I walked over to Jameson.

"A word, Cliff?"

"I'm not used to changing my plans after I've made them," he said, but motioned for me to follow him back down the hall.

"Look, Cliff. Szabo and I have a history of bad blood. He was under suspicion for murder some years ago and he blames me for putting him there."

I didn't see the need to bring up the whole thing with Susan. He'd think that I was reacting out of male rivalry when I really wasn't.

"The whale case, I guess you'd call it."

"Exactly. I have a hunch that he's still not very happy with me."

Jameson leaned in closer. "I'm not totally unreasonable. I was trying to separate Scott and Derek. I've only recently become aware of the their . . . er . . . a . . . relationship. I'm not the director of a gay cruise ship. I'm running an important science project here."

"Okay, okay. I can see that, but someone else can share his room. What about the big guy, Alan? I'm telling you, Scott and I are headed for trouble. And Danny doesn't seem to be very happy to be with Derek."

Jameson thought for a moment, then made his decision.

"People, people," he raised his voice and walked toward the others, still milling around. "I've been rethinking the cabin assignments. Alan, you're with Scott. Danny, you're with Tom. That'll leave Ben and Derek together. I want everyone to be happy while they're here, but someone has to make the decisions and that is me. Okay. If you've got your keys, we can get settled in. Ensign Zinko will lead the way."

"Sir, there is one other thing I forgot to mention," said the officer.

"Yeah, ensign. Well, spit it out!"

"Coast Guard regulations prohibit the possession or consumption of alcohol or controlled substances, except legally prescribed medication, aboard ship," he said, consulting a card. "These regulations also prohibit smoking within the interior of the ship."

"Shit!" said Salcido who was standing next to me.

"This is a good time to quit, Danny," said Jane.

"Easy for you to say!" he shot back.

"People, people. We're wasting valuable time," said Jameson. "Is that the end of your little spiel, ensign?"

"Almost, sir. Smoking is not permitted in the science labs or the fantail, where gasoline is stored."

"Where the hell is the fantail?" said Salcido, apparently the only smoker in our group, or at least the only person who cared about the nomenclature of the ship.

"That's at the rear, sir," said the ever-polite ensign. "Smoking areas are provided on the weather decks outside, port and starboard quarter decks only."

"This hold true during storms too?"

"Yes, sir, it does."

"Shit," muttered Salcido, who wasn't going to give this issue up quietly.

"Please use the butt cans provided," concluded the ensign.

"If not, your own butt will be in a can," deadpanned Jane.

Everybody laughed at that, including Salcido.

We got keys from Zinko, then followed him down the side corridor to our cabins. All of this took about 45 minutes, a lot longer than Jameson had planned. He grew increasingly impatient at the delays.

"Look, people. We're way behind schedule already. I'm pushing back our first meeting to 1900 hours in the lab."

"That's 7 p.m. to all you landlubbers," said Jane.

"After dinner," replied Jameson with a glare toward her for interrupting his rundown of procedures. She only smiled and walked into her room.

Salcido reached our cabin first and unlocked the door. He turned on the light and stepped in. I quickly followed.

"Not bad for government issue," he said after glancing around. I had to agree. The room held two beds, built one over the other into one wall, two desks, two chairs, and two metal clothes lockers. To the left of the door was a small head with a toilet, basin, and shower. We even had a porthole.

Salcido sat down on one of the chairs and immediately took out a cigarette.

"Mind?" he said, thrusting it toward me.

"It's the Coast Guard's rule, not mine," I shrugged. "They'll maybe keel-haul you if they catch you."

"What the fuck is that?" he said, looking momentarily worried.

"Oh, it's a pirate thing," I laughed. "I doubt you'll have to worry about it."

Salcido didn't dwell on my words for very long. He got out a lighter and fired up the end of a cigarette, moving over to the open porthole so the smoke would drift out.

"That ought to keep you from dying of secondhand smoke. So what's your specialty?" he said, puffing rapidly on his cigarette. "I mean, what will you be doing in our little group here?"

"I'll be doing PR stuff, you know writing press releases and background materials. I'm also the historian. I'll be keeping the permanent record of everything that happens. It'll be sent to our funding agencies and go into the libraries of the participating universities." I told him about my own research. "How about you? What will you be doing?"

"Jameson's got me listed as a technician," he said. "That means I can fix things. You know, stuff tends to break down when you get into rugged areas. I'm supposed to keep all the equipment working. I also know about communication. I'll be operating the satellite telephone and the backup radio when we're out in the wild."

"ALL ICE TEAM MEMBERS TO THE WARDROOM!" Jameson's voice over the intercom was so loud both Salcido and I jumped.

"Jesus!" he said, quickly extinguishing a cigarette on the edge of the porthole opening and throwing the butt out.

"ATTENTION! ATTENTION! ALL ICE TEAM MEMBERS TO THE WARDROOM!"

"Ice team!" sneered Salcido. "Leave it to Jameson to come up with a name like that!"

✦ ✦ ✦

". . . could be dangerous, but we're planning . . ."

Jameson stopped talking as Salcido and I entered the wardroom. Everyone else was seated around the table munching on sandwiches.

"Nice of you to join us," he said.

"We didn't . . ."

"Sit over there!" He motioned toward two chairs at the end of the large gray table.

My limited acquaintance with Jameson taught me that he liked to have the upper hand in everything he did. He wasn't interested in explanations; he just wanted subservience on matters large and small. Salcido and I grabbed sandwiches from the sideboard and sat down meekly. Jane filled two cups with coffee and pushed them in front of us.

"Okay. Back to business. For the benefit of the latecomers." Jameson paused and glanced at the two of us. I felt my face get red. Public humiliation worked every time I used it in my classes. It was equally effective here and I doubted we would be late again. I wanted to keep my job.

"I was saying before that we will spend the next week gathering ice samples, doing tests on them, then reviewing preliminary research results here on the ship. After that, we'll get ready for our expedition to Herschel Island. The ship will carry us there after conducting ice-breaking maneuvers. It'll drop us off and leave, we'll do our work on the island, then it will return for us in two weeks, and carry us to Point Barrow, Alaska, where we will disembark and fly back to the lower 48. Any questions?"

"I'm wondering about how cold it is likely to get," asked Szabo. "I mean it is late summer, but does that mean anything up here?"

"Spoken like a true California surfer," laughed Jameson. "I, too, worry about the cold. Although it is summer as you say, you've got to remember that we're all here at the mercy of the polar ice cap—thousands and thousands of miles of solid ice that extends from this coast to the north edge of Siberia on the other side. The ice can move in quickly and it sometimes has a mind of its own. Never forget that. What else?"

"Clothing," said Susan. "I wonder if we have enough?"

"Fine time to think of that," laughed Jameson. "You've all brought clothes on your checklist. I know because I examined your gear myself. I mean, we've got enough stuff to bring back the layered look big time: heavy shirts and pants, long underwear, a thermal layer of wool or polar fleece, parkas, waterproof gloves, and wool or fur hats. We also have the use of Coast Guard Mustang suits, special overalls that really keep the cold out."

"Sunglasses," said Alan Hopkins. "Don't forget sunglasses. There's enough glare from sun on the ice to keep you from seeing clearly. It could do some permanent damage."

"It's getting late," Jameson said after a glance at his watch. We'll start our background briefings at 0800 with Susan Foster's report on the Arctic. Tom will follow that with a backgrounder on Herschel Island and its history."

"You won't need your sleeping pills," I said. "I'll take care of that."

Everyone laughed at what I said, including Jameson. I followed Susan out of the wardroom.

"Are you hanging in there, Sue?"

"I guess so," she answered hesitantly. "I suddenly feel so lost. Scott's being a real shit. You and I are fighting again. Cliff put me in with Miss Teen USA. God, I see her and I see a body I always wanted to have."

"I doubt she's got as much up here as you," I said, tapping on my head. "There's more to life than a good body."

"Yeah, so they say. I used to be someone who could turn heads when I entered a room. Now look at me." She gestured down her body and I thought of Ben Aniak's remark about her big rear end.

"Besides, if you're worried about keeping Scott interested, Carmen Ames is not your competition. Derek Peters, that's who you're up against, or rather who Scott's up against even as we speak."

We both watched Szabo and Peters playing a mild form of what my students call "grab ass" as they walked down the hallway.

"I know, Tom. Boy, do I know," she said, tears in her eyes.

Susan never used to cry at all, even when she was in jail charged with murder. Sad that someone so unworthy of her could so easily reduce her to tears.

I returned to the cabin to find Salcido already snoring away in the lower bunk. Nice that we discussed who got what bunk.

As I got into bed, I heard the grinding sound of the huge anchor chain slowly ascending. Then the ship jerked slightly as a low hum filled the air. The *Polar Sea* was underway, carrying me to what promised to be the trip of a lifetime.

✧ ✧ ✧

Three

I could see an expanse of what we were here to study—ice— out the porthole of the wardroom. Breakfast was over, and had contained more food than I had ever seen in one place at such an early hour. I was stuffed with scrambled eggs, French toast, pancakes, ham, bacon and sausage, with biscuits and gravy thrown in lest we leave hungry.

Jameson's tirade about punctuality paid off. Everyone was in place as the brass-trimmed clock on the wall struck 0800.

"Good," he said. "You're all here. I'll save the lab assignments and some housekeeping announcements until the end of this morning's presentations. I'm pleased to introduce Susan Foster, a marine biologist of wide reputation, who will talk about the region of the world we shall be calling home for the next two months. Sue."

Odd that Jameson gave Sue such a buildup when she said he was using her to compile the research data of others. If he admired her so much, why didn't he give her a research project of her own? Susan got up and walked to the end of the table. As she did so, the lights dimmed and a projector came on. The scene behind her was breathtaking: white ice as far as the eye could see, topped off by dark blue sky. In the left rear of the photo, the black nose and dark eyes of a polar bear faced the camera. A map of the North Pole flashed next on the screen.

"The Arctic is the smallest of the world's oceans, 5.4 million square miles of water extending south from the North Pole to the shores of Europe, Asia, and North America. Nearly land-locked, the Arctic is surrounded by the landmasses of Europe, Asia, North America, and Greenland. It is connected to the Pacific by the Bering Strait and to the Atlantic through the Greenland Sea. A continental shelf lies under about one-third of the Arctic Ocean. The Arctic is subdivided into a set of three parallel ridges and four basins. The average depth of this ocean is 4,900 feet.

"The greatest inflow of water comes into the Arctic from the Atlantic via the Norwegian Current. Water also comes in from the Bering Strait. The East Greenland Current carries the Arctic's major outflow. The ocean's temperature and salinity vary seasonally as the ice cover melts and freezes.

"Ice covers most of the ocean surface throughout the year, causing subfreezing temperatures most of the time. The Arctic produces three forms of ice. Land ice enters the scene in the form of icebergs created when pieces of glaciers break off."

A photo of a huge iceberg appeared on the screen.

"River ice forms nearer the shore as rivers transport frozen fresh water into the ocean."

A photo of a river delta flashed on, the dark blue water dotted generously with ice.

"Sea ice occurs when seawater freezes. This is the most extensive form of ice in the Arctic. In winter, a permanent cap of ice covers almost all of the ocean surface."

A photo showing a large expanse of ice appeared on the screen.

"Some melting takes place in summer depending on air temperature, wind direction and current flow."

The next slide showed less ice and an expanse of muddy tundra with a blue flower protruding through it.

"The Arctic has often been called the birthplace of storms because it does affect the weather of most of the North American continent. It is the major source of very cold air that inevitably moves toward the Equator. In the middle latitudes, it meets with warmer air and causes rain and snow.

"Where ice covers the surface, little marine life exists. Marine life abounds in open areas, especially in more southerly waters."

"There seals . . ."

The appropriate seal slide came on.

". . . and whales . . ."

A whale's head broke the surface of frothy water.

". . . live, although both were hunted nearly to extinction before protective quotas were set up in the middle of the last century.

"Fish . . ."

A photo of a net brimming with fish flashed on the screen.

". . . in commercial exploitable quantities live in the warmer seas adjacent to the Arctic."

Susan paused to drink from a glass of water as the lights went back on. Everyone around the table listened intently to her presentation. Normally an audience of academic know-it-alls acts fairly blasé and uninterested. This gang was probably paying attention because they were actually learning something.

"Let's talk for a minute about the polar climate. It is characterized by persistent cold and relatively narrow annual temperature ranges. In winter, days and nights are practically indistinguishable: they are both dark. Continuous daylight marks the summers, along with dense and foggy weather, including weak cyclones with rain or snow.

"The terrain has a central surface covered by a perennial drifting polar ice pack averaging three meters in thickness. At times, however, pressure ridges can grow to three times that size. As I noted earlier, the ice pack, surrounded by open seas in the summer, more than doubles in size during the winter and extends then to the encircling landmasses."

Susan was rolling along nicely and she had her audience's attention. She seemed confident, prepared, and like the woman I once knew and loved. What had happened to her?

"Natural hazards abound, for example, ice islands that on occasion break away from islands, or icebergs that split from glaciers. The region is virtually locked in ice from October to June. The superstructures of ships even become encased in ice from October to May."

She looked up from her notes and took off her glasses.

"One last thing that I say as a warning to all of us who will be spending the next few months working in the Arctic. We need to remember that we are but temporary guests in one of the most fragile ecosystems in the world. The Arctic region recovers very slowly to even the slightest disruption or damage."

Susan gathered up her notes and returned to her seat. Even though she had given a good presentation, she seemed strangely defeated. Her shoulders slumped and her eyes were downcast in a manner that surprised me. The Susan I knew from years before was confident, almost feisty, in the way she tackled life. Even when she was accused of murder, she fought back and never gave up. It was hard for me to understand why she seemed so cowed, so subservient now. If Scott Szabo had made her into some kind of sexual slave, why did she put up with it?

I made a point of getting up and pulling back her chair.

"Really good presentation," I whispered. "You always did put me to shame."

She smiled halfheartedly and sat down next to me.

"Next, I've asked Alan Hopkins to tell us a bit about global warming and its effect on this region and on the ice we have come to study."

The tall, bespectacled scientist walked to the front of the table and slowly poured a glass of water.

"Thanks, Cliff. As you all know, our mission is to study ice and whether it is melting and what that will do both to the Arctic and the rest of the world. Because of that, I don't want to say too much lest our own efforts are prejudiced by studies conducted before our own.

"First, a word about global warming. There is great concern that changes caused by global warming are part of an Arctic-wide pattern that includes a pronounced thawing of the tundra and a retreat of the sea ice around the North Pole, at least in summer. Melting glaciers and rising snowfall are making the North Atlantic less salty.

"Warmer waters have caused a few anomalies in the animal world as well. For one thing, the caribou are thinner than they were in the past and so are the ringed seals. Arctic char that live in local waters are covered with scratches. We think this is because the water is more shallow due to climate shifts and the sharp rocks are no longer submerged. Beluga whales and seals don't hang around as much as they used to, probably because of the noise from increased motor boat traffic. The Canadian Inuits now eat meat from younger seals because they think the older ones are contaminated."

"Is that due to global warming?" asked Jane.

"Yes, wind and currents transport all kinds of contaminants from the industrialized south to the Arctic. These accumulate in the fatty tissues of animals here. Then people eat them and that can lead to health problems.

"But the danger is not only to people. Arctic char, ringed seals, and caribou are showing liver damage. Caribou have worms in their muscles and between their joints. The fat in Beluga whales is changing color. Hunters from all across the Arctic are reporting that more and more polar bears look emaciated, probably because their hunting season has been shortened by the shrinking ice cover. As the ice pack shrinks, they won't be able to get to their favorite prey, seals. Now, they hang around breathing holes and pick them off when they come up for air.

"Migration patterns are even being affected. Some natives think the walrus have moved farther north to hunt because it is colder. Some species have changed their calving grounds for the same reason.

"I should note that scientists have known about contaminants seeping into the Arctic for some time. The Stockholm Convention on Persistent Organic Pollutants is an international treaty signed by 150 countries that went into effect last year. It prohibits the production of a dozen toxic chemicals and aims to destroy existing stockpiles.

"But one man's solution can cause another man's problem. We in the southern regions think this is all great. Inuits here and Eskimos in Alaska worry about the ultimate effect on their tradition of hunting and using what they bring in from the sea and the frozen land to survive as a people."

"Amen to that," muttered Ben Aniak.

Hopkins picked up his papers and returned to his seat, amid nods of approval at his presentation.

"Okay, people," said Jameson who moved to the head of the table. "I know you want to have a coffee break but we have no time. We've got to move along. You can talk to Alan at some other time about his presentation. Just fill your cups when you need to and we'll move ahead to Tom's presentation on Herschel Island. Tom."

My long years in the classroom taught me the necessity of putting on a show as a way to attract and keep an audience. Although this group was way ahead of college undergraduates in knowledge and experience, I doubted they would spurn a little pizzazz. As I walked to the front, I signaled for the lights to be turned down and stepped to the podium as the first slide flashed on the screen.

"If we aren't careful," I began, "this is how we will look at the end of our stay on Herschel Island."

I paused as the projected image sank in: a line of the most bedraggled men imaginable, circa the 1890s, each wearing long beards, fur parkas, and heavy boots. The looks in their eyes bordered on derangement, as if they were about to crack up. They stood in front of a ramshackle building, high drifts of snow piled all around. Mangy, vicious-looking sled dogs lay at their feet.

The men and women around the wardroom table laughed, but not as heartily or for as long as I hoped. I pressed ahead anyway as another vintage photo appeared above our heads. This one showed the island in 1894.

"Well, maybe not quite that bad. Herschel Island was discovered in 1888 by Joe Tuckfield, who was sent by Charles Brower, the operator of a trading post at Point Barrow, Alaska, to look for whales in the eastern Beaufort Sea. We are in that sea right now on our way to the Arctic itself.

"Pauline Cove on Herschel Island is the only protective harbor between the Mackenzie River Delta in the Northwest Territories and Point Barrow, Alaska. The cove is deep enough to handle modern, ocean-going vessels and has the added advantage of being protected from the prevailing northerly winds and drifting ice pack. Its role as a haven for ships in the ice pack made Herschel a key port during the heyday of the Arctic whaling industry.

"Beginning in the 1870s, steam-powered whaling ships first ventured east of Point Barrow, but these early trips were not successful. As the numbers of whales decreased in the waters off Alaska because of expanded hunting, Brower and other whalers became interested in that eastern area.

"In 1887, Eskimos told Brower about seeing great numbers of whales in the waters of the Mackenzie River delta. This was enough for him to outfit Tuckfield with food and supplies for a year and a whaleboat to get him to the area. He departed on July 25, 1888, and returned on August 5, 1889, with information that would change the course of whaling history.

"During his winter in the delta, Tuckfield had found a lot of whales and a good harbor at Herschel Island, long named on maps but never really explored. This news electrified the whaling ship captains then operating in and around Barrow. Not only would they find abundant whales to the east but a natural harbor where they could anchor in case of storms or unexpected ice."

I paused to drink some water. Unlike many of my students at home, they were all paying close attention.

"The next year, the Pacific Steam Whaling Company sent a ship, the *Mary D. Hume,* and a crew with enough lumber and supplies to build a permanent station on Herschel Island. On September 18, the *Hume* and two other whaling ships, the *Grampus* and the *Nicoline,* were frozen in at Pauline Cove on the island, when an unexpected change in the weather caused the ice pack to move south. Although it was small, the harbor protected the three ships from the moving ice pack whose pressures could easily crush even the strongest of hulls.

"There was another side to life on the island, however. The isolation and harsh conditions turned the men into what one historian called 'rowdy, stir-crazy sailors.' And the whalers had a bad influence on the local natives as they turned the island into a kind of Sodom of the Arctic."

I looked at Ben Aniak and he lowered his eyes.

"That reputation brought Anglican missionaries to the island. In fact, their Mission House still stands, abandoned and decaying. Amid the debauchery, the crews worked hard. They built frameworks over the decks and hung sails from them for added protection from the cold. They could work in relative comfort on deck. Below, they kept stoves fired up with the abundant driftwood all over the area. They insulated the hulls from the crushing effects of the ice by cutting blocks of snow and banking them against the sides of the vessels.

"When the long night of winter set in on November 29, the 180 crewmen from the three ships were ready to spend the next five months in the Arctic's icy grip, 4,000 miles from their home in San Francisco, 400 miles east of the scant civilization of Point Barrow and 200 miles above the top of the world itself."

As a photo of an endless ice pack dissolved into a map of the North Pole, I gathered my notes and walked to my chair.

"But we're safe from ice now," asked Salcido, "aren't we?"

"As far as I know, we're okay," I laughed. "Winter arrives in November."

Next, Jameson turned to Paul Bickford, who was leaning against a side wall. As always, he was apart from everyone else.

"I've asked Paul to talk to you a bit about the role of security on this expedition. As most of you know, he is a private security consultant who served in the military."

Bickford walked to the end of the table and began passing out a stack of paper.

"Take one page and pass it along, please."

The others did as they were told as Bickford continued.

"All I have to say about security is listed. My main message for you is to keep all research findings to yourselves and your colleagues on what we call a need-to-know basis. We are in a pretty remote area, but that does not mean we should lower our guard. Many countries and individuals wish to see harm to the United States of America. As American citizens in a semi-official capacity, we must all strive not to become the weak link in what I like to call the chain of security. It begins with each of you and, sadly, could end with one of us."

Saying that, Bickford turned and walked out of the ward-room, much to the surprise of everyone at the table. We looked at one another for a few seconds before anyone spoke. Jane broke the silence.

"Cliff, is that all there is to security? Why can't we ask quest . . ."

Jameson held up his hand and ignored her.

"Thanks, Paul," said Jameson, speaking to a man who was no longer there. He resumed his place at the front of the room. "We must follow his advice and take as many security precautions as possible to keep our expedition secure. Now, I want to let you in on a surprise. We are adding a new element to our research project, one I hope you will enjoy. I would like to introduce the person who will be conducting a whale-tagging operation under our auspices."

All eyes turned toward the doorway, which remained empty for several tantalizing seconds. Then, a short, stocky man burst through it, followed by another man and a woman. Despite his short stature, the first man was an imposing figure with his full head of white hair, thick goatee and mustache and wearing black leather.

"This, my friends, is the eminent Russian whale researcher, Boris Belinsky."

Instead of joining Jameson at the head of the table, Belinsky walked around the table and shook hands with each of us, like a politician working a room.

"What's this guy running for—or from?" I muttered to Susan.

"I heard that, my friend," Belinsky said from down the table.

He walked to my side and paused in front of me. I didn't know what to do. As usual, my smart mouth had gotten me into trouble.

"I like a man with a sense of humor," he said after a few seconds of glaring. "I like a man who tells a good joke, even if it is on me. He, he, ha, ha, ha." Then he grabbed me, picked me off my feet and whirled me around.

"He, he, ha, ha, ha!" I joined everyone's laughter, even though it was at my expense. What the hell. It probably was a funny sight. He dropped me quickly and kept moving around the table.

"Boris, I need you to join me up here so I can tell our colleagues all about you and our plans to work together." Jameson was sounding impatient. He was clearly someone who disliked sharing the stage with anyone. Belinsky completed the survey of the room and walked to Jameson's side.

"Sit, sit, sit," he shouted, motioning to us with downturned hands. "Clifford, may I introduce my associates?"

Jameson nodded and impatiently pointed to his watch.

"Excellent. Dimitri Zukov has been my assistant for over ten years."

The tall, thin man who had been trailing Belinsky around the room stood up and bowed deeply. He was extremely pale, with deep-set green eyes that were not kind.

"Nadia Chernoff is my secretary and right arm—or is it left arm, given our long-standing political situation in Russia? He, he, ha, ha, ha!"

Belinsky was someone who had long ago been captivated by his own humor. Chernoff stood up and I realized for the first time that she was quite beautiful: black hair pulled straight back into a bun, setting off delicate features including extremely big, and extremely blue, eyes. She also wore black leather pants, which were as tight as the laws of physics allowed. A white wool turtleneck sweater clung in all the right places to a figure that was beyond voluptuous. The eyes of every man in the room undressed her. Even Scott and Derek were staring.

"Thank you, my dear. Is nice to have a good look, eh gentlemen? He, he, ha, ha, ha!"

Jameson cleared his throat. Belinsky took the hint and sat down.

"Thank you, Boris. I know we will all be looking forward to working with you, Mr. Zukov, and Miss Chernoff. Let me give you some background on why our new friends have joined us. Boris and I are old friends, having worked together in the 1980s on a joint National Science Foundation/Soviet Academy of Sciences project to map the North Pole. The funding got cut but we have kept in touch in the years since. When I organized this project, he contacted me with an offer to join us."

Belinsky was smiling and nodding as Miss Chernoff rubbed his shoulders. Now *this* was my idea of a good meeting! Yet it was too much for Jameson, who shook his head slightly. Miss Chernoff quit massaging and sat down.

"I have decided that we will incorporate a whale-tagging project into our ice research work. As we study the process of ice freezing and thawing, he will track migrating whales in order to tag them."

Jameson paused with a smirk, obviously happy with his surprise and, authoritarian that he was, equally certain that everyone would share his joy. He was wrong.

"I can't believe you would spring this kind of shit on us out of the blue," said one of the scientists, Alan Hopkins, who jumped to his feet and pounded the table. "You, of all people should know what happens when a scientific mission is diluted. I just can't believe you're doing this!" He sat down, shaking his head.

"What Alan means, I think, is that we all signed up for what we thought was a situation where we would be treated equally," said Jane, her former good humor now gone. "We will be stretched thin as it is, but now we must fit a totally new concept into our plans. This is too much, even for you!"

"A word, Cliff."

No one had seen Bickford reenter the room. He pulled Jameson aside and they spoke for several minutes. The diminutive leader kept shaking his head and waving his arms. Eventually, he pulled away from the taller man.

No one else spoke, apparently afraid of Jameson's short fuse. Contrary to my usual tendency to speak out of turn, I kept quiet too. Ever on the lookout for a good story, I was intrigued by this change in plans.

Jameson got red in the face, clearly resenting this challenge to his authority.

"I was under the impression that *I* was the one in charge of this expedition," he said haughtily. "I don't think I have to tell you who signed you up and who will sign your paychecks." He shot a glance at Bickford, who said nothing.

"I think what they meant . . . ," I started to say.

"You're not paid to think or be a spokesman for the others," interrupted Jameson. "You're paid to write stories that make me, I mean, us look good."

It seemed foolish to get into this. I didn't finish my sentence.

"So we've got that out in the open!" said Susan, her voice rising in anger. "The rest of us are only here to make *you* look good!"

This was turning into a real donnybrook, one that would do lasting damage. I tried to separate the combatants.

"Sue," I whispered, "you're not in any position to challenge him. You need this job. Don't give him an excuse to can you." She quit talking.

Jameson stood there seething. All this time, Belinsky sat in his chair, smiling and nodding, clearly enjoying the fracas his presence had created.

At that moment, as if on cue, Ensign Zinko appeared in the doorway. "Pardon me, sir, captain's compliments. He wanted me to tell you we reached the main pack ice. He thought you and your co-workers might like to join him on the upper deck."

The clatter of chairs was deafening, as everyone took the opportunity to get out of the room and break the tension.

✧ ✧ ✧

Four

The permanent Arctic ice pack is seldom more than 50 to 75 miles from shore, even in the summer. The varying air temperature causes its frigid mantle to move and shift like some kind of undulating monster.

As we reached the upper deck, the air felt cold on my face. We fanned out along the railing to gaze at the ice as if it were some exotic creature in a zoo. What hit me first was the color—an almost translucent blue/white that reminded me of a diamond. Looking at the unending expanse made me fantasize for a moment that I was in a desert, a desert where the usual unendurable heat had became unendurable cold. In the horizon at the end of the spectacular vista, the curvature of the earth stood out against the sky.

As the ship sped along just skirting the ice pack, I had the sensation of being on the edge of a dangerous abyss, where one false move would send me end over end to my death. I shuddered and pulled my parka more tightly around me.

"You look like you need a drink to warm up," Ben Aniak glanced around nervously, then pulled a tiny flask from his pocket, in direct defiance of both Jameson and the U.S. Coast Guard. I covered it with both hands and took a quick swig of very good brandy.

"My compliments to your bootlegger," I laughed, wiping my mouth and handing the flask back to him.

He quickly shoved it in his pocket.

"I am that bootlegger," he said with a smirk. "Hadn't you guessed by this time?"

"I don't suppose I'd thought that much about it. Does Jameson know?"

"Cliff Jameson knows everything," he said. "He runs a tight-ass operation here. Or hadn't you noticed?"

"Yeah, you got *that* right. But I'm surprised he lets it go on. I mean he'd risk a lot if his funding agencies found out."

"Let's just say I've got some insurance so it doesn't concern me."

"You mean you've got something on him?"

Aniak didn't reply. He laughed and moved away from me. No one seemed to be looking at either of us. They were concentrating on a large object moving along the ice pack.

A huge polar bear was having little trouble keeping up with the ship. His wide gait allowed him to cover an amazing amount of icy territory in a short time. Every once in a while the bear would glance to the side as if to check on his progress in the race with us.

"Now that is real confidence," I said to no one in particular.

"I never lose my feeling of awe," said Jane. "These creatures are the most magnif . . . Oh no, I can't believe it!" A look of horror crossed her face at something she saw behind me.

I turned in time to see Boris Belinsky raise a rifle to his shoulder. I started running towards him as he aimed.

"Stop!" I shouted as everyone turned. The sound caused him to hesitate just long enough for me to reach his side. His assistant, Zukov, tried to fend me off, but I dodged around him easily. I lunged at the rifle barrel causing it to fly up just as the weapon went off. Belinsky was so startled he didn't react at first. Zukov pulled me back roughly and seemed about to do worse. Out of nowhere, Bickford grabbed the smaller man and held him so tightly he could not move.

By then, we were surrounded by the entire scientific entourage and five Coast Guard officers with their guns drawn.

"Drop the weapon, sir!" said Ensign Zinko. Belinsky quickly complied. Everyone relaxed and lowered their guns. Bickford relaxed his hold on Zukov enough so that the man could probably breathe, but still not move around much.

"What is the meaning of this, Tom?" Clifford Jameson pushed through the crowd.

"Ask your friend, Belinsky, here. He was trying to shoot that defenseless polar bear out on the ice."

"Boris? Is this true?"

"Hunting is a noble calling in my country. Since the time of the czars . . ."

"The last czar has been dead for over eighty years," said the tall, powerfully built officer who appeared next to Jameson. "Allow me to introduce myself to all of you. I am Alexander Healy. This is my ship and you are here as guests of the United States Coast Guard."

He turned to face Jameson.

"Unless you can convince me otherwise, I am putting this man in restraints and in our brig until we reach port. It is a federal offense for a civilian to discharge a firearm aboard a ship of the United States Coast Guard. You, sir, are in direct violation of that order. As leader of your group, you are responsible for the actions of everyone you have brought along."

"I can't begin to say how sorry I am," said Jameson, suddenly becoming uncharacteristically polite. "If you arrest this man, you will ruin a major component of our scientific work here. He is about to attempt an important and unusual feat: to place tags on Bowhead whales while they migrate. If you lock him . . ."

"I don't care if he's discovered a cure for cancer. This man is a threat to the safety of my crew and of wildlife indigenous to the Arctic. There's also the matter of the concealed weapon."

"I did not try to hide this," said Belinsky. "I brought this magnificent gun with me in case I had the chance to use it to hunt. It was in an equipment case for ease of transport, nothing more. I had not meant to, as you say, conceal it, for dastardly purposes. I saw that creature and imagined his head mounted over my fireplace in St. Petersburg. A wonderful trophy, eh captain? He, he, ha, ha, ha."

Belinsky seemed ready to slap the captain on the back and bring out large beakers of vodka to celebrate.

"Boris, shut up!" said Jameson. "Captain, you've got to see that this unfortunate incident was an accident. I mean the gun would not have discharged carelessly had Mr. Martindale not jostled Professor Belinsky's arm. That caused the wild shot."

"And saved a bear," I said, suddenly energized by all the bullshit I was hearing. I needed to be in Jameson's good graces to continue on the project, but not at the expense of losing my self-respect. "Do you want this wild man around when we're going into the wilderness?"

Belinsky looked at me with hatred in his eyes but said nothing. Ever the loyal assistant, Zukov did the same thing.

"I can assure you," said Jameson, "that I will take full responsibility for Professor Belinsky for the short time we will be on board. You can lock his weapons up if you wish. I simply can't get by without his assistance. I mean, our work can't go on without his help."

Healy weighed his options before speaking again.

"I have your solemn promise that you will behave yourself while on this vessel?" he said to Belinsky. "No guns, no rough stuff? Just science?"

The Russian nodded.

"You have my word, captain, as a Russian patriot."

"Oh brother," I said in a stage whisper.

"Tom, you aren't being helpful," said Jane. "Why not let this play out?"

"Okay, okay," I continued ruefully. "I'll keep quiet."

"Ensign, take charge of the weapon and search Professor Belinsky's cabin for more. Also the sleeping quarters of Mr. Zukov, is it?"

He glanced at Bickford and the big man released his grip on the Russian.

"This is the only chance you will get, Dr. Jameson. One more incident and we'll return to port at your expense."

The captain turned abruptly and walked away. Ensign Zinko picked up the rifle and handed it to the other officer. The two of them walked toward the open doorway that led to our cabins.

The group dispersed to prepare for the next day's experiments. I spent the rest of the day bringing the official expedition history up to date. I waited to eat my evening meal so I could do it in peace. I really wasn't in the mood to talk to anyone.

I returned to my cabin and read for a while before heading for bed. My roommate, Salcido, was involved in an experiment. I hadn't seen him since morning. I must have fallen asleep right away because I don't remember the usual period of tossing and turning I always experience in a strange bed.

During the night, I was awakened by a strange dream. Someone was on top of me, rubbing my penis and my chest in a very determined way. I moaned with pleasure, not wanting to wake up all that quickly. A creak in the bedsprings caused me to open my eyes and realize that what I was experiencing was not a dream.

"What the hell?" I muttered, reaching over to turn on the reading lamp. Cool fingers gently gripped my hand and guided it to some very ample breasts.

"Not too fast, Mr. Thomas."

"Sue? Is that you?"

"No, silly man, it is Nadia. I can be your Russian princess. Did you ever have fantasy about sex with member of nobility?"

"Can't say that I have, but I'm not one to care about pedigrees," I laughed.

Nadia's hair brushed my face as she leaned down to kiss me. Before long, we were going at it like horny teenagers and I was enjoying every minute of it. In the middle of it all, I became vaguely aware of a whirring sound, but was too lost in my pleasure to pay much attention.

"Long live the Russian nobility," I moaned as I rolled off of her.

Just then, a camera flash went off and I heard the whirring sound again. Then, I identified it: the automated clicks of a motor drive as a camera captured shot after shot of me in one of the more compromising positions of my life.

My academic life passed before me as I contemplated the consequences of these photos being published. Scandal of any kind, even manufactured scandal, can derail a university career more quickly than anything. If you have tenure, which I did, you could be a so-so teacher or an average researcher, as long as you keep your nose clean. Of course, even tenure can't save you if you are involved in a scandal like this might become. Then it would become something we called *moral turpitude*. This definitely seemed to qualify for that designation. I had visions of Nadia and me on the Internet. While it might get both of us a few dates and proposals of marriage, it might also cost me my academic career.

Nadia Chernoff was comfortable enough with her beautiful body that she was in no hurry to put her clothes on. She got out of bed and sat on a chair. She lighted one of Salcido's cigarettes and took a long drag, smiling at me as she blew out the smoke. I scrambled out of bed and into jeans and a sweatshirt. She seemed in no hurry to run away.

"Your boss doesn't mess around with his enemies, does he?" I asked.

"You didn't like seeing perfect body?" she said, pretending to pout. "Many men would give anything to sleep with me. You got me for nothing."

"And don't think I didn't enjoy every minute of it," I said, still dazed by all that was happening. "I mean, until the camera started clicking, I was in heaven. Did you know about the photographer?"

She looked surprised that I would question her motives for coming to my cabin. She ignored my question.

"You do not like me?" she said, a big pout forming on her lips. "You like getting inside me."

"What is your boss's game? Does he intend to blackmail me?"

"I don't understand. What is blackmail? I know e-mail, but not blackmail."

"How old are you, Nadia?"

"Twenty-two."

"You have worked for Boris Belinsky for how long?"

"Six months. He is a friend of my father. We are very poor and my father gave me to Boris to save me from a very hard life."

"I thought you were a member of the nobility?"

She smiled. "A little joke to maybe convince you to want me more."

"Titles and tiaras don't mean so much in America," I said. "So where did you get your training as a research assistant?"

She looked at me blankly.

"What is tiara? What is research assistant? I assist him with more personal tasks."

"I'll bet you do. I think I get the picture here—no pun intended," I smiled. Her continuing blank stare indicated she didn't have the slightest idea of what I was talking about. "Put this on until you get back to your cabin," I said, handing her my bathrobe. "Is that where you left your clothes?"

"No. I dropped them just outside your door," she replied, throwing the cigarette out the open porthole.

I rushed to the door, glanced outside, and quickly retrieved a pile of her clothing. I threw them at her and she started dressing. I locked the door.

"Did you ever hear Belinsky say what he intended to do with the photos of us?" There was little doubt in my mind, but I wondered what she'd say.

She busied herself with straightening her hair, which had gotten disheveled in the rush to put her clothes on.

"Nadia. I need to know this. It's important."

"You know you are a very attractive man, Mr. Thomas. I could become your assistant."

She was smiling but still looked a bit blank. My questioning of her was going nowhere. I made one last try.

"I would like to know you better," I lied, moving behind her. I leaned over, kissed her neck and ran my hands up her body and cupped her breasts.

"You are a very lovely girl," I whispered. "I don't want to see you get in the middle of things you don't understand. Will you help me get those photos back?"

She jumped up, turned around, and slapped me.

"Okay. So you won't help me," I said, rubbing my cheek. "I think you'd better go. Be sure and tell your boss how good the sex was. He'll be jealous and maybe you can use that to get yourself a new blouse or some high-heeled shoes!"

She drew back to slap me again but I caught her arm just in time. I pulled her to the door. Unlocking it, I propelled her through it out into the hallway.

"Pleasant dreams, Nadia."

I slammed the door and put on a heavy parka. After a few minutes to allow time for her to depart, I left the cabin. I decided I needed a walk outside to clear my head.

Out on the main deck, I passed only a few sailors as I walked along. They nodded as I went by. Night duty required them to pay more attention to the world beyond the ship than a solitary pedestrian on board, however, so they gave me only a casual glance.

The early morning air felt good as it hit my face. My nostrils were soon filled with that wonderful sea smell so familiar to anyone who encounters it. I could taste the salt on my lips as I rounded the corner and left the protection of the ship's superstructure. The blast of Arctic air that hit me in the face made my eyes water.

I needed time to think. Belinsky was obviously getting ready to blackmail me and he had the means to do it. Even though he had set up my encounter with Nadia, the photos depicting it were probably graphic enough that no one would listen to my explanations. Another factor worried me: Jameson didn't know me very well and Belinsky was obviously an old friend. I had little doubt who he would back in any argument. For now, I decided to bide my time and see what Belinsky did with the photos.

✧ ✧ ✧

Five

All of us spent the next morning getting ready to gather ice core samples later in the day. The plan called for the ship to begin penetrating the ice pack so I went up on deck to watch the show. The vessel reached the ice pack and slammed against its edge. At first, the impact had no discernible effect. From far below in the belly of the ship, sounds indicated the ice was fighting back. It roared, screamed, and pounded against the thick hull, resisting the force with all its might.

But the ship would have none of that. After a brief pause, it backed up slightly, then rammed the ice again and again, eventually breaking through. As it did, shards of varying thickness would slough off and collect in special containers placed along the hull at the water line. After they were retrieved, these samples would be put in special refrigerators for use in future experiments.

As I worked around the others to observe and record their efforts, I didn't get the impression that they regarded me any differently than before. I mean they weren't giving me funny looks or smirking. For whatever reason, Belinsky and his two cohorts were keeping the details of their picture-taking session to themselves. In fact, I hadn't seen them all morning.

"Where's your friend Boris?" I asked Jameson when I saw him and Bickford watching the ice-battering operation.

"He's getting ready for his whale-tagging work," he replied.

"Did he say anything . . ." I was about to go against my earlier instinct.

"About what?"

"Er, a . . . when he planned to get started. I'd like to be there and observe for my record."

"Don't you read your daily schedule?" Jameson couldn't just tell me. He had to make an issue over every little thing.

"I guess I missed it."

"I don't have Carmen prepare those for her health, Tom." He glanced at his clipboard and turned several pages in a theatrical show of impatience.

"He will launch two Zodiaks at 0900 tomorrow and head to where the latest whale pods have been sighted. If—and it's a big 'if' up here in very hostile conditions—he finds the whales, he will commence his tagging operation right after that."

"Are you sure he won't just shoot them?" said Alan Hopkins who joined us on deck. "He's pretty handy with a gun."

"Alan, do I have to remind you again that you are on this expedition because I selected you," Jameson replied testily. "I can just as quickly un-select you. We need the money that Boris' experiment can bring in."

"I'm not sure I understand you, Cliff," I said. "You want to be connected to a country that let all those men die on that submarine without lifting a finger to save them? Or look how the government botched rescuing all those poor children in that school in Beslan. They're cynical and corrupt. What's more, I thought the Russian scientific establishment was broke. Their nuclear program is a mess. That whole Mir space station project was falling apart before they put it out of its misery. My God, it was like a once great Rolls Royce speeding down the highway on its wheel rims. I can't believe its marine biology projects would be any better funded."

Jameson didn't say anything for a minute or so, as Hopkins, Bickford, and I looked at him, waiting him out. He glanced around at members of the crew at work on the deck. All of them were now out of earshot. He motioned us closer.

"I wasn't going to mention this until later. I didn't think any of you had the need to know but you're senior people on the expedition, I guess. If you must know, we are going to receive a rather sizable amount of funding from the people who are backing Boris."

"I thought he had funding from the Russian government!" said Hopkins.

"Not exactly," said Jameson, his voice changing to a whisper. "Have you heard of the oligarchs?"

"That small group of men who kept Yeltsin in power. I guess he gave them exclusive control over most of the business and industry that means anything in return. They still own everything of value in the country."

Jameson nodded. Hopkins looked startled.

"What are you giving them in return, Cliff?" he said.

Jameson hesitated.

"Answer me, God damn it! You give me some straight answers!"

"Don't say anything to the others yet, but I'm allowing an emblem to be associated with the tagging."

"An emblem?" shouted Hopkins. "Isn't an American flag good enough for you?"

Jameson looked as if he would rather be anyplace else. As usual, Bickford said nothing and remained calm. I assumed he was in on everything Jameson was planning, although I did not know his precise role in the expedition.

"Is it some kind of corporate logo, is that what you're saying, Cliff?" I asked.

"The company is Siberoil, which owns a lot of the oil and gas fields in Siberia," he answered, finally. "The guy who controls that company has a Western view of the value of public relations and advertising. He thinks the company will gain prestige if its logo is on the tags Boris puts on the whales. He plans to use photos of the whale-tagging operation in a new public relations and advertising campaign."

"It's called product branding, I think," I added, ever the helpful professor.

"Does that extend to our clothing?" asked Hopkins. "What's next? Tattoos on our butts?"

"Sarcasm doesn't come naturally to you, Alan," Jameson said. "It sounds petty."

"I don't care how it sounds. I just can't believe that you'd sell us out like this. Worse, this probably isn't even legal. What did the university say?"

"I haven't mentioned it to anyone yet."

"My God, Jameson, have you lost your senses?" said Hopkins, getting more angry by the minute. "You could be arrested for fraud—and lose your position!"

Jameson laughed. "You are really naïve, Alan. I can see why your career has never gone very far. Besides, I don't think it will come to anything like my arrest." He scoffed at such a preposterous thought. It wasn't in his plan. "Especially if you keep quiet. I'm asking you both as friends to keep this to yourselves for now. Let's see how it all plays out. Let's wait and see how the project goes. If it's as successful as I think it will be, no one will care where the money came from."

"How much money are we talking about?" I asked.

"A million."

Hopkins seemed beside himself. He pounded the ship's railing with his hand and began pacing back and forth. "God, Cliff," he said. "When you sell out, you don't do it for peanuts. Do you really believe that the oligarch guy will be satisfied with a few emblems on whales? I never took you for someone with even an ounce of naiveté. This whole thing is really stupid."

"I'll ignore that insult, Alan, because I have a proposition for you. It's more important than my wounded pride. I am prepared to pay the two of you $30,000 each to keep quiet about what I just told you."

"I don't take kindly to bribes, Cliff," said Hopkins.

"Okay then, $50,000. That will go a long way toward paying for Becky's operation."

Hopkins' look of disdain slowly faded from his face.

"Alan's little girl needs a bone marrow transplant," explained Jameson. "Our insurance policy at the institute won't quite cover it all."

"You bastard," said Hopkins, tearfully. "You're a son of a bitch for even mentioning that." Then he walked away.

Jameson shrugged and turned to me with a smirk beginning to form on his mouth. Bickford seemed uncomfortable with the turn the conversation had taken.

"I doubt we'll need to worry about Alan's loyalty again," continued Jameson. "What about you, Tom? Have you got a price?"

I shook my head. The money didn't tempt me, but being on the inside did. I wouldn't compromise my ethics for money, but I would keep quiet and play along just so I would know what was going on. Call it the reporter's curse: the willingness to do almost anything to get the story. I liked being in a position of observing what would happen from the sidelines without my direct involvement. I wanted to remain neutral for now.

"You don't know me very well, Cliff. How do you know you can trust me?"

"When someone has been managing people for as long as I have, you get so you can read people fast. I hired you because I trust your abilities and your experience. I'm making this offer now because I trust your discretion."

"Fair enough. Let's do it this way. I come from a wealthy family so I don't need the money," I lied. "In return for my silence, you agree to place $50,000 in the scholarship account of my department. You also agree to give me unlimited access to all parts of this project. I need that to do my job anyway. But I also want to know everything you do—I mean all the decisions."

He looked at Bickford for only a second, as if seeking his approval. The big man did not make a move but possibly communicated something in his eyes because Jameson was decisive when he replied.

"Done," he said, looking out across the ice pack for a moment. "What will you do with the information?"

"A book, or article. I'm not sure. I find all of this fascinating. I won't publish a thing without your permission."

"Okay. That sounds fair enough."

I expected Jameson to demand that I sign something agreeing to those conditions, but he didn't ask.

"One other thing, Cliff. Keep Belinsky and his people away from me. I don't want to be hassled by them anymore."

"You've been hassled already?" he said, looking puzzled. His expression indicated that he knew nothing about the blackmail scheme.

"I'll tell you about it sometime. Just call them off."

"That'll be my job," said Bickford. "I'll keep 'em in line."

I nodded gratefully.

"So that's taken care of," said Jameson. "Let's get back inside. I don't know about you, but I'm freezing."

"I'm going to stay out a bit longer," I said, then changed the subject abruptly. "This view is really something."

The three of us shook hands and Jameson walked away. Bickford lingered for a moment. "I am your friend here, Tom, but if you interfere with me, I will have to go around you—or through you."

He spoke in a friendly way, but I had no doubt that fulfilling his mission, whatever it was, would come before establishing any friendship with me.

He disappeared into the same door Jameson had used. As I got near the bow, Alan Hopkins rejoined me.

"Sorry about your little girl," I said. "Cliff is really putting the screws to you."

"It isn't the first time. The phrase 'blind ambition' could have been coined for him."

He gazed out at the expanse of ice and was quiet for a moment.

"You know, countries have dreamed of sending ships from Europe to Asia all across the top of the world," he said. "Lots of explorers have given up their lives to find this Arctic short-cut. The few who made any headway at all were treated like heroes when they got back, like Lindbergh or the astronauts."

"Yeah, I guess so," I said. "But all I remember reading is failure after failure. I mean this whole way is crisscrossed with a maze of channels that are so frozen, nothing gets through."

"*That*, Tom, is the key to it all: ice. Nothing could move it except ice breakers and that has always been impractical for the continual flow of transport shipping companies need."

"And navies?" I asked.

"Navies, right. There is a strong military aspect to this, and I suspect that is where those Russian bastards come in. They're trying to make sure that any passage over the top of the world is open to them—or controlled by them."

"I doubt the U.S. Government would ever permit that," I said.

"If it realizes what is going on. We are such a behemoth we don't always react to things quickly enough. I expect that is why Paul Bickford is aboard. He looks like a spook of some kind—CIA, Army Special Forces, or something even more hush hush. You see how Cliff defers to him?"

"Yeah, I guess you're right," I replied. "He doesn't reveal much. I do trust him, though. Somehow, I'm glad he's along. But there is still the matter of the ice. Look out there. It doesn't seem to be any less thick than before." I gestured at the expanse of ice stretching in all directions. "Not this year, certainly. But remember reports last year of that tourist ship whose passengers discovered an ice-free patch of water near the North Pole. They said it was a mile wide. Global warming?"

"Precisely," said Alan. "It's no accident that the tourists were on a Russian icebreaker. Among them was an American scientist from Harvard. He told me the ice, which had been 6 to 9 feet thick on a visit several years before, was so thin that sunlight could penetrate it and plankton even grew under it. Am I sounding too professorial here? Stop me if I am."

"No, really. I am interested."

"Okay, but don't say I didn't warn you," he continued. "Because of global warming, the average surface temperatures are up about one degree over the last century. That's really fast when you look back at all the years the earth's existed."

"What you are saying fits in well with what we know are Russian friends have been up to," I said. "They want any and all data on ice to pass along to their government for future use."

"I'd say it's crucial to them," said Alan. "This is their backyard and they aim to beat us to it, no matter what."

I thought about this for a moment as I looked out as the ship rammed the ice again. This time the bow made it through effortlessly, turning the shards into tiny pellets as the ship made contact.

"Does Jameson know all of this?" I asked.

"He's a smart man. He's got to have figured it out."

"But maybe he's too blinded by his own ambition to care all that much."

"Maybe so," said Alan, shaking his head and walking away.

As I neared the doorway, I caught a glimpse of Belinsky's stooge, Dimitri Zukov, watching me from above. When he saw me recognize him, he didn't try to hide. He gave me a sharp salute and hoisted a small flask in a mock toast.

"*Za zdorovie,*" he yelled from his perch.

I ignored him and hurried into the dark corridor, hoping I had done the right thing about Jameson and the money. I remembered Bickford's remark about keeping the Russians in line. It was comforting to have him watching my back.

✧ ✧ ✧

Six

The following morning, seven of us set out in a Coast Guard tender to look for whales. Jameson had obviously made extensive arrangements for Belinsky's tagging project with the captain, he just hadn't bothered to tell the rest of us about it.

The sun was already high above the horizon as we clambered down the ladder to the boat, heaving on the churning water. The strong rays of light felt good as they touched my feet, but they did little to ward off the cold.

"This cold in August, I'd hate to be here in January," said Jane, waiting at my side for her turn.

I nodded and pulled my parka hood up a bit higher on my head. Below we could see the top of Jameson's head as he reached the boat. He looked up and motioned for the next person to join him. Hopkins, Peters, and Szabo quickly went over the side.

"Ladies first," I laughed, reaching for her arm to steady her as she stepped up and over the side. Soon she disappeared. As I waited for my turn, I felt two arms squeeze me and lift me up so that my legs flailed helplessly.

"Ah ha! Even tough guys like you can't keep their feet on the ground!"

Belinsky laughed at his joke and released me abruptly. As I dropped to the deck, it was all I could do to keep from falling flat.

"He, he, ha, ha, ha!"

He really enjoyed rousting me. He gestured for me to go next. As I did, he grabbed my arm as I prepared to descend.

"Watch your Yankee ass, my new friend," he hissed. "I would not desire that any unforeseen problem would be encountered by you on the open ocean."

"Interesting sentence structure," I said, smiling sweetly.

Belinsky let go and gave me a shove that might have sent me in a free fall had I not been holding on tightly. I climbed down to the smaller boat quickly. Belinsky and his sidekick, Zukov, followed. I did not see my would-be lover Miss Chernoff.

We all sat down on the wooden seats of the tender and Jameson signaled the helmsman to proceed. As we left the side of the ship I noticed that we were pulling two Zodiaks, small inflatable boats with outboard motors I had seen in operation before. They were very fast and maneuverable. From our briefing of last night, I knew that while the Russians would use one of the Zodiaks to come alongside and actually tag the whales, the rest of us would take turns observing the action from the other.

The prospect of speeding along next to a fast-moving whale of immense size was both exhilarating and frightening. Combine that with how the Russians felt about me and you have someone who felt less than secure. I couldn't get rid of the lump in my throat. In fact, the remains of my breakfast kept coming up to lodge in a little ball in the back of my throat. Why hadn't I selected oatmeal and toast instead of pancakes, bacon, and eggs over easy?

"The reports this morning were of a pod of whales about 10 kilometers south of our position," said Jameson as he gestured at a chart he was attempting to spread out on a flat space in the middle of the boat. The wind kept catching it and causing it to flutter like a flag. Finally, he gave up, folded it, and put it away.

"Take my word for it," he said, shaking his head.

We all sat facing each other in silence because the roar of the engine and the slap of the boat on the agitated water made it difficult to do otherwise. Most everyone stared at their feet. Belinsky and Zukov had another focal point. They glared at me whenever I caught their eyes. I tried to ignore them, pretending to whisper funny asides to Jane next to me. I doubt if she heard me, but she played along, laughing at intervals and elbowing me in the side.

The sun went behind a particularly menacing mass of dark clouds when we reached our apparent rendezvous point with the whales. We scanned the horizon in all directions. For the first time in several days, we were away from the pack ice, although chunks of it floated by intermittently.

Belinsky and Zukov stood up and took off their parkas, revealing wetsuits. They began to unpack equipment from large duffel bags stowed in the rear of the boat and lift it into one of the Zodiaks. They soon climbed aboard, untied the vessel, and fired up the engine. After a puff of smoke, the engine chugged alive and Zukov maneuvered the small boat away.

"Tom," said Jameson. "Let's go first, shall we? I need you to see this for your permanent history. You join us, Derek. Maybe you will learn something."

We followed his lead and stepped toward the second Zodiak, just as Belinsky and Zukov were pulling away. Because the tender had stopped, the sea around us became considerably calmer. I had put on one of the Coast Guard Mustang suits to keep out the cold. With it and my parka, I felt warm.

Jameson stepped aboard the other Zodiak and Peters and I followed. Luckily, the water was less choppy than before and I had no trouble sliding into place. Jameson started the outboard engine and we quickly pulled away from the tender.

I looked around for the Russians in time to see their Zodiak nearly out of sight to the southwest. Jameson gunned the engine in an attempt to overtake them. The plan called for us to cruise slightly behind and to the left of their wake. From that position we would be able to observe their work without interfering with it.

Both Belinsky and Zukov concentrated on their tagging. The latter steered while the former scanned the blue gray waters for whales. In 20 minutes Belinsky raised his arm and held up four fingers. We were apparently approaching a pod of four Bowhead whales.

At first I saw nothing but frothy water. Looking harder I could barely make out what looked to be a long, gray log. Then the log let out a spout of water. I pointed toward it and smiled at Jameson. He gave me a thumbs-up sign and slowed the engine.

"How big, would you say?"

"Maybe 45 feet long and 75 tons. A medium-sized one."

Zukov slowed the small boat as Belinsky rummaged around in the gear he had taken aboard. Soon, he got out a crossbow and hoisted it to his shoulder.

"What's he doing?" I yelled. "He's not going to shoot it!"

"Relax, Tom," said Jameson. "That's how he attaches the tag. Boris may be many things, but he's a committed scientist above all else."

"Tell that to the polar bear he wanted to kill yesterday."

"That was Boris Belinsky, the hunter. This is Boris Belinsky, the whale researcher. If he had been studying polar bears, he would have acted differently."

"If you say so," I replied, not really wanting to hear anything good about someone I really disliked.

Belinsky aimed and a small dark object shot through the air and landed on the back of the whale. It apparently attached itself because he raised his arm in a victory salute before rearming the crossbow for his next encounter. Zukov steered the small boat near the next whale, which seemed to me to be slightly smaller. Once again, Belinsky raised the crossbow and fired. This time, however, the tag did not attach and slid uselessly into the water. The Russian did not flinch, however. He merely reloaded his weapon and fired again. This time the tag stayed where it was supposed to be.

Belinsky sat down to rest and Zukov steered the small craft away from the whales. Jameson turned our boat around as well and slowed the motor to an idle.

"He put the tag on the top layer of blubber on the whale's back," explained Jameson. "The tag is really a tiny radio transmitter to allow us to track these guys and find out where they go once they leave here. You know they go south through the Bering Strait and a lot of them spend the winter in the Chukchi Sea in Russian waters. That's pretty much ice free. So it isn't so farfetched to have a Russian doing the tagging."

"Sure, as long as we can pick up the frequencies," I said.

Jameson's face fell and he frowned, as if he hadn't thought to ask about that rather crucial detail. "Of course, of course." He stared at the Russians in the other boat. "I've already arranged it."

The look on his face told me he hadn't done anything of the kind.

"Cliff, that would seem elemental. Why be involved if you can't use the data? Besides, do the Russians even have the ability to track anything via satellite? I mean the whole country's being held together by chewing gum and bailing wire, right?"

I had struck a sore spot, but Jameson would never admit that he had overlooked such a vital detail.

"Tom. Just stick to your note taking," he said huffily, pulling rank as he usually did in tight situations. "Last time I checked, *I* was the leader of this expedition. *You* work for me. You need to follow my directions and stay within your job parameters."

I started to ask him where the photographer was who would be recording Belinsky's exploits for the Russian ad campaign, but he cut me off with a wave.

I was appalled that Jameson could be so blind to the implications of taking money from the Russians. Not only was he allowing Belinsky free rein over a scientific project he was directing, he might not even be able to have access to the data, let alone have the wherewithal to receive it.

Because Jameson was stubborn and one of those people who was convinced that he was always right, I didn't reply. I sat down next to Derek in the boat as it bobbed up and down in the choppy water. He was watching Belinsky and Zukov in the distance as they prepared for their next tagging operation.

I could see the whales beyond their boat, apparently congregating to feed. They seemed undeterred by the earlier tagging operation. I couldn't make them out very well. About all I saw was a swirl of gray log look-alikes occasionally spouting and diving.

After he finished his preparatory work, Belinsky picked up his two-way radio.

"Why not . . . big shot . . . join . . ." his static-filled voice blasted out.

Jameson picked up his radio to reply. "Boris. I did not read you. Over. What was your message?"

More static ensued.

"Must be Russian equipment," I said nastily.

Jameson glared at me and stood up, shrugging his shoulders and holding his hands palms up. Then he pointed to his ears and shook his head.

Belinsky motioned for us to approach his boat and Jameson did so, starting the engine for the short trip. We sped to the other Zodiak in minutes and we soon were bobbing up and down alongside.

"Now then, Boris. What were you saying?"

Belinsky smiled broadly and pointed at Peters and me. "I said we'd like to take this big-shot writer and pretty young man with us so they could write good report. From here he could see how good we are. From here he could see how strong and brave are Russian men."

Saying that, he beat on his puffed up chest several times.

"I think that's a marvelous idea," said Jameson.

"No way, Cliff. I'm not going anywhere near that maniac." I leaned in closer. "He doesn't like me. I don't trust either of them."

Derek Peters seemed equally apprehensive.

Jameson shook his head.

"Tom, don't be dramatic. You know the world is not divided into people who like and dislike Tom Martindale. Everything does not revolve around you. Get your notebook and prepare to step into their boat. You'll have a great time. It'll improve your reporting. You're not afraid, are you?"

"Of course not!" I replied quickly. Peters shook his head a bit more hesitantly. I weighed the consequences of not going and decided I didn't have much of a choice. At least Peters and I could stick together. I stood up and got ready to climb aboard the other boat. Zukov was ready to help us across as we waited for the bobbing motion of the two vessels to get in sync. After several minutes, that moment came and I leaped across the narrow gap. Peters quickly followed. The boats were low enough to the water that I didn't fear falling in. Zukov was smiling so much that I saw for the first time that he had a tooth missing.

"Velcome, *Amerikan*," he said without much sincerity.

I sat down and watched as Jameson opened the throttle and sped away. I was nervous, although part of me thought that there was little these guys could do to me out in the open, with Jameson nearby and the others not too far away in the tender.

That was before the fog moved in.

I noticed it soon after Belinsky revved up the engine and we sailed off toward the whale pod. The wall of vapor was behind the area where the giant creatures were feeding so it didn't bother me. I concentrated on the action as Belinsky and Zukov changed places.

Belinsky took hold of the crossbow and attached the tag to the end. He looked out at one of the whales and aimed for its back. He drew and pulled the trigger and the small object flew through the air and penetrated the tough skin.

"Good *deel!*" yelled Zukov from behind me.

What they were doing was impressive. While I had reservations about these men as decent human beings, they did know their business. The whale-tagging operation was going very well.

"You impressed?" shouted Belinsky. "You think better of Russians now?"

I nodded and gave him a thumbs-up sign.

He continued the tagging process for about half an hour and five more whales. I became so engrossed in the operation that I didn't notice that I could no longer see either Jameson or the others in the Coast Guard boat. I also missed the onslaught of the, by now, fast-moving fogbank.

Within seconds, all I could see was the immediate area. I noted the fog and its clammy aura in my journal. It suddenly seemed colder and I shivered. When I looked up, both men were looking at Peters and me with strange expressions on their faces.

"You read popular American novels?" asked Belinsky.

"Sure, a lot of them. Why?"

"Do you know that book *Deliverance* and what happened to that one guy when those bad guys with guns surprised them in camp?"

"Yeah, so what?"

I didn't like the turn this conversation was taking.

"Dimitri."

I turned around to see Zukov unzipping his wetsuit and pulling it off. Before I could comprehend what was happening, Belinsky had pulled my arms in front of me and bound them with rope. Before I knew it I was face down and lying across a strut in the middle of the boat. I struggled but could not free myself.

I watched Zukov grab Peters, throw him down on the deck, and put his knee on his neck in a way that he could not breathe. Before long, Zukov was pulling off the outer shell of the young man's Mustang Suit first, then his underpants.

"Now you will feel the might of Russian manhood," yelled Belinsky. I caught a glimpse of his erect penis as he aimed for Peters. His aim was off, however, because of the rocking of the boat. I struggled to get free but could not move. Peters looked as if he had fainted.

". . . be serious . . . the others . . . see you," I gasped, to little avail.

"*Amerikansi* is pretty as young girl," said Zukov from behind Derek. "Must learn to just be relaxing and enjoying it."

"Hello, the Zodiak!"

The voice came out of the fog with a suddenness that startled all four of us. In an instant, Zukov pulled away from Derek Peters and Belinsky shoved me onto the bottom of the boat while he simultaneously untied my wrists. He pretended to help me to my feet but I pushed him away and he landed on his back hitting one of the ribs on the boat bottom.

By this time, the boat was rocking back and forth violently and this motion caught Zukov off balance. He was also having trouble with his zipper, one of those outsized ones with particularly jagged teeth. I was happy to help him out, easily grabbing the tab and pulling it up—fast. It was his bad luck that his penis was still in enough of an erect state that it got caught. He cried out as blood began trickling down his leg. I completed my task and brought the zipper all the way to the top, blood or no blood. I helped Peters pull up his pants and wrapped a parka around his shivering body.

The *Polar Sea* glided to within several hundred yards of us and dropped anchor. I waved my arms vigorously to make sure they had seen us from the ship. Its unexpected arrival had saved Derek from injury and a humiliation I didn't want to contemplate.

Soon, the gangway was lowered and I heard the sputter of engines behind us. Both the larger tender and Jameson's Zodiak soon moved next to us.

"We need to get Derek off this thing!" I yelled to Jameson. "Now!"

The Russians exchanged uneasy glances, then busied themselves picking up and stowing their gear. It was hard for Zukov to do much, because he was holding his groin with both hands.

"A bit seasick, Tom," laughed Jameson. "Not as much of a sailor as you thought you were, eh?"

"You might say that," I replied.

"How was it?" he yelled.

"Very exhilarating—so much so that I almost got tagged myself." I smiled at the Russians and they both looked away.

"Boris," Jameson shouted. "Why don't you go first to the gangway? We'll wait our turn."

The Russian nodded and Zukov started the engine and steered the small boat accordingly. Belinsky stepped next to me and pretended to be helping Peters and me get ready to disembark. He really wanted to whisper nasty things in my ear.

"You will be saying nothing of this!" he hissed. "As you can tell, we are very determined men. Do not get in the way, *Amerikanski*. We will not hesitate to do whatever it takes to achieve our goals."

"Why pick on Derek? He has done nothing to you."

"We can close eyes and pretend he is pretty girl. He, he, ha, ha, ha!

I let that subject drop.

"Why me, Boris? Why go after me?"

"You insulted honor of Russian nation."

"I did what? I don't understand. You mean when I kept you from killing that bear the other day?"

He nodded slightly, his eyes burning with hatred.

"You also insulted the honor of Russian *Spetsnaz* forces. I am officer in that proud organization. We do not take kindly to those who dishonor us."

"What kind of forces? I have no idea what you're talking about. How can I dishonor something I know nothing about? You seem to forget where you are. You are surrounded by Americans on an American ship."

My anger and frustration were overcoming my fear and humiliation. The presence of thousands of tons of ship stiffened my backbone as well.

"We have a long reach, Mr. Hot Shot *Amerikanski*. We never forget our true enemies," he said.

"As opposed to your false ones?" I answered sarcastically.

"Do not mock me. You do so at your peril. We know things about you I doubt you'd want the world to hear."

Belinsky's face suddenly changed into a wide smile, as if I had told him a joke.

"What things?"

"Your rape of a defenseless Russian girl, for one thing."

"Now that is a stretch, even for you," I replied.

I continued my bluff. "You're talking in real circles here. What you are saying makes no sense."

I had no choice but to play dumb in a bid for time to figure out what to do. I pressed on with my deer-in-the-headlights stance.

"You make light of this, professor, but we both know that certain photographs of this unfortunate deed will be terribly embarrassing to you if they become known. And there are other problems we might cast the light of day on."

"This just gets more bizarre by the minute, Boris," I said.

The Zodiak bumped gently into the small platform at the foot of the gangway, saving me from another confrontation with the Russians.

I helped Peters out, then sprang from the boat even before the tether was attached.

"Careful, sir," said the young seaman standing on the platform.

The water was lapping at the metal, at times overflowing it, at other times running off. A shift of even any inch would have sent me down. I wondered how deep the ocean was at this point.

Fortunately, the two vessels were in sync as they heaved in the choppy water so I spanned the gap safely. I nodded at the seaman and climbed quickly up the gangway. Susan was waiting for me at the top.

"How did it go?"

"Not all that great."

"No whales? I thought I saw some as we sailed up."

"Not that. There were plenty of them. The Russians tagged five or six of them."

"What was the problem, then?"

I pulled her into a doorway so no one else could hear us.

"Belinsky knows all about my little problem."

She looked shocked.

"Cut the act, Susan! How do you think he would come upon that juicy bit of information?"

"I can't imagine. I didn't tell . . ."

"I know you didn't tell *him* Susan. But you told your bastard of a boyfriend, Szabo. The same guy who'd rather sleep with *his* boyfriend than dive into the sack with you!"

She was crying by now, cascades of water pouring from her eyes, body-jerking sobs beginning to convulse her shoulders. Throughout our long friendship—including our brief time as lovers—Susan always had the ability to anger and confound me more than any person I had ever met.

"This crying stuff," I said. "It doesn't work with me now. You have done more to hurt me in the years I've known you than anyone else."

"I didn't mean to, Tom. You have to believe me!"

I leaned in so close to her our noses were almost touching.

"I wouldn't believe you if you said we were in the middle of the Arctic on a Coast Guard ship!"

"Is there a problem here?" said a deep voice suddenly. "Is this man bothering you?"

Someone had come out behind us from below, a tall muscular black seaman who could probably handle himself in a fight a lot better than I could. I stepped back, my arms outstretched and hands turned up, as if I were dropping a weapon.

"Butt out, Seaman . . ." I peered at his nametag, "Mortimer. The lady and I are old friends. This doesn't concern you. We were having a friendly discussion about . . ."

"Our rival theories of scientific research," Susan broke in.

"You're sure you are all right, ma'am?" He looked at her.

"Yes, Seaman Mortimer, very all right. But I thank you for your concern."

She smiled at the young man and he touched his cap before walking around us onto the main deck.

"This is madness," I said. "You make me crazy, that's what it is. Not crazy like crazy in love, but crazy like in how can you be so blind to life. Just tell your boyfriend to keep his comments about me to himself."

"You haven't really told me what happened, Tom. Maybe I can help."

"Help! Your kind of help I don't need! I'll handle this. I'm not sure how, but I'll handle it."

I stormed away without waiting for her reply. Knowing her, she would just stand there sobbing and I'd already seen enough of that particular act. My decision to join this expedition for the challenge and adventure of several months in the Arctic was rapidly turning into a nightmare. As I climbed down the metal steps to the next deck, Ben Aniak was coming up.

"Hey man, who's a laughingstock? I heard you talking to that Foster chick."

"It's really complicated, Ben."

"Too complicated for a dumb Eskimo to understand. Is that what you're saying?"

What was causing me to alienate everyone I encountered today? Was it something in the water or the stars?

"You said it, Ben, not me. But it's not that. I mean too complicated for me to sort out for myself, let alone try to explain to someone else."

"Yeah, I guess I see."

"So how is your work going, Ben? There hasn't been anybody to be a liaison with, has there?"

"No, not yet. I've been working on my notes for a presentation later, when we get to Herschel Island."

"What about the booze? You throw it overboard?"

Now I was the one dropping hints of blackmail. I'd keep quiet about the liquor if he'd keep quiet about what he obviously overheard.

"Okay, man. I hear you. I'll keep your shit to myself. Agreed?"

"Agreed," I answered, not wanting to know precisely what he thought my "shit" was.

"Later," he said, walking up the stairs.

Paul Bickford was waiting for me on deck as I got ready to duck below.

"I saw some of what happened, but I'd like a full report," he said, "when you've got a minute."

"Sure, right. Yeah. Just let me change my clothes."

He nodded and was gone. As I climbed down the stairs and neared my cabin, I felt the presence of someone behind me.

"What do you want?" I said to Nadia. "I've had enough of you and your friends to last a lifetime!"

She moved closer and opened her parka.

"Get some clothes on, Nadia! I thought we'd finished with this the other night!"

"This is for me and you, not Belinsky," she said softly. "I like you. I like sex we have together. Very nifty sex. You are kind man. More kind to me than I ever know."

"Is that a line out of your *Spetsnaz* playbook?"

I took her gently by the shoulders and turned her around. Someone else was standing in the corridor, in the shadows away from the light.

"Sir. I'll have to ask you to leave the young lady alone."

The ubiquitous Seaman Mortimer stood there, his mouth agape as he took in Nadia's naked body through the gap in her parka. I shook my head in disbelief.

"You have a way of showing up where you're not needed or wanted," I said.

"I'm just trying to get to my cabin, if you'll get out of my way." I ducked inside the door quickly.

This was spiraling out of control and I didn't like the feeling. The threats and counterthreats were making me physically sick. This was not the way I lived my life. I ran into the tiny bathroom and splashed cold water on my face.

✧ ✧ ✧

Seven

expected to toss and turn all night after all that had happened. But exhaustion set in and I slept so soundly that I
didn't hear Danny Salcido when he came into the cabin and
went to bed. He was standing by the open porthole smoking a
cigarette when I woke up. It took me a minute to figure out
where I was.

"Good morning. What time is it?"

"Quarter to seven."

I sat up on the side of the bed, just barely missing the ceiling above me. I ran my hand over my face.

"I really died. I didn't hear you come in."

"I didn't make it to our little home until after midnight. You
were sawing logs so I was careful not to wake you. I hear you
had some excitement."

"What did you hear?"

Had Belinsky blabbed after all? Was my embarrassment
common knowledge on the ship?

"That you guys found plenty of whales to tag. Did something else happen? Did I miss something?"

"Yeah, it sure did, but I'll fill you in later, just before I bring the roof down."

He was looking perplexed. I got up and started toward the bathroom.

"You finished in here?"

He nodded.

"What the hell happened out there?"

I ignored him.

"What time's the morning meeting?"

"0800."

"You've got that seafarin' lingo down pretty good. I'll see you there."

The shower felt good on my worn and battered body, even though the water was only lukewarm.

✧ ✧ ✧

If the events of the past few days had taught me anything it was that I could no longer be someone who worried about what people thought of me. Like a politician who worked the room to win the affection of everyone in it, I used to aim to please each person I encountered, whether they be students in a classroom or guests at a party. Now I had changed. It wasn't that I didn't care about my reputation; I had just decided that I couldn't worry about it every waking moment.

I walked into the wardroom with that change in my *modus operandi* in mind. I could look everyone in the room in the eye without hesitation. If they had heard something negative about me, it was in their problem, not mine.

I got coffee and a sweet roll and sat down next to Jane about halfway down the table. Susan was sitting with Szabo and Peters and none looked at me. The Russians, minus the lovely Nadia, had their heads together and were arguing heatedly in their native language at the far end. Aniak and Salcido were sitting together across from us, and Salcido raised his coffee cup in a mock toast. Paul Bickford was not there.

Cliff Jameson entered the room with a flourish, trailed by Hopkins and Carmen Ames, his secretary. I imagine that the chief swept into all rooms this way, so that heads would turn even if he was walking into his own living room. This day, the flourish came from the long parka he wore draped over his shoulders and, inexplicably, dark glasses.

"Hey man, dig those shades," said Salcido.

"Shut up, Danny," muttered Jameson as he reached a point opposite me and snapped his fingers. Carmen dutifully began to lay out binders and pieces of paper for her boss's presentation.

"Good morning, people."

The din of conversation continued a bit longer than Jameson wanted it to.

"People, people. Time is wasting. We need to get started."

The room gradually quieted.

"Thank you. As you know, our work has been going on for several days now. With the superb cooperation of the U.S. Coast Guard and the weather, we are right on schedule. The ice core samples have been gathered from various points along the ice pack. The whale-tagging work began yesterday and will continue for two more days. This means that we will be ready to set up our permanent encampment on Herschel Island by next Monday."

The people at the table smiled and nodded to one another, happy to be getting off the ship and living and working out-of-doors.

"People, people. Your attention again, please. Thank you. This time schedule coincides with the Coast Guard's need to drop us off and embark on their regular ice patrol along the Alaska coast, through the Bering Strait and back again. The ship will be back to pick us up in three weeks. That will be September 21, I believe. Right, Carmen?"

His secretary nodded and held up a calendar to show him the date.

"Right. Yes. Good. Some housekeeping details before I take your questions. As you know from Tom's presentation, Herschel Island is a reasonably habitable place: tolerable temperatures, existing buildings, the knowledge that people have lived there for long periods before. The last expedition to work there left two years ago. This may mean that we have a bit of a mess to clean up. The Coast Guard is prepared to off-load our supplies once we reach the island. Food, supplies, and lab equipment—I think I've thought of everything. The toilets and water system are working. It'll be up to us to open it all up and set it all up. The sooner we do this, the sooner we can get to work. I've got the duty rosters."

He nodded to Carmen who started passing around the appropriate pages.

"Okay. Now I'll turn to questions, although I doubt you'll have many."

Ever the believer in his own infallibility, Jameson really doubted that he had missed anything. I was happy to puncture that balloon.

"What about communication?"

"Oh yes, Tom. Good question. Danny, please fill us in."

This was the first time I'd seen my roommate without a cigarette in his mouth.

"Thanks, Dr. Jameson. All right, you guys, listen up! We've got top-of-the-line communications, from your conventional shortwave radio to the best cell phones money can buy. For extreme emergencies, we've got a satellite telephone."

There were murmurs of approval around the room causing Jameson to step forward. "Don't think you can use any of this stuff for idle chitchat, especially the satellite phone. It costs too much for us to use it for anything but official business. I wanted to have it in case we needed to reach the outside world. That's all. No calls to girlfriends or loved ones. I don't have the budget for high telephone bills.

"How about e-mail, Cliff?" asked Jane.

He nodded and again deferred to Salcido.

"Yeah, right. We have arranged to have the server on the ship handle your e-mails, as long as it stays within several hundred meters of us. And here's the good news: no charge to you or the expedition."

Again murmurs of approval drifted around the table.

"Those of you with your own laptops can log on as always except you'll need to set up new addresses using 'Polar Sea—no space—dot gov '. If you don't have your own units, I will set up a spare computer in a central location for that purpose. You can use it for two hours before and after meal times. Most likely I'll set that up in our dining hall. Another thing: back up all your data from your experiments on disks, then give the disks to me. I'm compiling a central control area for our research results, most likely a locked filing cabinet. Do that twice a week or anytime you finish counting up results."

He looked at Jameson and shrugged.

"That's all I have, chief."

"I'll have the only key to that cabinet," said Jameson as he looked around and waited for more questions.

"I guess we can . . ."

"I have a question," I said.

All eyes turned toward me.

"When will our Russian friends be leaving us?"

Jameson glanced at the far end of the table where the Russians sat motionless. He cleared his throat before replying, as if the words were hard to get out.

"Dr. Belinsky and his two co-workers . . . By the way, Boris, where is your lovely assistant, Miss Chernoff, this morning?"

"She was not in her cabin," he said. "I think she went for a walk on the deck."

"Very well. Please fill her in on all of this."

The Russian nodded.

"As I was saying, Dr. Belinsky and his people have kindly consented to join us on Herschel Island. They will be able to compile their data which they have agreed to share with us. They will also assist us in our own research endeavors."

"Is it proper to share proprietary data with security implications—I mean ice conditions—with representatives of another country?" I interrupted. "Let's face it. Their whole operation is a sham! For one thing, if this is PR for this Russian company, where's the photographer who is supposed to be recording the whale tagging? This whole thing is a subterfuge!"

"I resent the slur on our great nation," said Belinsky, his face reddening. On cue, Zukov resented it too and scowled accordingly. "I also resent this as a scientist. How dare you cast doubt on our motives and our work!"

My blood was boiling and I sprang to my feet. "How dare *you* try to compromise me by staging little incidents that try to ruin my reputation. I'm putting you on notice now in front of everyone in this expedition that I won't stand for it. And all of the rest of you." I paused and encompassed them all with a broad gesture. "You'll all know who to go after if anything happens to me."

At this moment, the door opened and Captain Healy walked in, followed by Ensign Zinko wearing a sidearm. I could see Paul Bickford standing in the passageway, just outside the door.

"I'm afraid I have some bad news for you, Dr. Jameson," he said. "One of your expedition members has been found dead in the fantail."

The looks around the table ranged from horror to puzzlement. Who was missing? We all counted heads and all the Americans were sitting around the table.

"Who did you find?" asked Jameson at last.

"Miss Nadia Chernoff."

Belinsky looked stricken. Although he didn't cry, he was clenching his jaw tightly to keep from doing so.

"I don't understand, captain," said Jameson. "Did she have an accident? I mean, fall and hit her head? Pass out? She was a young woman. I'm sure she didn't die of natural causes."

"I'm afraid it was murder. This was around her neck. Ensign."

At his signal, Zinko held up a long orange and black scarf with the letters "OU" on each end.

"Who on this voyage is representing Oregon University?"

No one said anything, but all eyes in the room turned toward me.

✧ ✧ ✧

Eight

"You can't be serious!" I said, as I glanced around the room at the grim faces looking back at me. "Why would I kill Nadia Chernoff? What motive would I have? I hardly knew her!"

Zinko started walking toward me, sidearm and all. I stood up.

"Now wait a minute! Stop right there! You are jumping to conclusions that are just plain wrong!"

As everyone remained mute, I began to wonder what life would be like in the brig. Did it have a porthole? Would they push bread and water through slot in the door once a day? Would I get seasick? Funny what your mind does as it contemplates total calamity.

"Cliff, are you just going to sit there?"

Jameson shifted uncomfortably in his seat. Belinsky seemed lost in his grief. Zukov got to his feet and walked toward the table holding the coffee urn, as if planning to pour himself another cup. In a flash, he wheeled around and threw the steaming coffee at me, then grabbed me by the throat.

"*Amerikan* dawg," he shouted.

Although Zinko and Salcido pulled him off me quickly, it took me several minutes to catch my breath. Another second and he might have damaged my larynx permanently. I kept coughing for a long time and when I tried to speak, it sounded raspy and unintelligible.

"Here is your killer, captain," I croaked, before going into a spasm of coughing. "This man is a lunatic! He has already attacked me physically several times and threatened my life. He's the one you should be arresting, not me!"

Healy signaled for Zinko to take Zukov out of the room and he did so, the Russian struggling violently until the ensign displayed a pair of handcuffs. I suppose they were originally meant for me.

Zukov's move had one positive effect. It shocked the others out of their collective stupor. Bickford stepped into the room and stood across from where I was standing.

"Captain Healy, Tom Martindale would never do what you're accusing him of doing," said Jane.

"Not in a million years," added Alan Hopkins.

"This guy is a righteous dude," said Salcido.

"You're wrong about this, sir, just plain wrong," said Ben Aniak.

I smiled weakly and nodded my gratitude at the four of them. I wanted to say something, but my throat was throbbing.

"What evidence do you have against Professor Martindale," said Jameson. "The scarf could well have been planted. How dumb do you think he is? I mean, to kill someone with such an easily identifiable item of clothing and leave it behind? Really, captain, that strikes me as preposterous!"

Jameson was rising to the occasion by jumping on his academic high horse to challenge this mere mortal of a Coast Guard officer.

"I had intended to save the explanation of evidence for a formal hearing later in the day," said the captain. "Mr. Zukov's outburst does make me wonder if I have the right man."

He turned to me. "Would you like me to lay it all out now?"

"Just . . . over . . . fast."

My voice sounded like a faulty cell phone connection. The words were coming out only sporadically. The rest got hung up on my damaged vocal cords.

"Very well then," he said. "Seaman Mortimer, you can come in now."

The young black sailor stepped through the door looking very nervous.

"Tell everyone what you told me about an incident you observed last night involving Mr. Martindale here," said Healy, gesturing toward me.

"Yes, sir. I saw him get into arguments with two ladies. Her." He pivoted toward Susan Foster who was sitting directly across from me. "And the dead Russian girl." He went on to recall how he had stepped in to offer his assistance to the two damsels in distress.

"Mr. Martin . . ."

"Martindale," said the captain.

"Mr. Martindale seemed pretty mad at both of them and I thought they might need my help."

I shook my head vigorously and tried to voice my objections. Try as I might, however, the words would not come out loudly enough to be heard.

"This man's voice has been damaged," said Jane from the chair next to me. "It's plain to see that he shouldn't be talking at all. He needs medical attention!"

"No," I rasped, motioning for her to lean in toward me so I could whisper in her ear.

"He asks that I convey his words to you. He wants to settle this now."

"Fine, fine," said the captain. "I owe him that."

For the next 15 minutes, I told my story through Jane— about how Susan and I had quarreled over old issues, including the breakup of our love affair; about how Nadia Chernoff had come onto me twice in order to blackmail me into silence about her boss's role in funding the expedition. I didn't leave anything out, deciding that too much was at stake to worry about hurting feelings or airing dirty laundry.

"Ms. Foster," said Healy, "is this true?"

Sue smiled at me and nodded, my old friend returning. "Mr. Martindale and I broke up many years ago, but there are still issues between us. They bubble to the surface every once in a while. The seaman was trying to be helpful, but I was not in any danger."

"Thank you, Ms. Foster. Anyone else want to speak. Dr. Belinsky?"

The Russian looked down at the table and said nothing.

"Dr. Jameson?"

Our great leader looked worried, his usual haughtiness replaced by fear that his deepest secrets were coming out.

"I do not intend to lay out the confidential arrangements of this expedition," he said. "I would be happy to talk to you about this in private, but not in such a public forum."

Thank you for your steadfast support, you prick, I thought to myself.

"I talked to Tom that night," said Ben Aniak. "It must have been right after he met Ms. Foster. He didn't look like no murderer to me. When I left him, he looked pretty beat, like he was going to hit the sack. And, yeah, I saw something else. I saw that Russian chick on the stairs. She passed me goin' down. She was a tease, you know. She let me see her tits for a minute. You know, her parka just happened to gap open as she went by me. I remember thinkin', 'Boy, would I like a piece of her ass'."

Aniak looked embarrassed.

"Sorry to speak about her in a vulgar way. But that's what I thought."

Bickford walked over to Healy and whispered in his ear. The captain nodded and the other man resumed his place leaning against the wall. Healy didn't say anything for a long time. He was obviously mulling over what everyone had said—and my fate. He acted as though what he had heard did not shock him. I suppose he encountered hundreds of instances each week where he had to judge human frailty and decide who was lying.

"I want all of you to write out statements about what happened last night regarding Mr. Martindale. Ms. Foster, Mr. Aniak, and you too, professor."

He looked at me. "You aren't off the hook yet, but this certainly isn't turning out as I anticipated. You can't go anywhere, so I'm not worried about your getting away."

He moved to the door, followed by the two seamen. "I'll need those statements by 0900 tomorrow."

After he left, Jameson quickly adjourned the meeting. I wanted to talk to Bickford to thank him for intervening on my behalf, but I could not find him. I really didn't want to see anyone else so I spent the rest of the weekend working on my statement for the captain. Along with everyone else, I got ready to set up operations on Herschel Island on Monday. We all avoided one another. Our work became a refuge from a terrible event, the murder of a beautiful young woman.

I borrowed one of the laptop computers and moved it to my cabin. In addition to writing a complete description of all our activities to date for the official record, I wrote several press releases detailing our work with the ice.

The Arctic ice pack undergoes profound changes every year. In winter, it is about the size of the continental United States. In summer, there is only half as much of it. Understanding what controls this annual freeze and meltdown is the key to predicting future climate change and assessing the toll of global warming, whether it be natural or human caused. From much of the information already known, scientists believe the Arctic is the key player in global climate change.

Our samplings have shown that the water had far less salt than normal, indicating that the ice was melting at an alarming rate, flooding the sea with fresh water. Scientists believe that the gradual warming of the planet through the so-called greenhouse effect will have the most dramatic impact on the polar regions. They have known for some time that the ice cap that normally blankets the Arctic has been shrinking, especially since 1990. But that doesn't mean that some years might not see an early freeze and an ice pack that looks like it has for centuries. From the cold I'd experienced on our trip so far, I suspected that this might be one of those years.

Another important factor here was the influence of weather in the north on weather around the globe. It is still unclear to experts how much change the greenhouse effect will cause. Some research shows that circulation patterns throughout the Arctic are shifting, contributing to weather changes in Northern Europe and across the Northern Hemisphere. This has resulted in more ice breaking up and drifting into the Beaufort Sea. Increased breaking of ice accelerates warming of the Arctic because more sunlight actually reaches the water, instead of reflecting off the ice. This raised temperatures.

Scientists need more data to predict what might happen to climate because of changes in the Arctic and I was quoting Jameson to that effect in one of my releases. It was all very interesting to me and I hoped to convey my fascination to the world at large.

I also included details of our overall mission and our impending move to Herschel Island. I cleared them with Jameson and the captain. Because I didn't want to talk with either of them directly, I left the releases with Carmen Ames. She returned them later in the day with minor changes.

"Thanks, Carmen. I'll give it to the Coast Guard for transmission and we'll get it into the hands of all those eager science writers around the world."

She lingered in the doorway. "Tom, gee. I hardly know how to say this."

"Best to just spit it out, I guess. Whatever it is." I smiled to reassure her.

"Well, er, do you really think you're in any danger? I mean, that's too awesome to think about. And who killed that girl? Gee, it makes me shiver. It makes me scared. Will I be next? Is there some kind of serial killer on the ship?"

She wrapped her arms across her body as if she was trying to ward off a sudden chill.

"I wouldn't worry about it," I answered. "You're too young to have enemies. You'll find as you get older that some people like you and some people don't. But even when people don't like you, they rarely try to murder you."

Her eyes got big as she failed to get my joke. Sick as I was of my condescending this-is-how-it-is-my-dear tone, I thought the truth would really spook her. Maybe we all were in danger.

"Wow. I know that's true," she said. "I've never thought about it, I guess. It's all so awesome!"

"Not the word I'd pick, but I guess you're right, Carmen."

She patted my hand.

"You'll be all right, Tom. Don't worry."

She turned and walked out of my cabin. I sat down at the laptop and quickly got on the Internet. Since my first confrontation with Belinsky, I was intrigued by his reference to *Spetsnaz*. I was sure it was a unit he belonged to, but for what purpose? And would that purpose have consequences for the rest of us now that he and Zukov were staying on.

I logged on, got up a search engine, and typed in "Russian Armed Forces." Over 500 entries came cascading onto the screen. My problem at this point was that I couldn't spell the word I was trying to look up. Was it *Spetsnetz* or *Spasnotz* or what? I eventually clicked onto a glossary in an intelligence web site.

I scrolled down to the S's and found what I wanted. It was spelled *Spetsnaz* and its mission was defined succinctly: "Special-purpose forces of the Soviet armed forces or KGB, trained to attack important command, communications, and weapons centers behind enemy lines."

I typed in the word and got an additional list of web sites specifically related to the unit. The more I checked, the more alarmed I became. The organization was a cross between the CIA and the Delta Force Army Rangers. While once a part of the KGB, it now operated under its successor, the FSB. The materials gave the impression of *esprit de corps* normally missing in the ill-treated, underpaid, unmotivated, and out-of-control Russian Army I had read about in the media. These guys seemed to have a sense of purpose and mission. They were often called upon to perform delicate tasks—usually in secret. What they often did was heroic but was seldom honored because of the secrecy required. Even dead Spetsnaz officers and men were buried without fanfare. They also had a sense of humor, if at times heavy-handed: the home page of the web site included a little animated man who periodically walked over and urinated on an American flag. I kept clicking my computer mouse and read on:

Spetsnaz is a counterterrorist unit of the Foreign Intelligence Service. Developed in 1981 as an infiltration unit, the organization trained its men and women for wartime operations like sabotage and carrying out intelligence missions in enemy territory. They were taught how to handle foreign weapons, including the languages needed to understand technical nomenclature. At first, the troops were inserted by air, even though they were capable of doing a seaborne insertion.

By 1987, the unit expanded into 500 members, and deployed to various hot spots within the old Soviet Union, mainly to perform covert entry missions for the KGB. However, the unit soon evolved into an antinuclear terrorist unit.

Early in the morning of 21 August 1991, Spetsnaz forces were assigned to storm the Russian Parliament building and seize key leadership personnel, including Boris Yeltsin. The officers in charge refused to take part in the action. This contributed to a failure of the coup against Mikhail Gorbachev which led, eventually, to the collapse of the Soviet Union.

On 24 October 1991, Gorbachev signed a decree abolishing the KGB. The Foreign Intelligence Service, including Spetsnaz, was reorganized as a separate organization incorporating most of the foreign operations, intelligence-gathering, and intelligence analysis activities of the old KGB First Chief Directorate.

In 1993, Boris Yeltsin, by now president of the Russian Federation, ordered Spetsnaz units to storm the Parliament building, called the White House. They were helpful in allowing him to crush another attempted coup and stay in power.

In the years since, the unit has dealt exclusively with antiterrorist missions and distinguished itself many times in various regions up the world.

Another reference called *Spetsnaz* a threat to NATO. An American air force officer wrote in a paper that while the West had long prepared for a conventional war with Soviet forces using thermonuclear weapons, that country—both as the Soviet Union and now as Russia—has been developing a third dimension of military operations using saboteurs, secret agents, and special forces.

"This third dimension of warfare essentially entails the use of military active measures that are special operations involving surprise, shock, and preemption in the enemy's rear echelons with the ultimate goal of winning a quick victory," said the paper. "The Soviet troops entrusted with fulfilling these preemptive actions are ' special purpose ' or ' special designation' (*spetsnaza chenoya*) troops, more commonly known as Spetsnaz forces."

The article went on to detail how these forces would operate. Prior to their use in combat, *Spetsnaz* forces would be prepositioned in enemy territory. They would be posted in embassies and consulates under the guise of technical personnel, guards, gardeners, and drivers. Other agents would pose as tourists, members of official delegations, members of sports teams, truck drivers, and ship or airline passengers. Once operations began, these undercover units would link up with regular forces in the target area and begin their work.

I scrolled up to the top of the article and noticed a quote from an Afghan rebel leader I had missed the first time through: "The *Spetsnaz* are the only Soviet troops who can think for themselves and make quick decisions."

I turned off the computer and pushed the chair away from the tiny desk in my cabin. I stood up and looked out of the porthole Salcido so liked as a way to vent the smoke from his cigarettes. The Arctic air hit my face with a coldness that made my eyes water. It was, after all, only August 31 and a bit early for very low temperatures. I blinked at first, but I gradually got used to the cold and soon found its bracing effect cleared my head.

What to make of Belinsky's reference to *Spetsnaz*? Was he one of their undercover operatives—a marine mammalogist by day and a saboteur by night? If so, this was no laughing matter. My encounters with him and his cohorts Dimitri and Nadia showed their ruthlessness. But why were they assigned to this expedition? What possible reason would their handlers in Moscow have for sending them to infiltrate our ranks? It had to be the ice. They needed the data our scientists were discovering about ice conditions.

Also, why had I suddenly become a focus of their wrath? Was it simply that I had insulted Belinsky's manhood when I knocked the rifle out of his hand, as he implied? God knows I have been known to piss people off, even without trying. Had he set me up to take the blame for Nadia's murder? Why go to all that trouble to get rid of me? If he was really trying to get a corner on the knowledge of ice conditions in the Arctic, why did he consider me such a threat that he allowed this hatred of me to get in the way of fulfilling his mission?

My paranoiac thoughts were interrupted by a knock at the door.

"Bickford. I looked for you earlier. I wanted to thank you for talking to the captain. I'm not sure why you have influence over him, but I'm glad. Are you some kind of . . ."

The tall man stepped in quickly, closed the door, and held up his hand to stop me in midsentence.

"You are getting into all of this way too deep, Tom," he said quietly.

"You aren't trained for this stuff. You are going to get hurt. I can watch your backside only so much."

"Why do I have the feeling that you are maneuvering everything like some kind of diabolical chess player?"

"Because maybe that is what I am."

Saying that, he turned on his heel and was gone.

After he left, I turned on the computer and brought up the home page of the Google web site. Although I usually only check my own skimpy listing, this time I typed in a new name: *Paul Bickford.*

My silent traveling companion had only a few more listings than I did, mainly dealing with the lectures he had given at the Army War College over the past five years. He had adapted a few as articles in military journals. Although Jameson had not used a military title in introducing him to the rest of us, it was obvious that he had been, or was still, an Army officer. Neither his branch nor his rank was indicated, however.

Before the Internet, few people outside a relatively small group of senior military officers would have found the article that I brought up on my screen. It was from an obscure military journal that often posted unclassified articles from official publications. One entry was of particular interest to me: his first person account of his assignment as an observer with a small Russian Army contingent in Chechnya, two years before.

ASSIGNMENT: PANKISI GORGE
GEORGIAN/CHECHEN BORDER
by Paul Bickford

    I had been lying in the snow so long my limbs were stiff and numb. It wasn't the cold that was getting to me. I was, after all, wearing the best thermal gear the army issued. Instead, it was the inactivity and the need to remain motionless for hours. Even in my training at Fort Bragg, where we once stood in neck-high water all night, I hadn't felt this impatient. But I was a lot younger then and thought only of the excitement of the moment, not the drudgery my line of work often involved.

    Getting by on the few calories in one MRE a day or biting the heads off of matches to get enough sulfur in the system to ward off mosquitoes? That, to my twenty-year-old mind, was cool. I was very proud that I had not been part of the 30 to 40 percent who did not wash out in the tough training. I was very pleased to make it into the most elite corps of the American military.

Although my training at Fort Bragg had molded me into one of the best Special Operations officers in the army, I had tired of a life that alternated between adrenaline-stoked danger and sheer boredom. I did not want to be a snake eater all my life. Five years out of Ranger School, I was contemplating a change in careers.

My partner on this mission, Eddie Zambrano, probably echoed my thoughts from an equally uncomfortable position several yards away. We had been friends since we both joined the army on the same day. We had even made captain a week apart two years before. Where I was controlled, Eddie was often out of control, at least in terms of keeping up a line of patter, no matter where he was.

A hand on the man lying on my other side shot up, palm down. He quickly drew it across his lips in the universal sign to shut up. Vassily Kazatin, a major in Spetsnaz, a Russian counterterrorism unit, spoke only when necessary. Although he seemed to like us, Kazatin had said on more than one occasion that we talked too much. On this special mission, with the enemy all around us, I had to agree. I frowned at my loquacious friend and drew a finger, not across my lips, but my throat. Zambrano flashed me a big smile.

The three of us were perched high above the main road through the Pankisi Gorge, the only link between the Republic of Georgia, now an independent nation, and Chechnya, still a part of Russia, about 30 kilometers away. The road, closed by winter snows until recently, was no super highway even in the summer. But recent warming temperatures had melted the heavy drifts enough to see the pothole-pocked surface in all but the shadiest of places.

The remoteness of the region had made it a safe redoubt for hundreds of Muslim militants fighting in Chechnya. Reportedly financed by Islamic charities and led by several fanatics, both homegrown and Middle Eastern, the insurgents had been fighting the Russians on and off since 1994. In the process, they had used the gorge as a route to smuggle men, weapons, and drugs from the Middle East. Their actions had destabilized the area and caused several thousand refugees to head into the seven small villages that dotted the valley floor at the south end of the gorge.

Chechnya had become one of the most lawless places on earth, despite the best efforts of the Russian government. Terror is a way of life there with kidnappings by masked men the rule, and the victims usually murdered. Kidnappings are so common, in fact, I heard that masks are sold from stalls by the roadside in the choice of camouflage or basic black. Some come with a hole for the mouth, as well as for the eyes. This is popular with terrorists who smoke. Merchants in the market also sell uniforms, boots, holsters, cartridge belts, and ammunition pouches.

The region could not be more precarious and it was that potential volatility that had brought us to this place on the ridge. The Georgian government wanted American help in keeping the Russians from invading their territory in search of the guerillas. The Russian government wanted the United States to stay out of a situation it considered its own to deal with.

As a result, officials from both countries had permitted this mission to assess things before any decisions were made. We were here to look things over with the help of Kazatin, an old friend. Although armed to the proverbial teeth, we were not supposed to draw and fire our weapons unless we were fired upon.

On ridges high above the deep chasm and outcroppings at various points on its rocky face, over a hundred Spetsnaz troopers waited too, their fingers on the triggers of their high-powered rifles. Soon, we heard the distant rumble of vehicles. The hundred trigger fingers tensed and so did we. The plan called for initial rifle fire to pick off the drivers, followed by rocket launcher strikes to pulverize the trucks and the munitions presumed to be inside.

But something went terribly wrong with the plan. As soon as Kazatin raised his gun to signal the start, men on their various perches began clutching their throats and chests and falling rapidly to their deaths. The Russian officer turned toward me, a look of bewilderment and fear on his face. I drew my pistol.

I turned to Zambrano who seemed about to speak but was then hit in the neck by a bullet. At first he stared at me, then down at the front of his body armor, being rapidly drenched with blood.

"Jesus, Bick, I'm dyin' here!" he whispered.

I crawled to his side and pulled his shoulders around so I could hold his head.

"Eddie, take it easy," I said. "You're going to be fine. We'll get you out of here."

"I don't believe you," he said. "But I love you for saying that. Huah."

And then he died.

My eyes filled with tears as I tried to shield Eddie's body with my own from the whizzing bullets that careened off the ground all around us. Some of Kazatin's men had joined us on the ridgetop and were forming a perimeter so we could move to a cave several hundred meters away.

One of the bigger men picked up Zambrano's body and ran toward the cave entrance. Kazatin, me, and the other commandos quickly followed. As we rushed for cover behind large boulders at the cave's entrance, several of the men slumped forward, blood spurting out of bullets holes in the backs of their heads. The Chechens had beaten us to the cave, easily anticipating Katazin's every move.

When the man next to me died, I rolled to one side and was able to conceal myself behind his body. Katazin did the same on the other side. From here, we could shoot anyone emerging from the cave in our own pincer movement, unless there were too many of them.

Just then, I heard a whirring sound to the west. Soon, the noise turned into a cacophony of grinding motors and rotors as a Russian helicopter swooped into view and landed in the only flat area on the ridgetop.

I got to my feet and motioned for Kazatin to help me lift Eddie's body. We picked up our fallen comrade and staggered toward the aircraft, ducking our heads to avoid the whirling propellers. The few remaining commandos followed.

As we made our break, I caught sight of a tall Arab in a white robe and turban standing on another ridge to the right. At his direction, the guerrillas turned and focused all their attention on us. They opened fire in a fusillade that sent bullets raining down from all directions. Some pinged off the metal shell of the aircraft. Others hit the exposed arms, legs, torsos, and heads of their intended targets. I got hit in the thigh; Kazatin in his left arm.

Miraculously, the men did not drop Zambrano's body. Helping hands hoisted us into the helicopter. The crew chief gave a thumbs-up sign and the chattering bird took flight once again.

As the helicopter took evasive maneuvers to get away, I looked back at the Arab in white. Oblivious to the gunfire around him, he stared at me with eyes so full of hatred that I finally turned away. When I looked again, the Arab and his men were gone from the ridgetop.

[EDITOR'S NOTE: For security reasons, the current rank and precise job classification of the author has been withheld. The topic discussed in this article is for instructional purposes only.]

✧ ✧ ✧

Nine

When I woke up at the usual 6 a.m. the following morning, I noticed immediately that the ship's engines had stopped. Salcido barely stirred in his bunk as I jumped down from my berth and walked to the porthole. The thin film of frost on the glass and metal frame made a cracking sound as I pushed outward and the small window opened.

Being this close to the Arctic Circle, we were already 1 hour into daylight. So far, however, the sun hadn't appeared. Fog enveloped the ship and the surrounding ocean surface. I was sure we were anchored off Herschel Island, but I couldn't see it.

As I smelled the wonderful sea air, with its aroma of fish and kelp combined, I began to worry. It boggled my mind that a benign summer assignment had turned into a worrisome tangle of international intrigue in which I had been accused of murder. I couldn't decide if I was really in danger or merely exaggerating a peril that did not exist.

I rubbed a hand over my face as if to ward off such thoughts. I was really working myself into a snit. Was I paranoid? Was I attaching too much importance to the things that had happened to me the past few days? I wasn't sure.

Just then, the fog lifted enough for me to catch a glimpse of the island. From my knowledge of the place, I calculated that we were anchored slightly north of Pauline Cove, the natural harbor that had made Herschel Island so attractive to whalers in the last century. I could see the treeless landscape, even the waves lapping the sandy beach.

This morning was one of calm, belying the normally windy conditions. The wind blows from the West and Northwest half the time, I had read. It was very common in winter for it to drive 30-foot-high pressure ridges onto the sand spit, burying everything. I recalled quite vividly the "Rule of 30"— 30 degrees Fahrenheit temperatures with 30-mile-per-hour wind causing exposed flesh to freeze in 30 seconds. I shivered at the thought.

As my eyes adjusted to the glare of bright light reflecting upon fog, the dim outline of a building became visible on the bluff overlooking the cove. This would be the Mission House, now abandoned and uninhabitable. Thank God for the prefab buildings set up away from the shore by the last expedition two years ago.

"What's so interesting out there?" said Salcido from his bunk. "What ya looking at?"

"Morning, Danny. It's the island. We got here sometime last night. It looks pretty interesting. Makes me feel like someone on a whaling ship 100 years ago."

"Shit, you seen one godforsaken research hole, you've seen another, if you ask me," he said, sitting on the edge of his bunk and lighting a cigarette.

He completely destroyed my visions of dreamy time travel. I picked up my towel and clothes and headed for the bathroom. "How you going to keep up your smoking without a porthole to blow the smoke out of?" I said before stepping into the tiny room.

"Hell, Jameson can't control the out-of-doors," he replied.

"Don't count on it!" I laughed.

✧ ✧ ✧

Jameson was his usual brisk self at the meeting an hour later. This was the first time we had gathered as a group since the morning after Nadia's murder.

"Carmen is giving you our schedule for the day. All of our equipment has been packed and put on pallets, and transferred by our Coast Guard friends to the beach. You are responsible only for your own gear. Tom, I'd like you, Scott, Derek, and Ben to be our advance party."

"Okay," I said, hiding my chagrin at being alone with people I didn't particularly like. "What about Paul Bickford?"

I wanted to talk to Bickford about what I had read about him in hopes he would tell me what he was doing on this expedition.

Before Jameson could answer, another voice rang out.

"I would very much like to be in that advanced contingent."

All eyes turned to Boris Belinsky who was seated in his usual spot at the end of the table. How would he function without his enforcer, Zukov? How could I stand to have him along on shore where he might make another run at me? I didn't say anything but I dreaded that possibility.

"I've got some things to discuss with you before we go ashore," said Jameson, turning to me. Bickford is tied up with the captain right now. We'll keep the assignments as I've made them."

For once, I welcomed Jameson's autocratic style. Belinsky nodded slightly but said nothing.

"Very well then, let's get to it," said Jameson, looking pleased that he was being obeyed. "I promised the captain that we would be out of his hair in two hours max."

On deck, I noticed that my duffel bags had been placed with those of the others at the top of the gangway.

"You run a first-class operation, Mr. Zinko."

The young officer smiled and touched his hat. "Sorry about the other day, sir. I was only following orders."

"Don't worry about it. Is Zukov still in the brig?"

"Yes, sir. He gets pretty violent from time to time. The captain's thinking about putting him in a straitjacket."

"Now *that* seems like an excellent idea," I laughed as I picked up my luggage and headed down the stairs.

"Safe trip, sir. We'll see you in a few weeks."

I reached the bobbing tender quickly and turned to watch the other three descend. Szabo threw his bag in my direction as he was halfway down. It landed at my feet but did not touch me. Both Derek and Ben held onto their bags all the way down.

"Sorry, old man," said Szabo as he stepped onto the tender.

"I'm not as old as I look," I said, trying to be nice in my best smart-ass manner. But I've always loved having the last word, especially with people I don't like very much. My attempt at humor was lost on him; he looked at me as if I was from another planet.

When everyone was safely on board and seated, the seaman opened the throttle and we sped away from the *Polar Sea*. At first, I didn't see anyone from our party watching from the deck. As I turned to look toward shore, however, I caught a glimpse of Belinsky, his binoculars trained on me.

It took less than 5 minutes to reach the pontoon-supported temporary dock. I was the first to step ashore and quickly tied the boat to the dock. The seaman cut the engine and helped us transfer our gear. He then helped us off-load the equipment we had brought. The bigger pieces would be brought ashore later in the day. Then, with Scott, Derek, and Ben standing next to me, the Coast Guardsman saluted and got back in the tender.

"Anything else, sir?" He looked at me.

"No. Thanks a lot. We're fine. See you later."

The four of us picked up our bags and trudged up the short incline to solid ground. After dropping it, we walked back down the hill and then lugged the rest of the equipment up to the top. We followed the map and walked to the cluster of buildings that would be our headquarters. I was anxious to explore the decaying Mission House structure on the spit but there wasn't time for that now.

Jameson had given me the keys to all the buildings, something that angered Szabo. He was the kind of person who worried about things like who was in charge. I normally wouldn't care who was entrusted with keys to a building, but I made a big thing out of this to antagonize him.

"Okay, let's see what we have here with these keys," I said in a taunting way. I jingled them a bit for effect before inserting the correct one in the lock of the first building. I opened the door and stepped into a big room, empty except for three long tables sitting at the opposite end. It was remarkably clean. Even the lights worked after Ben turned on the generator.

"This looks good," I observed, "not even a cobweb."

"Too far north for spiders," said Aniak. "Cold kills them."

We fanned out to look things over. I assumed Jameson would want the tables to be set up as workstations for computers and microscopes.

"Derek and Scott," I said. "Would you take these post-it notes and use this plan to show where the lab staff will go? We'll leave it packed for now and let the others actually set it up."

"It's cold in here," said Szabo, not responding to my suggestion.

"Yeah, you're right," said Aniak. "That's a wood stove over there. Let me round up some fuel." He walked out the door.

"All right, Derek. Here's your list." I handed the page and the notes to him, pointedly ignoring his great and good friend, Scott.

"You are such a shit," he said, grabbing the paper from Peters. I smiled but didn't respond to his outburst. Peters set about following the list, Scott plopped down on one of the bunks.

Ben Aniak returned with the arm full of driftwood, which he carried to the stove.

"This is what kept the whalers warm," he said, dropping the disparate pieces to the floor. "The beaches are full of it. The debris from the whole great North flows out of the rivers and winds up in the Beaufort. Must be half of it lands on the beach here."

"That's a relief," I said. "I think Paul Jameson's got some large space heaters in mind for permanent heat."

"Powered by what, moose tethered to a turning wheel?" laughed Szabo.

Peters practically doubled over with laughter. What Szabo said was mildly amusing, but not something to cause you to hold your sides so they wouldn't split.

"I don't like either of these fairies," Ben whispered as he walked by me. He put some wood in the stove and lighted a match. Before long, a fire blazed nicely.

"While you two finish up in here, Ben and I are going to check out the living quarters." Peters nodded but Szabo turned over on the bunk as we walked outside.

"That guy doesn't like you, Tom," said Aniak.

"I do that to people sometimes," I shrugged. "It's an old, and long, story."

"Something to do with that Foster woman?"

"Yeah, something like that."

"I thought he was gay? I mean he and that other guy are always prancing around each other. It gives me the creeps."

"Well, you're right, Ben, at least partly. Szabo swings both ways, if you get my drift."

"Yeah, I do. The other guy is harmless, but I still say you need to watch your back with that Szabo guy. He's bad news!"

Ben wasn't telling me anything I didn't already know, but I was tired of talking about it. We had work to do. I led the way toward one of the two buildings that would serve as our dorms. I unlocked the first door and stepped in.

The room was divided into sleeping cubicles, each with two bunks and clothes lockers. A large communal bathroom was situated at the far end on the left, with a shower room on the right.

"Good luck with getting enough water pressure to work all these toilets and the shower," said Aniak.

"I'm sure Cliff has it worked out. He wills things to happen, against all odds." I said. "The water wouldn't dare not come out in full force. He would throw a real fit!"

Aniak laughed and sat down on one of the bunks. I sat opposite him and started putting names on the post-it notes, consulting the master list as I went.

"This is the women's dorm. They're going to have a lot more space than we are. Put one of these in each cubicle, if you would."

He got up and did so.

"With all this space, they'll have room for plenty of hanky-panky," he laughed.

"Not with those three. Jane's too sensible. Susan's too uptight. And Carmen. Jameson is watching her like a hawk."

"Nadia, the Russian babe. Now there's someone I would have loved to fuck big time!" He looked slightly chagrined. "Sorry. I guess I shouldn't speak of the dead that way."

As I spoke her name, visions of her jumping on top of me in my bed floated into my head. When you have that kind of sex with someone, it's difficult to forget it.

"Yeah," I said, "she was a sweet girl. But she sold her soul and her body to Belinsky, I'm afraid. She'd do anything he told her to do,"

"Is that what got her killed you think?" he said.

"I don't know but I wish Jameson would get him off this expedition. I can't see why he's keeping him around, now that they've completed the tagging and he's done what he promised to earn that money."

"Money? What's that all about? I hadn't heard about any money."

"Don't you remember what I told the captain during my interrogation?"

He shook his head.

"I'm not sure of all the details," I lied. "I think he's getting some extra funding from the Russians for allowing them to do their whale work with us."

He shrugged and didn't seem to want to know more. I wrote Sue's name on a post-it note and stuck it on the bed I was sitting on.

"That's about it in here," I said. "Things look fairly clean. The ladies can spruce up after they move in."

I wrote the men's names on post-its and headed for the door. Aniak followed me out.

"I've never really thanked you for helping me out with the captain the other day."

He shrugged off my praise, so I changed the subject.

"When are you going to start doing your liaison work with native groups?"

"We have to find them to work with them first," he laughed. "Actually, Cliff wants me to take a boat once we've settled in and call on the small settlements along the coast near here. He wants me to interview them about their experiences with living with ice. I know people in some of these places but my face will get me in the door anyway. When you look like me you can only be Inuit."

"I'd like to go with you, Ben. It really sounds interesting. It would add to my research. I mean their ancestors must have worked with the whalers who lived on this island."

"I'd like to take you. Let's . . . a . . . see. If you want to know the truth, some of the people won't talk if they see a white face. I could check with them, but I can't promise."

"I understand. I don't want to interfere. Just keep me in mind, okay?"

"Sure, Tom. Glad to," he said, as we stepped back outside. "What the hell is that?"

I followed his outstretched arm with my eyes and saw something shiny in the tundra. We walked quickly to it.

"A motor bike up here? That's odd."

The bike was sitting upright on its stand, a driver nowhere in sight. Aniak felt the exhaust pipe and shook his head.

"Cold as a witch's tit," he said.

The bike was parked behind the building we were headed for, as if the person who had left it there was trying to conceal it in a low part of the rolling tundra.

"Must be inside," said Ben, running around to the door.

"Wait," I shouted. "It might not be safe."

Ben was gone, totally disregarding my alarm. As I followed him through the door, he began to wail.

"Oh my God, no. My poor Ezmeralda. God no. Please no."

When I reached his side Ben was sitting on the floor and cradling the head of a beautiful Eskimo woman. She looked serene, her long black hair cascading down across his lap. Although I saw no blood, she was not moving.

"Ben, Ben."

He ignored me and began to rock back and forth, tears running down his face. I touched his arm and it barely phased him.

"Ben."

I took his arm again, this time touching it slightly.

"Leave me alone!" He shook his head, as if to try to rid it of the scene before him.

"Ben. Who is this woman? Who is Ezmeralda?"

"Oh my God, no. Not Ezmeralda."

I needed help, both to deal with Ben and the body. I felt my pockets for a cell phone, but remembered I had handed it in for new batteries. I had no other way to reach the ship. I walked out the door.

"Scott. Derek," I yelled.

Nothing. I glanced back at Ben, still sobbing and rocking. "Ben, I'll be right back. Sit tight."

He stared straight ahead.

I ran out of the door and quickly retraced my steps to the first building we had entered. The door was open and I stepped into find the room in total darkness, the blinds closed. Something felt strange, what I couldn't quite tell. For one thing, I smelled something not present in the room when I was in it before: a combination of the damp, moldy tundra and human sweat. It was potent enough to make me gag.

"Scott. Scott. Are you in here? Derek?" I crept farther into the room, which appeared to be empty. I'd fished a flashlight out of my pocket and shined it under each table. I walked to each window and pulled on the blinds. Even open, they didn't allow a lot of light into the room, only thin shafts that revealed very little. I did see the post-it notes lying in place. They had apparently finished that task before disappearing. I got to the end of the big room and opened the door to the windowless bathroom.

"Scott. Derek. Are you in here?"

The light skittered along the floor, past the toilets and wash basins. The room was empty. I backed out of the room and turned towards the shower room behind me. The door wouldn't budge easily. I shoved it harder, putting my knee into the action. It seemed as if something bulky was blocking the door. Finally, it gave way and banged loudly against the wall.

I shined the light on the floor and caught sight of a boot, then a leg, then a hand. A shiver went down my spine. The beam of my flashlight illuminated what was obviously a human head. I knelt beside the body to get a closer look. Two eyes stared back it me, unblinking, unseeing. I touched a vein in his neck to confirm my suspicion that Derek Peters was quite dead.

I backed out of the room and turned to look for Scott. Was he dead too? I didn't know Peters so I had little to grieve about. Any death is a tragedy, but it is less dramatic when you don't know the person.

Scott Szabo was a different story. We had never been friends in the time I had known him. In fact, we had been adversaries for years, briefly during a murder investigation and a romantic rivalry years before, followed by a period when we didn't see each other at all. Now, there was a contentiousness between us that was even more vehement. In spite of this, I didn't wish him harm.

As I stepped out into the main room, something heavy hit my right shoulder with a force that sent me to my knees. It missed my head by inches, probably because the wielder of the object couldn't see very well in the dim light. I rolled to one side, away from the dark figure, then crawled under a table. The next blow hit the table with such a force that it split the thick wood. By the second blow, I realized that my attacker had an ax.

✧ ✧ ✧

Ten

"**D**rop the ax, buddy. Put your hands where I can see them."

The ax fell to the floor in front of me and someone walked over and leaned down to look at me.

"Are you okay, Tom?"

It was Ben Aniak.

"Ben. God, I'm glad to see you."

I struggled to my feet, hitting my head on the edge of the table as I got up. My shoulder was throbbing but it didn't seem to be broken. Ben moved toward the hulking figure standing in the shadows by the far wall, his hand in his pocket pretending to hold a gun.

"Just stay calm and sit down."

The man complied and Aniak brought his hand out into the open.

"Now cross your legs! I'm warning you! Don't make any quick moves. Jesus! Look at his head!"

I edged my way closer and peered at my attacker.

"Scott? Why did you go after me? What happened to you?" Szabo looked dazed as he ran his hand over his bloody face. I knelt down and got out a handkerchief.

"Watch it!" shouted Ben.

"He looks pretty calm," I said, dabbing at the blood on his face. Szabo seemed quiet enough and let me work on his face.

"Scott, can you remember what happened?" Szabo shook his head and looked at me, as if he was seeing me for the first time.

"You killed Derek! You tried to kill me!"

He pushed me away and tried to get to his feet.

"Take it easy, Scott," yelled Ben. "Stay where you are! Tom, just back away and quit the nursing duties. He's not going to die!"

"You killed Derek!" Szabo shouted again. "You killed my lover!"

Ben looked at me with a quizzical expression on his face, as if he was waiting for me to deny the accusation.

"This is too ridiculous to even deny. You were with him the whole time. I mean when this would have happened? Of course, I didn't do this. He's delusional. He's out of his head."

"You know it and I know it but will the others believe you?" He glanced at Szabo, now sobbing loudly. "Or him?"

"It'll take some time explaining, but I'll help them sort it out." I said confidently. In my heart, however, I wasn't all that sure. There had been way too many murders to suit me.

"We've got to get some help," I said, finally casting off my worry and trying to take charge again. "What happened to your friend's body?"

Ben's face became a mask of grief when I brought up the subject of Ezmeralda.

"I covered her up with a sheet. She was cold."

"So she'd been dead for a while. Who was she and why was she here?"

"A girlfriend. I loved her once and thought maybe . . ." tears ran down his face. "We were meeting to conduct a . . . little . . ."

"Never mind, Ben. We can talk about it later. I'm getting a bit nervous. We've got two dead people on our hands and a killer probably not too far away in the tundra. We've got no weapons to defend ourselves and no way to communicate."

At that moment, as if on cue, I heard the trill of the cell phone coming from a backpack in the corner.

✧ ✧ ✧

We stayed where we were for the hour it took for Jameson and the others to reach us. I had said very little to Susan when I answered Szabo's phone: "Two dead, need help now." What more did they need?

The three of us were sitting in the headquarters building when the rescue party walked in the door.

"My God, Tom. What's this all about? Hello, Ben. What the hell happened to your head?" Jameson was doing all the talking, as usual.

Szabo didn't say anything in reply, but pointed at me dramatically, like in a third-rate courtroom drama. Jameson looked at me, then Ben, then back to Scott.

"He's suffered a bad cut on his head," I said. "I think I stopped the bleeding but a medic better take a look at it. Derek's in the shower room—or what's left of Derek."

Susan, who had been hanging back until now, started crying. She rushed toward Scott and knelt by his side.

"So much for choosing sides," I muttered. But Jameson heard me.

"Is that what this is about?" he shouted. "Some kind of lover's revenge? I gave you more credit for professionalism than that, Tom."

"Cliff, it's not like that. I wasn't even in here when this attack happened. Ben and I were in the second barracks building, taking care of the other body."

"Other body? Someone else is dead?" Jameson was shouting and looking at us like we were crazy.

"Ask Ben. He knew her."

Aniak stepped forward, looking somewhat nervous. "Ezmeralda Savoonga. My old girlfriend. I loved her a lot."

"What was she doing here? Were you meeting her to give her some booze to smuggle ashore."

Aniak hung his head as the others looked at him questioningly. "I gave you one last chance and you blew it," said Jameson, quickly adopting the superior air he liked to assume in all conversations. "You couldn't resist getting back into your old role as a smuggler."

"He was carrying liquor to sell to the natives?" I asked, remembering the broken bottle in Ben's bag the week before.

"I'll handle this, Tom. Stay out of it!"

"Stay out of what?" said a voice behind us.

Captain Healy walked through the door followed by Lieutenant Madison, Ensign Zinko, and Paul Bickford. "We'll be taking charge."

Clifford Jameson blinked as if he couldn't believe anyone would have the effrontery to take charge of a situation he was trying to control.

"Madison, secure this area as a crime scene. Take that man into custody after seeing to his head wound," said the captain.

The lieutenant moved towards Scott who seemed dazed by what was happening around him.

"He came after you with an ax, correct?" the captain said to me.

"Yes sir, he did."

"We'll sort this out on the ship later. Zinko, check the rest of these premises."

"Captain," I said, "you will find a body in the shower room and another one in the barracks two buildings away."

He was unfazed by the news.

"Captain," yelled Jameson, "I must protest this."

Healy held up his hand to stop the scientist.

"Two bodies? You have the tendency to attract dead people, Mr. Martindale. Perhaps I am placing the wrong man in custody," he said, looking at me.

"I found the bodies. Or rather I found them with my friend, Ben Aniak, here."

"That's right, sir," said Ben. "We were together so we can vouch for each other."

The authoritarian hand went up again.

"A special hearing in Juneau will be sorting all of that out!"

"Juneau!" Jameson's face was crimson and he seemed headed for coronary on the spot. "You can't do this to me, captain. I am a . . ."

"*You* are a nuisance, *Mister* Jameson. I am in control here because the United States Coast Guard is the co-sponsor of your expedition. You and your people wouldn't even be here without us. This is a military matter now. And this makes three people who have died on your watch. I would be derelict in my duty not to investigate this thoroughly."

"I must protest your attitude," replied Jameson. There has to be a reasonable explanation for all of this. I can reach your boss, Secretary Hodges, on my cell phone, in seconds. He'll tell you . . ."

"I doubt you'd want to wake him, *Mister* Jameson. I calculate that it's 0300 hours in Washington, D.C., right now. I doubt if you'd get much benefit from a call to a very groggy Secretary of Transportation. Besides, I report to the Commandant of the United States Coast Guard, Admiral John Baxter, and take my orders from him."

"I . . . er . . . you can't..."

Jameson sputtered for a few more seconds, then quit talking.

"Madison, put that man in plastic handcuffs, then go with Mr. . . ." The lieutenant tied Szabo's hands behind his back.

". . . Mr. Martindale to the other building and secure that location as a crime scene. Just a minute."

A radio cracked to life in his pocket and he pulled out. I couldn't hear all he said, but only a few words: "man . . . soonest . . . bodies . . . armed." He turned to the rest of us who had remained mute throughout much of the strange tableau playing out the past half hour.

"I've called for reinforcements while we sort this out."

He nodded to Madison and the officer and I walked out of the room.

"Whew. That guy is really something!" I said, as we started toward the other building.

"Yes, sir, he is that!" said Madison with a mixture of admiration and fear. "You don't mess with the big man. He's like his great-great grandfather."

"Great-great grandfather?"

"Maybe even another 'great' in there. He was Captain Michael Healy, who was a legend up here from 1886 to 1895. We read about him at the Academy. He commanded the Barkentine steamer, *Bear*. In his years in the Arctic, his primary duty was to apprehend seal poachers and murderers. He took his work very seriously and had the nickname 'Hell Raisin' Mike Healy.' He was a bit brutal in disciplining his men, though, and in the way he handled the people he arrested. Got him in some trouble but he was vindicated later. In those years, the Coast Guard was called the Revenue Cutter Service. We've got an icebreaker named for him now. A proud man who was outspoken and I guess always trying to prove himself."

Madison leaned closer to me, then whispered, "I guess because he was black in an era when few captains were of that race."

"A bit overbearing, was he?"

Madison leaned in again and looked around conspiratorially.

"You've got to realize that the *Bear* was the largest cutter in the Arctic service so it really was the symbol of America's sovereignty in Alaska. As captain, Healy was kind of the symbol of the symbol, so to speak. I mean his word was law. But it went to his head. Any long voyage is stressful, even today. But then it was worse. Crew members fought from time to time and balked at the captain's orders. For his part, Healy didn't feel he could tolerate any breach of discipline. So he dealt harshly with anyone who disobeyed him."

"And how did that go over with the higher ups?"

"Not well. Healy was court-martialed twice for his treatment of crew members. He was acquitted in one trial but twenty-five officers of the Revenue Cutter Service pressed charges in another trial and he was found guilty of excessive drinking. He lost command of the *Bear* and dropped to the bottom of the captain's list. In 1920, though, he was reinstated and given command of another ship."

"Fascinating stuff. You've really done a lot of homework."

"Self-preservation, I guess. I'd studied a bit about Healy in history class, but when our captain took command, I looked up the rest on the Internet. It's all there."

"Does he know what you know?"

"God no! He wouldn't like it. I've kept it to myself. I don't know why I've told you. You won't say anything about it, will you?"

"No. I promise I won't."

"You seemed interested and I thought it would help you deal with the captain better."

"I'm not really looking forward to it if you want to know the truth. Besides I'm not in charge of what my boss likes to call an 'expedition.' Clifford Jameson is."

"Yeah, but the captain doesn't like him. I've seen how he reacts to people he doesn't like. He disses them. He acts like they aren't there. I'll bet he'll pick you to deal with, no matter what the professor says."

"He's already asking Paul Bickford to take over, it seems to me. What do you know about him? Is he some kind of spook?"

Madison looked even more worried than before.

"I can't . . . it wouldn't . . ." He paused and cleared his throat. "That is a national security matter, sir, and I can't answer. I still think the captain will rely on you if things get tight."

"I hope you're wrong, but if you're right, it'll help to know this stuff. Thanks."

We resumed walking toward the building when I thought I saw some movement several hundred yards away in the tundra.

"Did you see something moving out there?"

Madison shook his head.

"No, but I was looking at you. Maybe it was a reflection of the sun against the uneven ground. It's a weird terrain, the tundra. It looks flat but it's got all kinds of nooks and crannies. Besides, everyone connected to the ship and your group is back there."

He motioned toward the main building to our rear.

"This is an uninhabited island, you know. Just polar bears and foxes and a lot of little ground critters."

"Yeah, you're right. My eyes were playing tricks on me."

We got to the door of the barracks and Madison stopped me with his hand.

"What's the matter?"

"Oh, nothing. I just wanted you to tell me what happened in detail before we go in. For my report. The captain will boil me alive if I leave anything out."

"It's not too complicated. Ben Aniak and I were looking through all the buildings to set them up for the others. We were checking out how clean things were and assigning bunks. That kind of thing. We walked into the building and found the body. Actually, Ben found the body because he was first through the door. He started yelling ' Ezmeralda, oh no, ' or something to that effect."

Madison paused in his note taking and motioned me to enter the building. It was darker than when I had been here earlier in today because the light had shifted. I squinted to get my bearings.

"He walked in and found the girl lying right over there."

I pointed to where I remembered Ben had been standing.

"Where? I don't see anybody."

"Maybe Ben moved it for some reason. He was pretty upset."

I quickly looked in each cubicle while Madison walked to the bathroom and shower at the rear. He came out and shrugged.

"Nothing in there, sir. Are you sure we got the right building?"

I knew what I had seen. Hell, I even had a witness. But when a body comes up missing, it is fairly hard to convince someone else that one existed in the first place, especially if that some-one was a hard-nosed guy like Captain Healy. The lieutenant read my mind.

"I won't insult your intelligence by questioning whether you and your friend found a dead woman here," he said. "But I'm worried about the captain's reaction."

"You mean you think he won't believe this?"

Madison nodded.

"What will happen then?"

The lieutenant glanced around as if he expected the mercu-rial captain to be listening in on our conversation. He lowered his voice to a whisper.

"He seems to believe you so far. I mean he ordered the other guy handcuffed, after all."

He waved his hand as if to recall a scene we both witnessed.

"And?"

"The captain is very literal and exacting. Most career military men are. You told him there was a body. He believed you to the extent that he sent us to find the body. Now, there is no body. I'm not sure what he'll do."

"About me?"

"Yeah, exactly."

"Well, we've just got to find the body or a trace of it."

I had visions of myself being transported to Juneau to stand trial for some infraction or the other instead of Scott Szabo. He would love to trade places with me in court. And he might, ax or no ax.

"Okay, but where do we start, sir?"

"Please call me Tom, lieutenant."

"I'm Phil."

"Good, Phil. Let's try to figure this out together. How much time do we have?"

"Not a lot. The captain's going to be getting suspicious of this delay any time now."

"Can you call him and buy some time?"

"I'll try, sir."

"I'm going to look around outside while you do."

I remembered the motor bike we had seen before we found the body. Had it been moved too? I ran out the door and hit the ground at a fast pace. Walking wasn't easy because of the ground, which was a combination of mud and molasses. I found the spot where the bike had been lying; the grass on the tundra was bent in a perfect outline of its dimensions.

Looking further, I noted a narrow tire track heading out to the south away from our encampment. At first, only the track was visible. Then several yards away, I saw two sets of foot-prints. It was as if the people pushing the motor bike—and, presumably, carrying the body—had been careful to walk in the tire impressions. The further away they got, the less careful they were of leaving anything behind.

I began to run in the direction of the tracks, forgetting completely that the people I was pursuing were apparently capable of murder. I headed toward some vegetation and soon reached a small rise. There weren't any trees because of the spongy ground. It stunted the growth of what plant life there was. These gnarled midgets more closely resembled medium-sized bushes.

In a few minutes I got beyond the growth and stopped to get my bearings. The tracks ran out because the tundra hardened into a hardpan resembling cement. I saw no sign of life in any direction. The only thing breaking the monotony of the view was another grove about a half mile away. A slog through the tundra seemed fruitless at this point. And a little dangerous. I was unarmed and uncertain about who might be waiting out there. My foolish bravado had its limits.

I turned back to face defeat and the captain's certain accusations and punishment. Just then, the sun's rays broke out of shadow and glinted off something shiny on the ground. I bent down and picked it up. At first the metal object meant nothing to me as I turned over in my hand.

Then I saw familiar word: "Siberoil," the Russian company that was paying for part of this expedition.

✧ ✧ ✧

Eleven

"I'm waiting," said Captain Healy, "for you to give me one good reason why I shouldn't throw you both into the brig for lying to me."

Madison and I were standing in front of the captain, who was glaring down on us in all his official glory. I felt like a student being hauled into the principal's office for copying someone's test answers. I hated the feeling.

"Yes, sir, I can see why you'd think that, sir."

Madison was unwilling or unable to say anything that his senior officer might construe as insubordination. He was going to remain quiet, even if it ended his career. I'd have to step in.

"With all due respect, captain, you aren't listening to what we're saying."

Healy looked as if I had punched him in the face.

"*I* am in charge of this interrogation, Mr. Martindale."

"Yes, you are, captain, but you're doing this at the expense of the truth."

"The truth is my only goal here. The truth is our friend."

"And it will set us free, blah, blah, blah."

Jameson had been standing behind the captain all this time and when he heard what I said, he started shaking his head wildly and gesturing like an umpire ruling a player out. Of course, he didn't utter a word. I pressed on, figuring I had very little to lose. I was, after all, a civilian.

"You are standing on dangerous ground here."

"With all due respect, captain. You need to let me tell you what happened. If you'll do that, I think you'll see that you are jumping to conclusions here that are at odds with the facts."

The captain waved his hand dismissively but allowed me to continue.

"There was a body in that building. Ben saw it. I saw it. Somebody moved it before anybody else could see it. I found some tire tracks in the tundra from the young woman's motor bike. Then I found footprints. Then I found this."

I handed him the Siberoil emblem, which he glanced at perfunctorily.

"And what does this prove?"

I looked at Jameson who looked as if he wouldn't like my answer, whatever it was.

"It is an emblem of the Russian company that is paying the expenses of our expedition."

"Shit," said Jameson as he sat down hard on the nearest bench.

Healy whirled around and walked over to the sheepish-looking scientist.

"You mean to tell me that the United States Coast Guard is party to a scientific enterprise that is being paid for by a foreign government?"

"I tried to tell you about it the other day, but . . ." I said.

"Foreign company, actually sir," mumbled Jameson.

"What?" yelled the captain.

"I said," Jameson cleared his throat, "I said Siberoil is a foreign company, not a government."

"That's not totally true," I added, ever the helpful execution-
er when it came to someone I felt needed bringing down to size.

"Siberoil is owned by one of the richest oligarchs in Russia
today. Like all those people, he got that way because the Yeltsin
government let him loot an important natural resource."

The captain shook his head.

"I don't know where to begin to sort this out. I'm not used
to being lied to."

"I didn't actually lie to you," said Jameson. "None of this
came up before today."

"You lied to the United States Coast Guard. That's the same
thing. I represent the United States Coast Guard in this part
of the world. I am sick of this whole mess. Believe me, I have
better things to do with my time than sort this out. I have a
good mind to leave you all here for a few weeks. You all
deserve one another."

At this moment, Ensign Zinko approached the captain and
whispered something in his ear.

"Tell him I'll take the call in the other room."

Healy got up and signaled for his communications man and
Bickford to follow him into the bathroom at the end of the
building. Zinko and Madison moved toward the room until
the captain waved them off.

"God, Tom. Do you realize what you've just done here?" said
Jameson, the rage apparent in his voice. Everyone else crowded
around the two of us as if to keep us from coming to blows.

"*I* didn't sell out to another country, Cliff."

"Sell out?" Jameson lunged at me but Hopkins caught his
arm before his fist connected with my jaw.

"Whoa, Cliff. Just calm down. Hitting Tom is not going to
solve anything. We need to concentrate on how to salvage our
work. We need to remember that we are professional scientists
who happen to have some personal differences."

"It's way beyond that," I scoffed. "I've reached the point where all I want is to be off this expedition. I don't think I can work with any of you any longer."

"I'm afraid you will have no other choice," said Healy behind me. We all turned to face the captain and his entourage as they walked from the rear toward us.

"The decision on what to do with all of us has been taken out of my hands," he said. "I will be giving the order to have the rest of your equipment and provisions off-loaded this afternoon. Also, the rest of your company will be brought here as well."

"Why? You can't . . . ."

"I have my orders, Dr. Jameson."

"You are leaving us stranded here?" I asked, incredulously.

"I am doing what the plan called for all along."

"That was before three murders," I said.

"Two murders are all I know about. We have one body only here—plus Miss Chernoff on the ship."

He gestured toward the back where Derek's body had been brought, encased in a body bag.

"I will take these remains to the ship until we decide how to dispose of them. This case needs to be investigated properly. I can't do it now."

"I can do anything I want to do," he said. "I have my orders, Mr. Martindale." He snapped his fingers as if to end any discussion. Zinko and Madison rushed to his side and the three turned to leave the room.

"I have to return to my ship immediately."

Jameson, who had been reacting as if he were in a trance, finally said something.

"When will you come back for us?"

The captain stopped and looked at the bewildered scientist.

"Our agreement called for you to stay on this island for three weeks. That would make our pickup date on September 21. I see no reason to change that now."

"But that was before the murders," protested Jameson.

"Mur-*der*" replied Healy. "Singular. I've seen one body and I'm removing it now."

"I can't believe you're leaving."

"I have my orders. Zinko. Madison."

The captain left the building followed by Zinko and Madison. Bickford lingered for a fraction of a second and I rushed over to him.

"I wanted to talk to you. I read your article in that military journal. Are you here to . . ."

He looked surprised.

"I didn't expect it to be posted. It was classified. It would be better for me if you don't tell anyone what you read. I'll tell you this much because I think you need to know."

The big man glanced around to make sure the captain was gone.

"We've just gotten orders to join several other ships in the Bering Strait. We've had a report of Russian special forces invading Little Diomede Island. All ships in the region are to proceed there in full battle mode. No civilians. That's why the captain's leaving all of you here. I know he'll be back for you. I'm just not sure when."

"Why can't you stay with us? You're not Coast Guard. You could be a real help if we are in danger."

"Not *if* but *when*," he said. "Watch your back."

"What have you heard beyond what I already know?"

"I was talking about them."

Bickford pointed to the door, through which walked the Russians as if on cue. As Bickford turned and strode from the room, Belinsky and Zukov threw their gear onto the floor and grinned at the rest of us. When he thought no one else was looking, Zukov brought a finger across his throat.

✧ ✧ ✧

True to his word, the captain saw to it that his men transferred our equipment and supplies to the area outside the first building. I threw myself into the physical labor of the unloading so I wouldn't have to think about what I had come to think of as "my plight."

I had signed on to this expedition for the challenge and the adventure. Now, however, a series of bizarre events had made me fear for my own safety. For one thing, the Russians didn't have my best interests at heart. But was their boorish behavior a prelude to something truly harmful? Who was responsible for the three deaths? Who would be next? And why was I the only one who seemed worried?

I felt totally alone and without friends. Susan and I had been intimate, but she was clearly under some kind of spell with Scott. Jane, Alan, Danny, and Ben were friendly, but I hardly knew them, nor they me. And Jameson? He was interested only in exerting his authority and saving his own ass. Given what Bickford had said about the danger, I couldn't figure out why he had left. He was supposed to be handling security for the expedition.

We finished our work by about 7 p.m., then ate our evening meal in silence. Salcido had gone to chef's school sometime in the distant past so he happily assumed that duty for the duration of our stay on Herschel Island. We gorged ourselves on fish tacos and he hinted at other special dishes to come. While we might eventually be relegated to foraging off the land and catching fish from the sea, right now we would be well fed.

Most everyone was lost in his or her own thoughts as we ate. I sat with Jane and Alan. Susan was with Scott, whose hand restraints had been removed. Ben helped Danny serve and clean up. The Russians sat at the far end of the room doing more smoking and laughing than eating. Maybe they don't eat fish tacos in Russia. They certainly weren't mourning Nadia Chernoff that I could see. Jameson chose to dine alone, except for the hovering presence of Carmen Ames, who spent time preparing the agenda for our upcoming staff meeting. The jerk wouldn't even let her eat.

We drifted to our sleeping areas about 7:30 p.m., to unpack our gear and relax. I picked a cubicle as far away as possible from the two Russian men and made sure that Danny, Ben, and Alan were between me and those two vandals. I was somewhat relieved when Jameson installed a tentlike enclosure around his area, effectively blocking Belinsky and Zukov from getting to me without walking over him. For his part, Scott was to be locked in a small room at the other end each night. Oddly, he didn't protest this arrangement, acting benumbed to all that had happened. Given Zukov's attack on me, I wanted him to be similarly restrained, but Jameson wouldn't listen when I suggested it. I didn't bother to ask him about Bickford because I doubted he would answer my questions.

We convened for our first staff meeting on the island at 8:30 p.m.

"We are meeting under circumstances I would never have predicted," he said solemnly. "Before we begin, let us bow our heads in tribute to Derek Peters, whose tragic death is sad for us all."

The assembled group followed his suggestion and the room was completely quiet except for the hum of the generator outside the door.

"Very well then, thank you," he said, signaling an end to our tribute.

"What about Ezmeralda Savoonga?" said Ben, his face a study in anguish.

"Who?" asked Jameson coldly.

"For God's sake, Cliff," I said. "His girlfriend. She's dead too. Why can't we honor her as well?"

"I wasn't aware there was any proof of her death," Jameson said haughtily. "I mean, no one located a body."

"You are an idiot!" I shouted, throwing to the winds any fear of being fired. After all, where would Jameson find a new historian—slash—public relations man in the Arctic?

"I'm going to ignore that remark for now," he said.

"Ignoring what I said doesn't make it any less truthful," I added. "You can put aside the fact of that murder, but I . . ."

"Who says it was murder?" Jameson said.

I looked around at the others, who sat around the makeshift conference table as if they were suddenly struck mute.

"Doesn't anyone else have the slightest tinge of worry that we may become a victim of some deranged Arctic madman?" I screamed.

"Calm down, Tom," said Hopkins. "I think you're getting carried away about this."

"Okay, okay. So I'm a bit overexcited," I said, pushing my arms away from my body in a gesture of distancing myself from everything I'd heard here. These people brought professional detachment to a new level.

"We need to get on with our work," said Jameson in his best "show-must-go-on" voice. "We've only got a few weeks before the Coast Guard picks us up again."

"I'm like Tom," said Jane. "I'm a bit unnerved by these incidents." As a true team player, though, she wasn't going to utter my word, *murder*.

"Jane, Jane," said Jameson soothingly. "Would I put you in danger? We've worked together for a long time. Have you ever known me to disregard the safety of the people who work for me, the people I have been privileged to lead?"

"Oh, p-l-e-a-z," I muttered.

If Jameson heard me, he chose to ignore it.

"Very well, then," he said. "I think we should move on."

"You need to address the issue of security," said Alan Hopkins. "I'm with Tom about this."

"Alan, have you ever known me to ignore matters vital to an expedition?"

"Maybe not, but I don't think you are taking this as seriously as you should. Listen to us!"

Jameson blinked but did not react as negatively as he did when I said something.

"All right, all right! I get the message! Carmen."

His ever-obedient secretary tugged a large footlocker over to where Jameson was sitting. He pulled out a key and opened the lock hanging from the front.

"I brought these along in case we needed them," he said.

Jameson held up several rifles and what looked like five pistols.

"That should do it," he said. "That should satisfy you guys."

"It's not a question of satisfying us," I said, "it's a question of safety."

"Whatever," he replied. "Alan, I'm putting you in charge of the weapons. You devise a security plan."

Hopkins nodded and pulled the footlocker over to his chair. I felt relieved because I trusted him completely. I made a mental note to talk to him about the Russians and my doubts about them. For one thing, I was certain they had their own weapons tucked away.

The meeting continued for another hour with Jameson discussing work schedules. I would have looked forward to it had I not had the lingering fear of what unknown person might be out there waiting for the chance to move in. I wound up with a schedule I liked. I was to be given research results as they were compiled by the others to incorporate into my main report. I was also to look them over as potential sources for stories I would prepare as news releases.

✧ ✧ ✧

After breakfast the following morning, I set up a little office in my cubicle. I used a drafting board placed on two stools as a desk. On it, I put the laptop computer and pads and pencils. I dug up my research files and my reference books out of a duffel bag and I was in business.

No one had anything for me to compile that soon, so I spent the first day editing the diaries of the Arctic explorer and troubleshooter, Charles Brower. Although I knew he had spent time on this island 100 years before, I hadn't read his words very carefully before. As I looked over his reminiscences, the parallels to our present circumstances were eerie. Although he wrote of danger, courage, and isolation that couldn't exist in this time of instantaneous communication and modern modes of transportation like helicopters, the climate hadn't changed all that much.

Before very long, I realized that while Brower was able to cope with any danger or adversity caused by men. When he came to ice, however, he wasn't so certain, such as the time the local hospital burned down.

The Arctic usually does things in a big way. Once the elements get out of hand, nature goes to limit. The hospital embers were hardly cool when Nature showed what could be done with frozen water. As if jealous of all that its fiery rival had accomplished on the hospital, suddenly ten million tons of sea ice, driven by a southwest gale, came surging in to finish the rest of Barrow. They thundered against the anchored ice along the shore. They shoved across the sand spits and up the slopes beyond. They squeezed and pressured it into fantastic masses which towered 75 feet high.

All in 20 minutes! Then when there seemed no hope left for any wooden structure, the pressure ceased as abruptly as it had started and the fleeing populace, not yet adjusted to loss by fire, came back to survey its loss by ice.

I placed these old pages aside and got up to walk over to look out the window. The clear blue sky cast doubt on any theory of adverse weather conditions anytime soon. It was, after all, only September 2. I knew the ice pack was out there, many miles to the North. It would advance southward in a month or so and begin to pose a threat in late October or November. What's more, Brower was talking about Point Barrow, several hundred miles to the West. I hadn't found any similar references to ice here on Herschel Island. I was convinced that my worries here were of men, not the elements. After all, global warming would keep temperatures way up.

I walked back to my desk and picked up another sheet of the old diary pages, those marked "Herschel Island" in that old scrawly handwriting people used in the past.

> *I had seen the insidious creeping action of ice too often not to call [the] captain's attention to the danger. But instead of steaming south . . . he seemed to think it safe to tie up to a large [ice] floe, apparently grounded. So here we stayed, while drifting ice gradually packed in solid on all sides.*

I read on about the obstinacy of the captain on that expedition and his tendency to ignore all advice and warnings. That certainly sounded like Jameson. But this was winter, way past the present date. We would be long gone by the time the ice pack formed.

I looked at the date on this entry: September 10, 1897.

✧ ✧ ✧

Twelve

hree days later, I had the first encounter with the Russians since we landed on the island. It happened as I was walking to lunch in the main building. I had gradually relaxed because Ben told me the Russians were spending their days doing practice runs in their Zodiak.

"Good morning, *tovarich.*"

Belinsky came up on one side of me and Zukov on the other.

"I don't need a Praetorian guard," I said, trying to ease my growing apprehension.

"What is this *Praetorian* you speak of?" asked Belinsky.

"Nothing. Just a figure of speech."

He shrugged and we kept walking.

"What do you want?" I asked, abandoning any pretense of civility.

"Is that a way to address old friends?" said Zukov, his gold teeth showing through an insincere smile.

I stopped, trying to slough off the fear I felt every time I looked at these two.

"Look. We have to live and work side by side in a very small area. I don't like it to any better than you like it. Just stay away from me and we'll get through this."

Zukov made a move to twist my arm behind my back. I whirled around and broke free, then turned to face him.

"Stay back," I shouted, holding up my hands as a shield. "I don't intend to say anymore about how you tried to blackmail me last week and what you tried to do to Derek Peters. Let's just let it pass."

Zukov started smiling again, as if recalling their attempt to humiliate me on the boat really made him happy. He made a back and forth movement with one hand down hear his crotch.

"Nadia tell me you not so good in sex department," he said. "She need Russian man with better equipment." He kept laughing and continued his simulated groin action. That made me mad and I took a swing at him, but Belinsky deflected my arm.

"You bastards really liked your little episodes, didn't you?" I shouted. "What is it, some kind of Cold War envy? You have to humiliate an American every once in a while to forget what a lousy country you come from?"

I was really going now, venting my anger at these two as well as the whole mess I found myself in. The men had put their arms down but were moving toward me very slowly.

"You can't even keep your own men from being slaughtered in Chechnya or drowned in a nuclear sub or killed in that Moscow theater. You couldn't even save those poor little kids in that Beslan school. You care more about preserving power for the few than really helping the many. You like having something to hold over me. You like humiliating people like Derek. I think you like having sex with other men, now don't you, Zukov? How do you say *faggot* in Russian?"

Neither man said anything. They kept walking closer to me.

"You used Nadia as a whore to get something on me. Did you kill her because she was unsuccessful in her mission?"

Zukov lunged at me with a knife, which I managed to dodge before I fell over Belinsky's protruding foot. The younger man was on top of me in an instant, his right hand raised above his head, so as to get better velocity for the knife he apparently intended to shove into my chest.

Out of nowhere, Aniak and Salcido grabbed his arms and pulled him off me.

"You okay, Tom? Did this little Red prick hurt you?" asked Salcido.

"No. I'm all right."

I got to my feet and began brushing off my clothes.

"This man attacked my assistant," said Belinsky. "He also insulted the memory of my secretary."

"Let's move this inside and get Jameson involved," I said finally, to break the impasse.

As a group, we began walking to the main building, with me in the lead, followed by Belinsky. Aniak and Salcido kept Zukov further back, each one holding tightly to his arms.

I opened the door and led the way into the large room. The smell of vegetable soup filled the air and made me realize I was hungry.

"Just in time," Susan called out to me from one of the tables we used for our meals. I had forgotten my roll on the muddy ground. My clothes were a mess.

"Tom, what the hell happened to you?" asked Jameson, causing everyone else to look at me and the phalanx of people behind me. He sensed that something was wrong and a quizzical look came over his face.

"I . . . er . . . fell over someone's foot."

"Your man brutally attacked Dimitri Zukov, then insulted the memory of my secretary, Nadia Chernoff. I demand that he be disciplined immediately or our arrangement of cooperation is off! That also will mean an immediate cutoff of funding!" said Belinsky.

Jameson blinked several times as if he were having trouble taking this all in.

"Slow down, everyone!" he said, gesturing with his arms as if he were an umpire making a ruling at first base. "I need to know what happened!"

"It's fairly easy," I said, "I was walking to lunch when these goons . . ."

Jameson held up his hand. "I'd like to hear what Boris has to say first."

"Great! Take the word of a gangster like him over me."

When he heard me say "gangster," Zukov tried to break away from Salcido and Aniak. They tightened their hold on him.

"Hurling insults will not get us anywhere, Tom," said Jameson.

"Why do I suddenly feel like all of this is my fault?" I said.

"Now tell me, Boris. What is this all about?" Jameson continued.

"It's of no great importance to our overall work here," he replied.

We all looked at each other with amazement.

"What gives?" asked Salcido. "One minute you're after his balls, now you're not interested?"

"What happened, Belinsky?" said Alan Hopkins, who had been quiet up to this point, sitting to one side as if weighing which person to believe.

Belinsky smiled and looked at his watch.

"You do seem to be doing what we call in my country an 'about face'," said Jameson, who also looked perplexed.

Belinsky said nothing but walked to the window, then nodded at Zukov.

"It is now 1153 hours and I am taking control of this expedition and this island in the name of holy mother Russia," he said.

"What the hell?" I muttered.

"You will keep silent, professor!"

"This is absurd, Belinsky. We outnumber you!" shouted Hopkins who was moving toward the big Russian.

"That is where you are wrong, Dr. Hopkins."

At that, Belinsky pulled a silver whistle from his pocket and started blowing on it. The high-pitched beeps even drowned out the hum of the generators.

Carmen and Susan screamed as the doors at both ends of the building burst open and men in black Ninja suits soon filled the room. I counted ten and they were all carrying Kalishnikov rifles. Their faces were hidden by ski masks.

This was one of those moments when I'd like to think in advance that I would do something heroic to save the day, and all of us, from these marauders. The truth was I couldn't move.

"Allow me to introduce Major Gregor Kirov."

A tall lean figure stepped forward and pulled off his hood. He clicked his heels and smiled. Kirov could well have been the model for a poster depicting the virtues of the new Russian man. He had delicate, almost feminine features and a full head of blond hair.

"At your service," the young major said.

Cliff Jameson was having none of it. He might betray us individually and treat us shabbily, but no one was going to take his expedition away from him.

"I must protest these actions, Boris, and demand that you stop all of this nonsense immediately," he said. "If you stop now and withdraw these men, I will forget that any of this ever happened. We can get back to work as if nothing happened."

Belinsky apparently grew tired of what Jameson was saying. Or maybe he needed to set an example for the rest of us. He took a rifle from the man standing near him and smashed its butt across Jameson's face.

Amid Susan's loud screams, our fearless leader fell to the floor, blood spurting out of his broken mouth.

✧ ✧ ✧

A half hour later, we had all been herded into the shower room of the second building. Jameson was unconscious, but still breathing. The ever-resourceful Danny Salcido was working on stopping the bleeding using various supplies from the first aid kit.

The women clustered around him to help in whatever way they could. The rest of us were standing together a few feet away trying to figure out what was happening to us.

"It's still kind of murky in my mind, but I'd guess something like this," I said, quietly mindful of the man guarding us just outside the closed door. They probably didn't speak English, but I didn't want to take the chance.

"These men are *Spetsnaz*, kind of a combination Navy Seal and Army Rangers. Belinsky referred to them once in passing last week," I continued.

"Why land here?" said Hopkins. "Why bother with us?"

"I'd guess that good old Boris holds some kind of rank in that organization so he's commanding these men in whatever mission they've been sent to carry out."

"But what?" said Szabo, who I hadn't heard speak since we found Derek's body.

"I'm not sure, but I'd bet it's got to do with our research and that Russian oil company paying some of the freight here. You remember I found one of their emblems when we were looking for whoever took Ezmeralda Savoonga's body."

At the mention of his fiancée's name, Ben Aniak's eyes filled with tears.

"Sorry, Ben," I said, and draped an arm over his shoulders for a minute to give him moral support. "This squad has obviously been waiting on the island for us to land. Maybe they were hanging around here when Ezmeralda surprised them. They killed her to keep their presence quiet. Maybe Derek saw them too, I don't know."

I glanced at Szabo for his acquiescence.

"But I was practically with Derek the whole time. Then the lights went out. I'm not sure what happened after that. I can't believe they could kill him so fast."

"These guys are trained assassins, Scott," I said. "The little bit of research I did on them on the Internet convinced me of that. Maybe Derek surprised them, like I said."

"Whatever they're after, I doubt they'll need us," Hopkins added, a grim look on his face.

"Shhh," I said, a finger pressed to my lips. "No need to alarm the ladies yet." I glanced at them and they all seemed to be concentrating on Jameson. "If I could figure out what they're after, maybe we could decide how to react."

The three men looked at me like I was crazy.

"Bear with me, guys. If Boris thinks we're withholding other information from him, he'll keep us alive until he gets it."

"As if he'd tell us that," said Szabo with a scoff. "Yeah, right. Okay, Mr. Commando, let's have it."

"Shut up, Scott," said Hopkins. "Have you got a better idea? Let's hear what Tom has to say."

"I'm not sure what I have to say," I laughed. "I'm thinking out loud, I guess. I wish I knew how Paul Bickford fits into this."

At that moment, the door opened and Major Kirov walked in, followed by one of his Kalishnikov-toting men.

"If you will be pleased to follow me," he said. "We will go to bigger building."

What he said came out *yavilplztfolami*. I understood him, but only by listening carefully.

"We've got to an injured man here," I said, gesturing toward Jameson and people clustered around him. "I'm not sure we can move him."

Kirov looked at Jameson and then to me.

"*Yavilplztfolami*," he repeated, still smiling.

"I'm not sure we . . ."

He held up his hand to stop me in midsentence. Then he snapped his fingers. Two more men entered the room and walked over to Jameson. Kirov pointed a forefinger at the prostrate scientist, then hooked his thumb toward the door. The burly commandos picked up Jameson and carried him out. The rest of us followed them out of the room.

When I stepped outside the building I was struck by a distinct change in the air. It felt a lot colder than when we had gone inside four hours before. The sky was bright and clear, the sun still shining. Given the steadily shortened days however, its rays were not having as much effect on keeping things warm. I shuddered a bit at feeling the cold and grabbed my arms in a futile gesture of warming myself. We trudged to the main building and Kirov stepped aside to allow us to enter.

"*Yavilplzinterhier*."

We did what we were told, then, gasped audibly at the sight awaiting us. The entire room had been turned upside down, with storage boxes overturned, files strewn all over the floor, office supplies thrown around. Several commandos were sitting at computer keyboards entering various passwords that did not seem to be working. With their dark hair and dark complexions, they looked very different from the Nordic-looking Kirov.

Belinsky motioned for us to gather around the conference table. They even sat Jameson down, his head lolling to one side, the bandages around his mouth saturated with blood.

"You probably wondered why I called you together here," said the Russian in a display of how cool he had become during his time in America. "He, he, ha, ha!"

As if on cue, Zukov nearly doubled over with laughter.

"This man needs medical attention or he's going to bleed to death," I shouted.

Zukov started toward me, apparently itching to hit me and make my mouth match Jameson's. Belinsky held up his hand and the younger man stopped.

"We all need to spill a little blood for things we believe in," he said. "Can you change his dressing again?" He looked at Salcido, who pulled out his first aid kit and went to work on Jameson again.

"While he tends to this wounded man, I want to introduce a distinguished guest from some much warmer climates," said Belinsky.

As he spoke, a tall, lean man stepped out of one of the rear rooms and walked to the Russian's side. His gold-trimmed robe was so white as to make me wonder how anyone could stay so clean in the muck and mire of the Arctic. His beard was long and carefully combed and his turban wound in perfect folds around his head. He was followed by two men similarly, if not as elaborately, attired. They were carrying rifles and had pistols stuffed into the sashes around their waists.

A closer look revealed someone who had had a tough life. A scar ran from the corner of his left eye to the ear on that side of his face. That eye had a fixed look that comes from being artificial and dead. The other eye, though real, was almost equally devoid of life. He looked at us with pure hatred as he passed by. The Arab, as we all referred to him from then on, walked with a limp. The way he favored his left leg made me think it was prosthetic.

It was not a stretch to imagine that he had suffered these serious injuries on one side of his body while fighting the Russians in Chechnya. Islamic militants including Arabs had been making life miserable for Russians in that breakaway province for years. But why was he here and how did he fit into Belinsky's plans?

"Let's get to the matter at hand," said Belinsky, looking at the rest of us one by one. "One of you, or maybe all of you, has some important information that I wish to possess."

"Wait a minute," I said. "I think we deserve some answers before you go any further. Who are these people? We won't tell you anything if you don't give us answers!"

"It will be best if you do not, as you Americans are fond of saying, 'play dumb.'

"*Tovarich*," said Zukov, motioning to me. "I will find out if this one is really as dumb as he looks."

"I'm smart enough to know an asshole like you when I see him!" I said, puffing myself up in righteous, if misguided, anger.

"Tom," muttered Hopkins next to me, "don't make it worse by taunting them."

"Your friend is right, professor," said Belinsky. "Would you wave a red flag at a bull? I may be, how do you say, hung like a bull, but I am much smarter."

He pointed to his head and then burst into peals of laughter. As always, Zukov joined in.

"My young associate, Dimitri, would like to pound you with his fists, but I will protect you."

More laughter.

"God, Belinsky, can we just get on with it and cut the comedy act," I said calmly, trying to mask my growing fear with bravado.

"Enough!" said the Arab, who looked quite out of place in this frigid environment. He snapped is fingers and one of his men draped a fur parka over his shoulders. "You told me these Americans would present no problem." He spoke perfect English without an accent of any kind.

"They will not hinder us for long, my friend. We will get on with our main business. We have searched the files for some information I very much need to possess."

The Arab and his men relaxed and moved off to one side of the room of observe.

"What kind of information?" asked Hopkins.

"Certain information you have gained on the formation of the ice pack in the Arctic," Belinsky answered calmly.

"So that's what this is all about," I said, shaking my head in understanding as this final piece of a puzzle fell into place. "Your government needs these research results so it knows when it can send ships freely across the top of the world."

"Not exactly my government, but elements in it," said Belinsky. "And our Muslim brothers are supporting our endeavors by helping us carry on the fight in our homeland in Chechnya."

"So you are Chechens, Boris," I said. "That explains a lot. So if the plan works, you will have another way for terrorists to get into the United States. What are you going to do, hold Alaska hostage, or invade us from the North?"

I said this half in jest, but neither Belinsky nor the Arab was smiling.

"My God," said Hopkins. "You can never pull that kind of thing off!"

A smile crossed the Russian's lips.

"Not immediately or perhaps never. Let us just say that some associates in my government want to keep their options open," he answered, a look of pride on his face.

"So no more feeling ashamed of a floundering nation?" I said, glancing at both Belinsky and Zukov. As usual, the latter was ready to grab me by the throat. His boss touched his arm and shook his head.

"Yes, you are correct, professor. We are now able to be proud to be Russians again and in alliance with our Muslim brothers we will . . ."

"I would not burden these people with too many details of our plans," said the Arab. "They are, after all, infidels and bitter enemies of Islam."

"Yeah, after you slaughtered our people on 9/11," shouted Salcido. "What do you expect? You fuckin' rag heads deserve to be strung up by the balls."

Now it was Bobby's turn to be hit. The Arab nodded to one of his commandos and he promptly kicked Salcido in the groin. The women screamed as he doubled over and fell to the floor.

Belinsky paid scant attention to any of this. His eyes looked dreamy as if he was contemplating his role in whatever new universe he was trying to construct.

"But that is the future," he said, the sound of his own voice bringing him back to reality. "We have more pressing concerns today. Who among you will tell us about this final ice data— this crucial ice data?"

We all looked appropriately perplexed. In my case, I really didn't know. My role was to report on the findings later. I had no part in gathering that material, nor had Jameson or any of the others confided in me. I knew Scott, Jane, and Alan had made forays onto the ice to set up instrumentation. Susan had then compiled it. Ben and Danny had support jobs that put them out of the direct scientific flow of information. Carmen was Cliff's secretary. Whether her role included the typing of his findings I wasn't sure.

"You've observed our work for several weeks, Belinsky," I said in a stall for time. "I'm surprised you can't take an educated guess."

"My old friend Clifford has been careful in shielding this research from me. I could not pry on the ship. I needed my men to back me up. Which brings us to our present point. Dimitri."

Zukov got up and I braced for another encounter with him. Instead, he walked to where Jameson sat slumped in his chair, his eyes closed, a quiet moan coming from his mouth. As we held our collective breath, the muscular Russian stood over the semiconscious man as if he couldn't decide what kind of pain to inflict on him.

"Belinsky, for God's sake, he's already injured," I said, taking a step toward the two of them. In an instant, a rifle-toting commando pushed me back. No one else moved.

Zukov pulled off the bandage and, with an eyedropper, calmly deposited a drop of something into the open wound near Jameson's mouth. He began screaming in agony immediately.

"Peroxide tends to sting a bit when it hits damaged skin," said Belinsky. "It will sting even more when placed in the human eye."

"You'll blind him for life!" I shouted, trying to step around the guard who was restraining me. No one else was moving a muscle and I can't say that I blamed them. "How do you know he has what you want?"

"Are you volunteering to reveal the information I want, professor?" he said. "Are you ready to, as you Americans say, 'spill the beans'?"

"I would if it would make you leave him alone. He's in no shape to tell you anything. By now, he's probably unconscious."

We all looked at Jameson who, indeed, had passed out. Zukov let him fall unceremoniously to the floor.

"Who else would know about this data I seek?" Belinsky said in a transparent attempt to make us believe he was thinking out loud. "Dr. Jameson is very close-mouthed about everything and very, how do you put it, territorial about his prerogatives as the leader of this expedition. I'm not surprised that he didn't confide in any of you."

He glanced around the room and no one engaged his eyes. It was like in childhood where none of the kids wanted to be picked by the teacher to read an essay in class.

"I haven't got the time to interrogate everyone," he continued. "I will concentrate on Dr. Jameson and his secretary, the lovely Miss Ames."

I looked at the tiny, red-haired Carmen, who never seemed so defenseless and vulnerable. A look of absolute terror came over her face. Belinsky snapped his fingers and the other commandos began to ease the rest of us out of the room. Except for a few instances of arms pulled away from attempts to restrain them and cries of "I can do this on my own" or similar language, the group filed out of the building like zombies. We were too outnumbered to resist.

"I know where the data is hidden," I shouted as I was led away, the last to leave the room. "I know what you are trying to do with the ice data. You're trying to take over the top of the world."

Belinsky walked over to me and stared into my eyes for a long time. Then he slapped me hard, in a blow that caused me to stumble backwards a step or two.

"That is a ridiculous assumption, professor. You make wild guesses but you do not know the truth, do you? Clifford talked to me about you," he laughed. "He told me you talk too much to be trusted. He gave you nothing. Your attempt at heroics gained nothing for your friends. Take him away."

Because it was pointless to do otherwise, I walked out to join the others.

About an hour later, the rest of us were sitting around on the beds in the women's dorm. The building was surrounded by commandos but none was actually inside with us. Suddenly, the quiet was broken by one high-pitched scream. We could only guess at the horrors Carmen was being subjected to.

I glanced around the room. Susan was sobbing softly. Jane was dry-eyed but her hands were white from gripping the edge of the bed frame too tightly. Alan Hopkins looked grim and kept cracking his knuckles. Aniak and Salcido paced the outer perimeter of the room, as if their fury couldn't be contained any other way.

Only Scott Szabo seemed untouched by the gravity of the situation. He sat off by himself clipping his fingernails, the nail remnants falling one by one to the floor in front of him.

"We've got to do something," said Salcido, "even if we get hurt trying. I can't let Carmen suffer anymore."

Szabo yawned loudly.

"You've been trying to get in her pants the whole time we've been up here," he said, a big smirk on his face.

Salcido ran to Szabo and started shaking him. As Hopkins and I pulled him off, Salcido hit Szabo hard in the jaw, knocking him onto the floor.

"Stop, you're killing him!" shouted Susan who rushed to comfort her boyfriend. A twinge of jealousy hit me when I saw her reaction.

Szabo was rising slowly to his feet rubbing his jaw and moving it back and forth to test its viability.

"Is it broken?" I asked.

He shook his head and sat down.

"I don't think so."

Susan sat beside him and put one arm around his shoulders.

"Drape this over him so he doesn't go into shock," I said, throwing her a blanket.

Hopkins had walked Salcido to the other end of the room and he was talking to him in low tones. Whatever he was saying, it seemed to be working. Salcido calmed down.

"I don't see what all the fuss is about," said Szabo, still trying to decide if his jaw was seriously damaged. "I was just saying what I thought. I'm entitled to my opinion. Last time I looked, this was a free country."

I walked over to Szabo and knelt in front of him so we would be eye-to-eye.

"You don't seem to grasp the facts here, Scott. Derek is dead. Carmen is being raped over and over. Cliff is being tortured and may die. What is it that makes that so hard for you to understand?"

He blinked but didn't say anything.

"You don't have a soul or a conscience," I muttered and walked away.

"What are our options here?" I said to the group. "They've taken away our cell phones, our radios, and our weapons. They've got two of our people. There is no help within a thousand miles or so."

"And the weather is getting bad," said Jane, who was standing by the window. "I wouldn't be a bit surprised if we have a blizzard tonight. Whatever happened to global warming?"

✧ ✧ ✧

Thirteen

ometime during the night, someone shook me out of a
fitful sleep. I was dreaming of the Oregon Coast. I could
see my house, but I couldn't seem to get to it. It was one
of those dreams where you can't walk because your legs are
mired in quicksand.

"Tom, Tom. Wake up!"

Ben Aniak had his hand over my mouth to keep me from
crying out. My bed was away from the others so they probably couldn't hear us. Ben was taking his turn at what we were
calling guard duty, to make sure we wouldn't be surprised by
the Russians.

"Ben. What's going on?"

"My cousin is here."

"Your cousin is where?"

"Back there in the shower room."

I blinked, trying to figure out how Ben and his cousin had
gotten into my dream of the Oregon Coast.

"Get up. We need to talk to him."

I rose to my feet and followed him into the shower room. I closed the door and turned to see a young man who could have been Ben's twin.

"This is Alfred."

The young man smiled and we shook hands.

"How did you get in here?"

"He came up through that trapdoor over there," said Ben. "He doesn't talk so much, so I'll explain. We know this island. We played here as kids."

"You got by the guards?" I asked him and he nodded in reply.

"Some of them are drunk and others are sleeping," said Ben.

"So much for the discipline of the most elite corps of the Russian military," I scoffed. "They're a farce."

"Yeah, but they've got a lot of guns," answered Aniak. "Anyway, Alfred got in and we both think we can get out the same way, if we do it before daybreak."

"But where do we go after we get away from here?"

"Alfred and several of his mates have Zodiaks waiting for us on the other side of the island. We can head back to Tuk."

"Why would he take these chances for us, a bunch of strangers?"

Alfred smiled as he listened to Ben's answer.

"Because he's my cousin and because I have something he wants."

"The booze," I said. "You *were* smuggling liquor! That's why your fiancée was here waiting for you and why good old Alfred here came back. For a shipment of demon rum."

Aniak nodded and smiled.

"You got it, partner! I've also got something else. The thing the Russians are looking for."

He fumbled around it in the pocket of his parka and pulled out a computer disk.

"You sly fox," I said, laughing and shaking my head. "How'd you get that?"

"Yesterday I was talking to Cliff and he interrupted our conversation to tell Carmen to put the data from the ice research onto one disk for safekeeping. I watched her do it, then dropped the disk in my pocket when she wasn't looking. I'm not sure why. I guess I'm just naturally light fingered."

"Don't apologize, just hang onto it and don't tell anyone else."

As we talked, I formed a plan in my mind to get all of us out.

I pulled out my own disk and exchanged it with Ben, after adding new labels to both.

"You got any ideas, Alfred?" I turned to the pleasant-looking young man standing next to Ben.

"If you round up your guys, I'll get them out of here."

"What about the might of the Russian army?" I asked, only partly in jest. "She-it," he sneered. "It won't be hard to outwit them. Get them up, get them into parkas and boots, and send them to me."

I did what he said as quickly as possible. I walked around to everyone and woke them up, whispering instructions and pointing toward Ben and Alfred at the rear.

Only Szabo grumbled at the plan, probably because I had come up with it.

"Okay, Scott. You're free to stay. Roll over and catch a few more winks."

He got up and joined the others after I said that. The old me wished he would stay behind and get beat up by the Russians. The new, "great leader" in me knew I had to treat everyone the same, even a bastard like Szabo. But I still didn't trust him.

When everybody had assembled, I filled them in on what I thought we should do.

"Can we make it to Tuk that easily?" asked Hopkins.

"Will we freeze to death?" added Jane.

"What we gonna eat?" said Salcido.

Aniak talked about the route, the food supply, and the importance of speed to beat any bad weather.

I saved the hardest question until last, and I raised it to clear the air, not because I expected a satisfactory answer.

"Do any of you have a problem leaving Carmen and Cliff behind? I've thought about it constantly and I just don't see a way to rescue them and still get away ourselves. We can send help back for them later."

"Yeah, right, and the tooth fairy will find me up here too," said Szabo. "You never liked Jameson anyway. This is a convenient way to get rid of him and take over. Don't the rest of you see that?"

I didn't answer, although I could barely keep quiet. I could feel the muscles in my neck and back tighten. Somewhere behind my eyes, a headache was forming.

"For God's sake, Scott," said Hopkins. "Are you going to be a prick until the end? If you've got a better idea, let's hear it. If not, shut up and listen for a change, or don't new ideas easily penetrate that empty California surfer head of yours?"

"Leave Scott alone!" shouted Susan, still quick to defend her boyfriend, no matter how much he dumped on her. Both Scott and Susan moved into a corner, she with her arm around his shoulder, he with a hurt look on his face.

"I don't see that we have any other choice," said Jane. "I mean to leave poor Carmen and Cliff behind. I've known him for many years and he's a friend. But I think it would be silly to try some heroics here when whatever we do would get us killed. I can't say Cliff wouldn't want us to try. I think you all know he isn't exactly the martyr type."

"No, he's a selfish bastard," added Salcido. "We all know that."

No one disagreed or said anything else on the subject of leaving two of our party behind. The more we talked and thought about it, the more it became a given.

"Are we set then?" said Ben, after a few moments of silence. I nodded and walked to the women.

"Alfred is going to take you out first. Don't say anything at all. When you get out from under the building, he says you'll find the tundra less flat than it looks. There are crevices and gullies everywhere. You'll be crawling along on the most direct route away from camp. When it's safe, Alfred will signal you to stand up and run like hell to where some of his buddies are waiting for us. Am I right, Alfred?"

The taciturn Eskimo nodded and motioned for the women to join him at the trapdoor. I hugged Jane and she hoisted her rather bulky figure into the hole.

"I'm not built for derring-do," she laughed, before dropping from sight.

I didn't want to touch Susan or even see her again. It took all the self-control I could muster not to turn away as Alfred helped her navigate the small opening in the floor. She glanced at me only at the last minute. Tears glistened in her eyes as she disappeared through the floor.

"All right, they are on their way," I said. "We'll wait a few minutes and then follow them out. Ben knows the way. I'll bring up the rear. Like I said to the ladies, at some point we'll just have to run like hell. We don't have much more time until daylight. Let's do it."

As the men walked to the trapdoor for their turn at dropping out of sight, I decided to check the main room one more time for anything that we might use. We were dressed as warmly as we could. We'd filled our canteens with water from the showers. I scavenged all the high protein biscuits, power bars and apples I found in the eating area and stuffed them in my backpack.

Through a slat in the blind, I could see the dozing sentry leaning against the porch railings. I hoped Ben had been right about the other commandos stationed around the buildings. I had no idea how long we had before Belinsky sent someone to check on us. Probably not more than an hour or two.

I decided to impede his progress as much as I could. I didn't dare slide the bolt across the door, because I was afraid its snap would wake up the man on the porch. Instead, I pushed two filing cabinets slowly across the floor so they would be in position to keep the door from opening easily. I managed to move the first cabinet easily. When I got the second half the way I wanted it to go, however, a high spot on the floor snagged the corner of the metal file, causing one of the drawers to open. The noise it made was magnified by the quiet of the Arctic dawn. Without waiting to see if the sentry was awake, I closed the drawer and finished pushing the cabinet into place.

I couldn't resist a peak through the blind. A single eye blinked back at me. I staggered away and ran to the shower room. The sentry was yelling as I slipped through the door to the permafrost below, "Halt! *Amerikanski!*" or something that sounded like that.

Ben was waiting for me as I hit the ground.

"Quick, Tom! We've got to get going!"

"Yeah. Did you hear that shout?"

Ben had already rushed off and I had trouble keeping up with him. We cleared the building and started running in a kind of half crouch. I felt like an outsized spider or Groucho Marx on a bad day.

We made good time in getting away from the camp. The guard was still shouting but his voice grew faint. Apparently, he and his fellow commandos were not following us, or at least not yet.

We reached the others who were waiting with Alfred in a section of the tundra that dropped away into a crevice. From a distance, their heads blended well with the vegetation.

The sun was up by now, flooding the plain with its harsh early morning light. As my adrenaline levels receded, I realized how cold it was. All that running and excitement had warmed me up so much I hadn't noticed.

"We're freezing our butts off," said Salcido.

Jane and Susan looked blue. Hopkins and Szabo looked grim.

"How could it change so fast—I mean the temperature," I said. "It was warm yesterday."

"The season of change is upon us," said Alfred, who had spoken so little that everyone looked at him as he spoke, like he was some kind of Arctic oracle sent to explain everything.

"Yeah, you got that right," added Ben, who spoke in less rarified language. "This is the Arctic, man. What can I say? It happens."

"What happens?" I whispered.

"Ice," he replied. "I can feel it in my bones."

"In early September? Seems pretty early, from what I've read," I said.

"Not this year, I guess," he said. "We best be moving along."

I didn't ask Ben any more questions but took my cue from the urgent tone of his voice.

"Okay, everybody. The sooner we get going, the sooner we'll get out of this mess." I looked at Alfred. "How far to the Zodiaks?"

"One half hour."

"Let's get the hell out of here!"

I nodded at Alfred Aniak and he stood up and started walking fast, the others following behind in single file. They all had parkas on and were carrying backpacks. At least outwardly, they looked well equipped. How they would fare when things got really tough, I couldn't be sure.

After about 20 minutes, I could see a gentle rise in the tundra ahead and guessed that the ocean would be on the other side of the bottom of a slope. The others disappeared over the hillock for an instant. As they reached the top, I saw them scampering down the incline like children, slipping and sliding on the surface. Odd they would fall back quickly on permafrost, I thought. Just then, I too lost my footing and began my own rapid descent. The ground under me was solid ice.

When I reached the bottom, the others were laughing as they got up and brushed each other off. For a moment, they had turned into children enjoying the first day of winter. My heart sank as I looked around at the solid ice offshore. I looked around for the Zodiaks and the young Eskimos left to guard them.

I saw two dark blobs several hundred yards away on the frozen beach and Ben and I started walking in that direction. I saw the red from the men's slashed throats before I saw the men themselves in much detail. I noticed that the ice pack had completely enveloped the small boats that were to spirit us away to safety. We were not going anywhere very quickly.

At that point, Susan let out one of the most terrifying screams I had ever heard. Ben and I turned in time to see a party of men walking toward us from the other direction. They were dressed in the black outfits of the *Spetsnaz* commandos, carrying their machine guns. They had their hoods pulled over their heads, except for the man in front.

Dimitri Zukov was grinning and pulling a pistol out of his holster.

✧ ✧ ✧

Fourteen

ukov walked directly to me and tried to hit me across the mouth with his pistol. If I hadn't ducked in time, I would be missing all of my front teeth. The force of his thrust threw him off balance and he stumbled slightly to one side.

"It's all in the footwork," I said, foolishly trying to bait him. I braced for another assault. Zukov regained his footing, raised his pistol and pointed at my head. Jane screamed and cried "No!" Everyone else looked grim but remained silent.

Although I'm not a brave man, I do have dignity and that trait kicked in as I stood to face my possible demise. I wasn't about to cry or beg or fall to my knees in prayer. Zukov aimed the gun at me and placed his finger on the trigger. I closed both eyes and wondered if I would feel much pain.

"*Tovarich!*"

I opened my eyes to see that Zukov had lowered his weapon and turned around. The commandos standing in a semicircle behind him parted and Boris Belinsky strode into view. He walked up to Zukov and slapped him in one direction, then the other. Zukov's eyes flashed but he said nothing. He snapped to attention and backed away.

Ah, the wonders of military discipline.

"I apologize for this outburst, professor," he said to me.

"Sure. Great. Apology accepted," I mumbled, trying hard to steady my knees, which were beginning to feel weak.

Alan Hopkins rushed to my side to steady me. I quickly regained my equilibrium and nodded my thanks to him.

"What do you intend to do with us?" I shouted after Belinsky's departing form. Scared as I was, I was still the leader of our motley crew.

"You are our prisoners, of course," he said. "I am waiting for my orders from Vladivostok. I imagine they will be sending helicopters, if the weather cooperates. It is hard to say how bad it will get. It is much colder than our meteorologists predicted."

"You do realize that we are American citizens on our territory," I said, trying to maintain my show of defiance. "If you kill us all, the full might of the United States Government will come down on you. I don't think your country wants to be party to an international incident. This has greater implications than your own desire for glory."

"This is Canadian territory, professor," he hissed, ignoring my taunt. "I don't think that government will care anything at all about a group of nobodies who are not their citizens and who are probably trespassing anyway. We are not afraid of the so-called might of the United States Government. Ha! We possess the might of the great Russian nation!"

"Will you tell me about Jameson and Carmen Ames?" asked Jane Baugh, who didn't seem afraid of Belinsky and his henchmen. "Are they in good health?"

"My dear Miss Baugh," he replied, "I'm afraid they are both unable to join us now."

"You bastard," yelled Salcido. "You killed them."

I shook my head at him to calm him down a bit. I needed to try to distract Belinsky's attention.

"So you got what you wanted from them, then decided to leave them alone and attend to their medical needs?"

"Unfortunately no, professor. They gave us nothing. We searched them but did not find the certain computer disk I thought one of them possessed. That's what I hope you will have the good sense to give me now."

"I'll be happy to give you everything I have, Mr. Belinsky," I replied. "I am the historian and record keeper for the expedition. I have a great deal of information gathered together for my final report. You are welcome to have what I have."

I pulled a disk marked "Expedition Record" from the pocket of my parka and held up for him. He glanced at it briefly, then handed it back to me.

"This is mere public relations verbiage. It would not do me any good. You may keep it as a souvenir of your fruitless journey here to the great Northland. Although I doubt you'll be able to play it where you are going."

Ben's and my ruse had worked—so far. I put the disk back in my pocket, feeling pretty good about myself. Belinsky nodded at Major Kirov, his more decent second in command, and the young officer began to line up everyone else, women on one end, the men on the other. He then patted the men down but left the two women alone for the time being.

Hopkins was first. The big man stood stolidly at attention while Kirov pulled opened his parka and ran his hands up and down his shirt and pants, as he looked for the missing computer disk. His pockets yielded several paperback books and some notebooks and pens.

Szabo was next and he didn't object to the search of his body either. The commando performed a similar frisk but found nothing in his pockets. It was the same story with Salcido, although he seemed on the verge of resisting the whole process. He tried to pull away even though the man searching him had a rifle.

"For God's sake, Danny," I yelled. "This is no time to be macho!"

He calmed down.

Ben's turn came. We both knew he had the disk marked "Ice Data Research Results." When they found out how innocuous the information on it was, the Russians would probably kill us all.

At that moment, Ben's cousin, Alfred, tried to take a gun from the commando nearest to him. The man clubbed him in the face. Hearing the commotion, Zukov turned around and shot the young Eskimo in the head. The woman screamed as Ben started to swing at the Russian. Belinsky restrained him at the last minute.

"Not so fast, my young friend," he said. "You cannot help your fellow Eskimo now. I doubt you want to join him in the great beyond."

Ben Aniak quit struggling and looked utterly defeated.

I looked at the women who turned out their pockets on their own to show they didn't have the disk. Jane and Susan seemed relieved to be off the hook. Both looked strained but Susan, especially, was on the verge of collapse.

For some reason, Belinsky decided to have Ben searched again. He motioned to the commando nearest him, who patted his legs first, then opened his parka to check out his upper body. The man finished the task, turned toward Belinsky, and shook his head. Belinsky said something to him in Russian and he started focusing on the parka. He went down one side with both hands flat.

"*Nocne.*"

He patted down the other side in the same way.

Nothing there either.

I relaxed and so did Ben.

Belinsky motioned to the man to look in the back of the parka. He pulled the coat off and ran his fingers up and down the fabric. In a few seconds he stopped and pulled a knife from his pocket. He swiftly cut a hole in the fur lining and reached a hand in to retrieve what was in there and pulled out a small gray diskette. He held it carefully and handed it to his boss. Belinsky broke into a broad smile and gave a thumbs-up sign to all his men. In his mind, his mission was complete. But what would that mean for the rest of us? I dreaded the answer.

Belinsky held up the diskette to read the label.

"Ice research results, 2002–2003," he said aloud. "I am very pleased."

"That ought to give you a nice promotion," I said. "What are you now? I've never seen you in uniform."

"I am a colonel," he answered proudly. "I serve the state in whatever way I can. I do not do these things that I do to be rewarded."

"That's hard to believe, colonel," I said.

Hopkins grew tense and grabbed my arm. "Don't, Tom. It'll make things worse if you bait him."

Zukov looked longingly at me, no doubt contemplating another chance to work me over. Belinsky held up his hand to stop his thuggish assistant.

"I realize what you are doing, professor, but I do not care. I am so pleased with our efforts here and I refuse to let you spoil it for me. I cannot wait to give this to my superiors. I only wish we had time to run it through the computers back at camp and prepare printouts. I must speed this to our headquarters and let our experts work on this vital data."

He looked at the sky as it began to snow.

"We need to move out of this area before the weather deteriorates."

During the entire time the search for the disk had gone on, it had turned colder. That the ice had closed in around the Zodiaks was a sign that things were taking a turn for the worse. No one had anticipated the arrival of winter so early. I recalled the historical accounts of the winter of 1897 on this same island, but brushed off comparisons to today. This was, after all, the era of global warming. As Belinsky snapped his fingers and barked orders to his men, I wondered if bad weather would make it easier to escape or more difficult.

The commandos formed us into groups of three and marched us back toward camp. Everyone seemed in good enough shape to make the trek so I didn't object. We needed to get back in the shelter and heat of the structures on the other side of the island. From there, after we had had some food and water, we could plan another escape. I wasn't sure how we would accomplish this, but I knew we would have to try.

The drastic change in the weather was even more noticeable during the walk back to camp. The wind stung my face and my feet felt frozen even through my heavy boots. Given the cold—and everyone's generally downbeat mood—I decided that any attempt at escape now would fail. We would have to wait until the timing was better.

This time, Belinsky split us up: Hopkins and Szabo with Jane; Salcido, Aniak, and Susan with me in a separate building.

The warmth of the room started the process of thawing us out. Food had been set out on the table—rolls, some kind of meat, and bowls of soup. We all forgot our fear and the cold and ran to the table to dig in.

Major Kirov followed me into the room and pulled me aside. "I will be in lead position of you in this building," he whispered. "If you cooperate with what we ask you to do, no harm will come to you. I want you to know that I am professional soldier, I am proud member of *Spetsnaz*, one of the most elite of all Russian military units. The men are under my command, they will not harm you. But you must do what we tell. We must strike bargain on that factor."

"Your English is pretty good, major," I said. "Where did you learn it?"

"I went to school in Canada," he replied, a pleased look on his face. "My father was cultural attaché in Ottawa for many years."

"Well, my compliments to you, major. Most Americans simply don't have the ear, or the interest, to learn other languages. We expect everyone to speak English."

"Yes, I would consider that a form of cultural imperialism."

"I like that phrase."

"Professor Martindale, I admire your obvious intellect and envy your position as a university professor, but I did not come here to this godforsaken place to speak of these things. You have not answered my question."

"What question was that, major?"

"The one about your agreement not to try to escape."

"Oh yes, you did say something about that."

Kirov stepped closer and put his face next to my own.

"I am not playing games here! If you do not follow instructions, I will be in disgrace and the colonel will replace me with Dimitri Zukov, someone I think you already are knowing too well."

"That thug!"

"Keep your voice down! Don't let anyone hear you say that! We could all get into much trouble if you maintain an attitude such as you just uttered!"

"Okay, okay, I see your point. As much as I like sparring verbally with our mutual friend, I guess caution dictates that I behave myself," I sighed. "We are really outnumbered."

"Good. I am pleased that you are turning into such a cooperating individual."

Kirov spoke well, but he still talked in a rather stilted way from time to time, like an English-Russian phrase book gone wrong.

"I will be a cooperating individual, I promise," I said, smiling sweetly. But this cooperating individual would still be spending every waking minute trying to escape.

"Very well then. I will leave you to your dinner. I hope you enjoy the delicious victuals."

I covered my mouth and turned my head so he wouldn't see my smile.

"My grandmother called food 'vittles,'" I said. "That's a new word to add to your already formidable English vocabulary."

"Thank you, professor. I consider that big compliment coming from you."

Our mutual admiration society was getting to be a bit much under the circumstances.

"One more question, major. What happened to Jameson and the girl, Carmen Ames?"

Kirov looked sad for a moment and averted his eyes.

"You did not hear these words coming from me," he whispered, "but both of them are dead."

I controlled my impulse to hit him or curse loudly or do something to display my rage. I didn't like Jameson but I didn't wish him dead either.

"Zukov?"

Kirov nodded his head.

"I fear so. He is not someone to underestimate. The colonel at times seems unwilling to restrain Zukov's darker impulses. I know I would not like to meet him, how do you put it, in alley that is dark."

"Where are the bodies?"

"They are wrapped in sheets and lying in the shower room of the main building. The onset of this cold weather will help preserve them."

"Does he plan to bury them here?"

"I am not certain of their disposition. He does not keep me informed of all aspects of our mission here. I follow orders and my responsibilities do not extend to that task."

"I can't see how you can be involved with all of these shady characters," I said. "You are a decent man, a professional soldier."

"I do not wish to discuss. I cannot say anything further, except for one factor I will tell. My mother was Chechen."

"And she was harmed in some way by Russian forces? She was killed, raped?"

"Stop," Kirov shouted. "You must cease these questions of yours! I have said enough up to this point for my very own good!"

"All right, all right, but tell me this. How will Belinsky explain their deaths? Frostbite? Food poisoning?"

"Perhaps it is his hope that he will not have to explain them at all."

"You mean if he removes the bodies and takes them to Russia, no one will be the wiser? But we all know what happened. What if . . ."

"I realize that you were once reporter, a person paid to ask questions all the time, but I think the time has come for you to think about having some food and getting some sleep," said Kirov patiently. "Just remove these other damaging thoughts from your mind and think only of immediate tasks. See to your people and have a good night."

The major stepped away and walked out of the room without saying another word. I hitched up my shoulders and tried to look calm as I walked toward the others.

"Tom," said Susan, in a tone of concern she hadn't shown since we saw one another on this trip, "I've saved some food for you. It's amazingly good."

Ben and Danny were shoveling food into their mouths at a rapid rate. We ate in silence and I didn't say anything about death or escape. I was too tired to plot or strategize. I needed sleep, and after that, time to think.

A distant sound woke me during the night and I got up. I looked out the back windows and saw a faint light two buildings away. I dressed in dark clothes and, on a hunch that it would not be secured, slipped through the trapdoor we had all used the day before. Once on the ground, I could see the entire encampment. Except for the sentries I knew were at the front door, no one else was visible.

I easily ran to one building, then to the next one, which had been our work area. I looked through the window and saw several commandos hunched over computers, still trying to figure out if the data was viable. Where were Belinsky, Zukov, and the Arab?

I glanced toward the largest of the original buildings on Herschel Island and saw another light. Reaching it, I tried a rear door and it opened easily. I stepped into a small entry hall with doors on both sides. Ahead through an arch was a larger room, with another door at the end. It was from this room that the light was shining. I moved quietly to the door on the left and saw a wooden ladder. Climbing up I could see that it led to a narrow catwalk that overlooked the big room below. I held my breath and inched forward, hoping a loose board would not betray me.

The Arab was pacing back and forth directly below me. He seemed to be agitated. Belinsky was seated at a table across from Zukov.

The Arab spoke in Russian.

"I do not like it that these Americans are getting in the way of our plans," answered Belinsky, switching to English.

"You told me it would be easy," said the Arab, also choosing to speak English. "You told me it would be no problem for you and your men to get the ice data from this bunch of amateurs. Now, there are complications and I am behind schedule. For the love of Allah, nothing can stop us from our quest!"

"I must remind my distinguished Arab brother that the noble Russian force, *Spesnatz*, is directing this operation," answered Belinsky.

The Arab switched to Russian.

Belinsky held up his hand.

"With all due respect, your Russian is not as good as you think," said Belinsky. "Let us use English for the practice it will give us."

The Arab seemed angry at this putdown and stopped pacing.

"I said that you do not grasp the complexity of where we find ourselves. You may have a Muslim mother but you are not really a son of Allah. You cannot be trusted, I fear, to carry out this mission for the greater good of our cause."

"That is not for you to decide, my dear brother."

The Arab disappeared from view and returned to throw a stack of photographs on the table in front of Belinsky.

"I am not interested in photographs of your trips around the word," he said haughtily. He glanced at them, then picked one up to examine more closely. "Where did you get these? Who is this man?"

"Feigning ignorance does not become you, colonel," said the Arab. "You know perfectly well that these photographs are of you and one of the Americans in this camp until yesterday. Do not play the fool with me, colonel!"

Belinksy hesitated before he spoke again.

"Very well," he said at last. "He is an American special operations officer named Paul Bickford. He has been under surveillance of our own security service on and off for years. He has retired from the military but is on this expedition to provide security. For a job only. I attach no special significance to his presence here."

"Why do I think you are lying, colonel?"

"As a true partner in this enterprise, you are entitled to know everything," said Belinsky. "I have never actually met him but do know that he was along as an observer in Chechnya several years ago. His fellow officer was killed in an ambush in Pankisi Gorge, I believe. That is all I know of him. I think his presence here is an inconsequential accident."

"*Allah-u Akbar,*" said the Arab. "God is great. You told me the truth, for once. I did not want there to be any bad blood between us."

Quite suddenly, I decided that I was probably stretching my luck on the catwalk. If they discovered my presence, they would kill me. I tiptoed back to the steps, descended them, and slipped out the door. My head was full of questions about Bickford and the Arab and what their connection would mean for our survival.

✧ ✧ ✧

Fifteen

It was even colder the next morning, but the strong sun made it seem less so. I saw it streaming through the window before I sat up in bed. At first, I forgot about the seriousness of our situation as I contemplated the day ahead.

It was 6 a.m. by my watch. The others were still sleeping.

"Git op! Git op!"

A commando burst through the door yelling at the top of his lungs. I was back to reality in a hurry.

Susan, Danny, and Ben jumped up and staggered around in the confusion that comes with you are awakened from a sound sleep. I was already standing by then, wishing for a shower and a change of clothing. That was out of the question, but I hoped for the chance to dab some water on my face. Was brushing my teeth out of the question? Probably so.

Major Kirov strode in like a teacher about to lecture his students.

"Good day to you all," he said, cheerfully. "I am pleased to offer breakfast, a rather modest repast, but food nevertheless."

"God, Kirov," I sneered. "You make it sound like we're staying at a resort."

Susan frowned as if she feared my tone would cause everyone more trouble.

But Kirov smiled and led two other men carrying containers of food to the table.

"Major. I appreciate this, I really do. But could we go to the bathroom before we eat?"

After taking care of our various needs, we sat down to breakfast together. Kirov watched us like the proud owner of a bed and breakfast. The rolls, jam, and what I would call porridge were surprisingly good. We washed it all down with strong black tea.

"My compliments to the chef," I said, gesturing with a piece of roll before I stuffed it in my mouth.

Susan glared at me again. I suppose I should have been as sullen and gloomy as she was, but the sun had lightened my mood. For some reason, I now had hope that somehow we were going to get out of our current predicament alive. Salcido and Aniak ate in silence, taking their lead as to how to act from me.

"Where'd you get all this food, Kirov?"

He smiled and puffed up his chest.

"As the most elite unit in the Russian military, *Spetsnaz* provides for its men in every way. We arrived here with sufficient foodstuffs to last several months. We even brought a cook. As you can see, he is a very fine cook. You are guests of the Russian state so we are only too happy to feed you in the same way that we ourselves are fed."

Ben Aniak frowned.

"Does this cook wind up with a lot of garbage?"

Kirov looked puzzled.

"Anyone who cooks creates garbage. I mean, one cannot utilize everything when one cooks: eggshells, flour, vegetable skins, and so on and so forth. Why do you ask?"

"What is he doing with this garbage?" Ben persisted.

"I cannot answer with any certainty that question," said Kirov.

"Why *are* you asking, Ben?" I interrupted.

"Polar bears," he said. "They can smell garbage miles away."

Kirov scoffed.

"My dear sir, we are on an island here, or have you forgotten that factor?"

Ben kept eating, then looked at me to gauge how far he could take this.

"Go on, Ben. I have the feeling we all need to know what you know."

Ben pushed his plate away and took a sip of tea. He was enjoying his role as the center of attention.

"Polar bears roam all over the Arctic at will," he said. "They are adapted physically to live in one of the most harsh environments on earth. They can survive for years in the glacial ice of the Arctic Circle where temperatures get down to 50 degrees Fahrenheit. They subsist only on seal meat. They've got a double layer of fur. Underneath are 4 inches of blubber. This prevents heat loss from their bodies. They've got broad, almost fluffy paws that are like snowshoes, plus short claws that grip the ice. Their long noses are ideal for poking into ice holes. Then, they pull out the seals. Those suckers can smell something 20 miles away.

"They are a protected species, permitted to be hunted only by my people. Because they are protected, their number has multiplied. There may be as many as 20,000 of them in the hundreds of thousands of miles up here. There are probably several hundred of them within a mile of us right now."

"Impossible!" said Kirov. "We have not seen even a single one in the days we have been here! And, as I said before, we are on island here."

"Major, these guys are smart and they swim like fish. They use their big feet to paddle around faster than the eye can see. They live on eating seals and they have learned to conceal and camouflage themselves to do so. I've seen one submerge completely, swim to a seal sleeping on the edge of an ice floe, then surface to seize the prey so fast the seal couldn't get away. If they don't want us to see them, we won't see them. But all the people up here have brought food with them and when they dispose of it, the bears smell it and move in."

"You said swim, Ben?"

"Yeah, I did. That's why our being on an island means nothing. They wouldn't need to come far to reach us."

"And hell, you only have to remember those iced-in boats yesterday to know there's an ice bridge forming around us," added Salcido.

Kirov was looking more and more alarmed. The two commandos who had remained in the room were impassive, probably because they didn't understand English. Rising to the rapt attention of his audience, Aniak continued talking.

"Polar bears are normally not as aggressive as, say grizzlies, but they are curious, especially about anything that differs from their normal world of white. I mean, they usually see snow and ice. Once their curiosity is piqued, they are determined and fearless until they find what they're looking for."

"Do they eat people?" asked Salcido.

"Not as a staple of their diet," said Aniak.

Kirov gulped.

"So the garbage would attract them, even if their stomachs were full of seal meat?" I asked.

"Sure, the garbage would bring them right in," said Aniak. "They'd wonder what the smell was and they are always interested in something good to eat. That's why the garbage has to be carefully handled."

"That is not my department, unfortunately," answered the major.

"Do you think you might mention it to the colonel?" I said. "If you don't, I will!"

Kirov looked alarmed as if this suggested violation of the chain of command was more than he could comprehend.

"No, I would not wish you to do this," he said, holding a hand up. "I will inform him regarding what your friend has uttered to us. It is my duty to do this thing."

He was well on the way to convincing himself to talk to Belinsky about the bear.

"God, Kirov, is the colonel that paranoid that he wouldn't want to hear bad news? I mean is bad news a sign that the person telling him is this loyal? That is perverted!"

"Keep your voice down, I implore you," he said, glancing nervously at the two other commandos in the room. I followed his gaze.

"Do they understand English?"

"I do not think so," he said. "I consulted their files before bringing them along on this detail. One can never be sure about anything."

Salcido picked up two buns and walked over to the men in question, who were standing by the door.

"You two are dirty cocksuckers," he smiled.

I held my breath and Susan looked as though she might faint. Kirov's jaw was clenched so tightly the tendons in his neck were showing.

The commandos looked at one another, then laughed.

"*Tovarich*," they said, each accepting a roll from Salcido.

"I guess that little mystery is solved," he laughed. Everyone in the room relaxed. The air expended from four sets of lungs sounded like the tires on a car that had all gone flat at once.

"Jesus, Danny," I laughed. "You sure know how to grab everyone's attention."

Salcido shrugged and sat down to finish his meal.

"I think we can converse with ease, major," I turned to Kirov. "Care to defect and take us with you?"

He walked quickly toward me and slapped me hard across the face. Susan screamed and the two commandos brought their guns up.

"I cannot permit such blasphemous phrases to come forth from your mouth!" He leaned in closer, a scowl on his face. "Look angry, professor. We must put on a show for my men. It will look good when they report to the colonel."

"I don't have to *look* angry, captain, I *am* angry," I said as I rubbed my throbbing jaw. "I didn't see that coming."

"I would not leave my beloved homeland to the Dimitri Zukovs of the world. He is someone who I consider aberration to new Russian military. Not a professional. I need to stay to see that those with better natures do prevail."

"Nice speech," I answered. "I wish you luck."

I sat down feeling disgusted, at myself and our predicament. I waved him away.

"Let's just get on with this," I said. "What is next on your leader's agenda?"

"I believe we are waiting for transport," he said.

"To where?" screamed Susan. "Are we being taken to Russia?"

"Perhaps so," said Kirov. "I am not, as you say, in the know on the complete plan."

"I believe that would be kidnapping," I said. "In my country, there are laws against it."

"We would consider it protective custody," said a voice at the door as Colonel Belinsky strode into the room flanked by Zukov and four more commandos.

"Protection from what?" I said, standing up to face the entourage. "The only thing we have to fear is all of you people."

"Tom, no!" yelled Susan. "Keep quiet for a change!"

"Your former lover is correct, professor," hissed Belinsky. "Your attempts at vainglorious heroics are foolhardy."

"Now there are some phrases to add to your English lexicon, Major Kirov. Really first rate phraseology."

"Are you mocking me, professor?" asked Belinsky.

At the word *mocking*, Zukov started toward me, no doubt itching to smack me around a bit more. I braced for the impact of his hand. How far away from permanent brain damage was my poor old head? Belinsky snapped his fingers once again and Zukov stopped. I knew, however, that one of these days, the colonel would let his assistant work me over again and no one would stop him.

"We must not harm our guests, Dimitri," he laughed. "At least not at this time."

At this point, another commando rushed through the door and whispered something in Belinsky's ear. He looked surprised and repeated one word aloud. "*Medbed?*"

What had he said? I was sorry I had taken only Spanish in college.

Oblivious to who was holding machine guns on who, we all ran to the door and fanned out in a confused semicircle on the tundra. Several hundred yards away, a large polar bear stared back at us. He was standing up and cradling a body across his outstretched front legs. We no longer needed an English translation.

All of us—the macho commandos, the harried captives— were rendered speechless at the scene. Jane, Alan, and Scott were standing in front of the other building and they soon joined us in front of ours. The commandos kept their weapons raised, but seemed in no hurry to use them.

The bear stood completely still for what seemed like a half hour, but was probably a minute or less. He sniffed the air with his huge black nose and squinted at the strange creatures hovering on the periphery of his vision through eyes that seemed too small for the rest of him.

Somewhere in the deep recesses of my mind was the kind of stray fact that reporters and college professors horde for later use: bears don't see very well but have a keen sense of smell. The actions of this giant were proving my memory right.

Even though he frightened the hell out of me, the bear was magnificent. His yellowish white coat glistened in the sunlight. I could see his large paws with their long, curled claws almost caressing the body of the Arab.

"Belinsky," I whispered, "your vainglorious leader looks pretty dead to me."

"Silence!" he said, a bit too loudly because the bear raised his head and was more interested in what we were doing than he had been before. Belinsky ignored me and kept looking at the bear. His men did the same thing. I suppose he was trying to tell if the man was still alive, although the blood on the claws indicated otherwise. The way he was holding the man made it impossible to tell because we couldn't see the head. His white robe was covered with blood and his turban lay behind him on the ground.

This strange standoff continued for another minute or so. I wondered if the bear would eventually tire, drop the man, and walk away. He did none of these things and seemed possessive of his prize. He would not give it up easily, if at all.

Although the sun was shining brightly, the air was cold. Before long I began to shiver because I had come outside without a coat. My compatriots were equally uncomfortable.

Then, I heard a commotion to my left and looked over to see Scott Szabo running toward the bear waving a blanket.

"Scott, no!" I yelled.

He ignored me and sprinted along toward the bear, which still stood motionless and mesmerized by another strange creature heading toward him. After several more seconds, Zukov raised his pistol and fired, the bullets hitting Szabo in the neck. He spun around and looked at me with a quizzical look on his face. In our long acquaintance, he had usually blamed me for everything that went wrong. He was dying with the same mindset.

Susan screamed and fell to her knees sobbing uncontrollably. In her long love affair with this man who had once been her student, she had flouted convention in both the academic world and her relationship with me. And, it had cost her dearly. In the end, even though Szabo had turned against her, I guess she really loved him.

Jane moved to comfort her as only a slightly older and more motherly woman could. I didn't have the strength or the inclination.

"That was cold-blooded murder," I said to Belinsky. "You and your chief goon will pay for it somehow!"

"And who will make us do this 'paying'," laughed Zukov, who was edging slowly toward me before Belinsky waived him off.

The bear must have been getting tired because he dropped the Arab he had been holding all this time. We all watched it fall like a rag doll, hoping to see some movement.

"Use your head, colonel, for once, and let him go," I whispered. "If you wound him or miss, he'll charge us or kill this man. He seems about to run away. I think he's getting tired of us. Let him live. Do something decent for a change."

Ben Aniak chimed in from the rear.

"My people consider the bear the symbol of everlasting life and endurance," he said. "If you let him survive, the great spirit will let all of us survive. Listen to Tom. Let this great creature live."

The bear looked like he had heard my words and taken them as a suggestion. He turned away from us and I held my breath, hoping that the Russians would hold their fire.

Suddenly I heard a short shrill cry from behind the bear, and soon a small bundle of white fur scampered into view. Another errant thought popped into my head: this had to be a female bear. That explained her fierce reaction to us. Mothers avoid all danger, including adult male bears who sometimes attack cubs and eat them. I had heard that mother polar bears can be so protective of their young that they have been known to rear up and leap at helicopters flying overhead.

As I contemplated this wonderful scene out of the pages of *National Geographic*, Zukov found a way to ruin it and add to the carnage. He raised the same pistol he had used to kill Scott and shot the bear cub. His tiny body, at one moment brimming with life, was blown apart by the force of the bullet.

At first, the bear seemed not to fathom what had happened. She looked at the baby and finally at us. When Zukov raised a machine gun, I lost my composure and any sense of fear.

Without saying a word, I lunged for him. I managed to knock the gun away from his intended target, but it went off anyway, hitting Colonel Belinsky in the head, killing him instantly. Zukov looked confused at what had happened, and so did the men. When he regained his senses, he aimed the gun at me and put his finger on the trigger.

The bear let out a roar at this time, however, and Zukov turned his head long enough for me to grab a gun from the nearest commando. I wasn't sure I knew how to fire it but I was determined to try, even if it killed me.

Major Kirov beat me to it. He shot Zukov in the heart and he fell at my feet, a thin stream of blood trickling from his nose.

The bear took this period of distraction to pick up the body of the man she had so tenderly guarded earlier. She held it up for inspection, then bit off his head in one big chomp. It rolled toward us like a ball. Even in death, the Arab's eyes seemed filled with hatred for us all.

Then the bear dropped the body and walked to the lifeless form of the cub. She roared another warning, then grasped the cub by the scruff of the neck and carried it over the hill out of sight.

I wondered if any of the commandos would follow the bear to shoot her and act out their revenge. They had been strangely quiet throughout this entire bloody tableau. When I turned to look for them, all but one of the commandos was gone. That figure turned and pulled back the hood of his parka enough for me to see his face. Nodding slightly, Paul Bickford quickly joined the others in their hasty and cowardly retreat. Their weapons lay where they dropped them. In their haphazard retreat, the men left a pathway of deadly iron. As I looked at the rifles, I noticed a neatly folded sheaf of papers. Amid all the tumult, I had only a few seconds to glance at them.

AFTER ACTION REPORT REGARDING
CAPT. PAUL BICKFORD, U.S. ARMY, 17 DECEMBER 2001,
0700 HOURS, NEAR TULAK, AFGHANISTAN

Although he had been in Afghanistan for only 24 hours, Capt. Paul Bickford, a U.S. Army Special Operations officer, was already leading a squad of men into battle. They were outside a small village southwest of Kabul in an area so desolate that it looked like the moon, except that it was covered with constantly drifting sand. He was grateful for the map and for the presence of Vassily Kazatin.

Bickford imagined that the six noncommissioned men waiting with him behind the sand berm were wondering why a mili-

tary officer from another country—a country that was once the most hated enemy of the United States of America—was anywhere near such a sensitive mission. But Kazatin was not here on Bickford's whim. He was here with the approval of the highest levels of the U.S. Army. He had been stationed in this region during the ill-fated invasion of Afghanistan by his country, then called the Soviet Union, in the 1980s.

Kazatin would blend well with the locals because he spoke perfect Dari and looked a bit like they did: a dark beard, wild hair, a hook nose, and penetrating green eyes. He had instructed Bickford to dress similarly: long, billowy pants, a cotton shirt, a long wool vest, and the traditional Afghan hat, called a pakol. *Although Bickford did not have a beard and looked much too healthy to be local, they hoped he would pass, if he didn't open his mouth.*

Vassily's presence made Bickford's men nervous, nonetheless. For now, Bickford had decided not to tell his men anything about the Russian's background. It was his own little test—to see if they trusted him enough to accept his authority and obey his orders, even if they questioned his judgment.

Bickford trusted Kazatin completely. They shared the same interests, had similar goals, and even had the same birthday. They had gotten to know one another six months before when both had been assigned to a multinational Special Ops task force in East Africa.

Today's plan called for Bickford and his men to secure the fort and then set it up as a forward base of operations for two companies of Army rangers set to arrive the next day. With the small fort abandoned, their task would probably be fairly easy. But nothing in Afghanistan was ever as easy as it seemed on the surface. Bickford and Kazatin were to go in first, leading horses and keeping their revolvers out of sight. The others would follow as soon as it seemed safe.

At Bickford's signal, he and Katazin stood up and walked toward the only entrance in the steep, sandy ramparts that protected the fort from invaders. They walked through the opening and were soon standing in a large open space that looked like a parade field. Only a few buildings remained standing at the rear of the enclosure.

As they approached one of the buildings, they noticed a camel and some goats standing out front. They exchanged quizzical glances because the area had been declared clear after the last reconnaissance flight. To be on the safe side, the two split up as they approached, Bickford on the left, Kazatin on the right. Once there, they looked through the filthy windows before ducking down again.

Inside, five women in burkas were stacking Kalashnikov rifles and RPGs into neat rows on several long tables. Presumably, they were getting them ready for transport. Bickford was surprised by the lack of guards, but assumed the remote location had lulled the enemy into complacency.

As he and Kazatin broke in the door, he uttered the pre-arranged signal—a one-word "huah"—in his tiny radio mike. The men behind the sand berm would be joining them in the fort soon.

One of the women screamed and backed away from the advancing men. The other four stood their ground and pulled revolvers from under their garments. Only they weren't women. The men started firing wildly before diving for cover behind the table.

Bickford and Kazatin were on them in a flash, pulling them to their feet. Two of them gave up without a fight, one taking a swing at Vassily before he hit him hard in the stomach. The man nearest Bickford aimed and cocked his pistol ready to fire, but it jammed. Bickford hit him in the face.

The two of them easily dispatched the men, and turned their attention to the other Taliban commando who had just darted out of sight into a darkened room at the back. They ran to the opening, then stopped to glance in before entering.

Bickford nodded and both tucked their heads around the corner. In that instant, they saw no one inside. To be safe, however, they threw a tear gas canister in and donned gas masks. They would grab the man when he emerged. But he did not come out.

Bickford looked back to see his men leading the other four Taliban away, all walking under their own power but two with blood on their faces. They would be picked up and taken by helicopter to the main American base at Kandahar for questioning. He signaled for two of his men to remain behind; both put on their gas masks. Then he and Vassily stepped through the door and into the room. They scanned the space with flashlights but it was empty, with only an upturned chair, a table, and a primitive bed inside.

As they neared what appeared to be a trapdoor in the corner of the room, a single shot rang out from below. Bickford opened the trapdoor quickly and dropped another tear gas canister into the hole. When it hit the floor below, however, it exploded, sending both Bickford and Kazatin backwards, then scrambling out the door.

As they waited for the fire to die and the gas fumes to dissipate, Bickford thought only of his plan. He and Kazatin had spread maps onto the ground while the other troops stood guard. Everyone started eating items from their MREs, and Bickford even made coffee. He had not once thought about what happened to the commando below. His task was to accomplish his mission, no matter what. Whoever got in his way had to be eliminated.

After an hour, he sent one of his men, a big Texan named Dennis Flanders, down into the hole to bring up the body. Flanders appeared 5 minutes later with two small shapes under each arm, tears running down his face. He laid them on the ground.

"This is what was down there, sir, along with a woman."

As Bickford got to his feet, he saw the small shapes were the charred remains of two tiny children.

"Oh my God," he moaned. "What have I done."

The following week, local herdsmen reported to Army scouts the strange tale of a tall Arab and his men who arrived at the small fort looking for his family.

He and his men rode down from the hillside and into the enclosure and dismounted. Using flashlights, they searched the buildings but found no one inside. The Arab smelled the remnants of smoke in the small room at the rear of one of the buildings. He opened the trapdoor carefully and was overwhelmed at once by the smell of burnt flesh. He put his hands over his nose.

"Oh Mina, no! My god, not my Mina."

As he started to climb down the stairs, one of his men caught his arm and shook his head, motioning him to go outside.

The Arab ran out into the courtyard, his body shaking with grief. The rest of the men were standing around three mounds of earth near the rear wall. He sank to his knees and started digging in the ground of the largest mound. Before long, his fingers were bleeding as he clawed the dirt of this makeshift grave. When he got to his wife's body, he lifted it and let the earth fall away from the white shroud encasing her.

"In the name of Allah, why has God forsaken me?" he wailed. "Why has he taken away all that is dear to me?"

After his men had dug three new graves, he said a silent prayer and nodded for his men to fill in the holes.

"I will avenge these deaths no matter how long it takes," the Arab shouted.

Then, the nomads reported that he stumbled toward his horse and rode away into the dry dust of the desolate Afghani plain.

✧ ✧ ✧

Sixteen

I felt like a character in one of those movies where the group of people are invited to an isolated island by a crazy millionaire and then begin dying under mysterious circumstances. There was no mystery about the circumstances of all the deaths we had seen. Except for the one caused by the bear, they were deliberate. I did not have time to figure out the meaning of the Bickford's narrative. Jamming it into my pocket, I decided to keep it to myself for the time being.

"Let's get inside and sort this out," I said to my sober-looking compatriots. Somebody had to take charge and I didn't want it to be Kirov. Jane, Susan, Danny, Ben, and Alan turned toward the building. The major fell into line too. For the time being, we left the bodies of Belinsky, Zukov, and Szabo where they were.

The warmth of the building felt good when we stepped inside. The others were sitting around the dining table watching me walk toward them. Even Kirov was following my lead.

"We are in a hell of a mess, Tom," said Hopkins.

"You've got *that* right, man," said Salcido. "You got any great ideas?" He looked at me.

"I guess I better get some fast," I laughed hesitantly. "Are you with us, Kirov? Do you want to defect? I think we can make a good case for you to get political asylum."

The major looked down the floor, a glum expression on his face. "I do not know what I must do," he said. "I have given my whole life to serve Russia. I am proud of my involvement in the *Spetsnaz* but I cannot sanction what Belinsky and Zukov did. We are trained as men of honor, not killers."

"Kirov, how long will your men stay away from here?" I asked. "I mean how much time will they stay frightened of the bears?"

"I cannot answer this question. They tend to act like wandering sheep without anyone to lead them. As you can notice, in their great fright at seeing the bear, they left all weaponry behind."

"Are we all to be picked up?" I asked.

Kirov hesitated. He would, after all, be revealing information that was classified. An answer to my question would indicate whether he was with us or still an adversary. The officer looked around the room, making a calculation that would change his life. No one moved. It seemed that everyone appreciated the importance of the next few seconds.

"Colonel Belinsky was to call for helicopters this afternoon," he said, at last. "One for me and my men, the rest for all of you."

"And where were these helicopters coming from?"

"We were using our largest icebreaker, the *Marshal Stalin*, he said.

"What a comforting name," muttered Hopkins.

"Will the men wait for the helicopters? Did they know about this plan?"

"I can only guess, but I would imagine that is so," he said. "They saw their leader killed. They saw his chief lieutenant killed. I doubt they care what fate happens to befall me. They are highly superstitious. They want to be rescued only from this great white beast. I am sure his size will only grow in the retelling of this saga."

"Can they communicate with the ship in any way?"

He shook his head.

"I have these means of communication only."

He held up a small two-way radio and a cell phone, which he handed to me. I gave it to Salcido.

"Good. I think we've found our way of escape. If we clear out of here this afternoon, we can reach the Zodiaks and try to get to Tuktoyaktuk by tomorrow. As we go, we can try to reach the *Polar Sea* by our satellite phone and see if the captain can help us.

"If I can get it cranked up," said Salcido. "I'll try." He walked off to tinker with the equipment.

"We need to gather all the cold weather gear from all the buildings, plus all the food and backpacks. Jane and Susan, you do that. Ben, pick up all the Russian guns outside."

"Alan, you and I can deal with the bodies."

The bearded scientist got up and walked outside as well.

"Major Kirov, you've got to decide whether you will be going with us. We'll be back in a while."

When I got outside, snowflakes brushed my cheeks. Was I crazy to leave the protection of the building and take these people into a boat ride to God knows where? I felt the Russians would come back eventually and take us with them to the ice breaker. To me, we were following a path of lesser evils.

We wrapped Szabo, Belinsky, and Zukov in sheets and carried them to the main building where I hoped the Russians would find them when they came in search of us. While in that room, I looked around for any valuable records and found a book tucked in the bottom drawer of Jameson's desk. He was keeping a personal diary in an old-fashioned ledger. In a casual leafing through its pages I noticed entries detailing payments to Jameson from the Russian company Belinsky worked for. I tucked them into the pocket of my parka. They would be useful in helping us explain all of this to the investigation I was sure we would eventually face. I had the disk containing the scientific data, so I felt comfortable that I had the important stuff safely secured. I patted my jacket pocket to confirm its presence.

"Paul and Carmen are back there," said Hopkins as he walked from the shower room. "Pretty badly beaten up, both of them."

"We need to put Szabo in there too. We can't carry them. We can't bury them in this permafrost. Let's wrap them like those guys and hope we can retrieve the bodies later, after we're rescued."

"You really think that's going to happen?"

"We've got to act as though we all do," I answered. "What other choice do we have? It's what will keep us going. Buck up, Alan. There's no other way. Better cover your nose."

"I guess you're right," he said, not looking all that convinced.

Dealing with the bodies was one of the grimmest things I'd ever had to do. Hopkins took care of Jameson while I dealt with Carmen Ames. I approached her body slowly because I was afraid of what I might see if I looked too closely. Her beautiful face looked peaceful. It didn't reflect the horrible things that had undoubtedly happened to her. I was certain she had been raped, probably more than once. A red mark on her throat indicated she died by strangulation. Anything beyond that, I didn't want to know because there was nothing I could do about it. She was dead and we were going to have to leave her; that was that.

I picked up her body as gently as I could and placed it in a sleeping bag I found in one of the lockers. Then I carried her to a cot and laid her on it. I put her passport and her wallet in an envelope and then clipped it to the sleeping bag. I wanted whoever came to claim the body to know who she was. Then I did the same thing with Jameson's remains.

I stared at Scott Szabo's face for a long time before zipping up the sleeping bag. We had clashed the entire time we had known one another. He had changed from a fawning graduate student into a professional and personal rival during those years. I dragged him into the shower room.

"I don't know what else we can do for now, Alan. I think we'd best get out of here. I don't know what to fear most: the cold weather or the Russians."

"Both, I'd guess. You know, none of this seems real. I've worked with Cliff for years. He could be pigheaded and prone to making bad decisions. I mean, bringing these Russians in on this operation for the money was crazy."

He shook his head.

"That caused this whole mess. What was he thinking?"

"Yeah. It's hard to comprehend."

I put on my coat and looked around to see if we could scavenge anything else for our trek.

"We've got to get moving. There'll be plenty of time for postmortems later on."

"You're right," he said. "Let's do it!"

We closed the door on this scene of death and hurried along to the third building. Everyone would be there now and we could get organized for our journey off this island.

For me it couldn't happen soon enough.

✧ ✧ ✧

There was never a question in my mind that Major Kirov would go with us, not as a prisoner but as a colleague. He had saved our lives and I felt I owed him for that.

Everyone was sitting around the room waiting for us to return. They stood up and began to heave their packs onto their backs when they saw us.

"God, Tom," said Susan, "it took you long enough!"

"Nice to see you too, Susan," I snapped. She probably blamed me for Scott's death. Oddly, though, she didn't ask me about his body.

I turned to everyone else, feeling a bit odd in my new role as a leader. I decided I would get by if I treated them like university committee members. If you're the chairman, you succeed best if you act like a benevolent despot: let them talk but make all the important decisions yourself.

"I guess we've got all the food and water we can find," I said. "Ben's got the maps and he knows this area."

Aniak nodded and held the maps up in the air.

"Danny, did you get the satellite telephone working?"

"No way. It's dead! All I got is this."

He held up the Russian cell phone. Salcido held the phone to his mouth and ear. "I hope it speaks English," he laughed.

I pulled Kirov to one side for a word in private.

"You are going with us, major? We've been through a lot together. I feel I can trust you, even though we're pretty far apart on a lot of things. I know you'll have no trouble getting asylum. I'll testify about what you did for us."

"I have spent much time thinking about this moment," he said, sadly.

"Don't tell me you aren't going with us?" I shouted. "That's craziness! How can you not go!"

"I cannot desert my country in its time of need," he answered. "I must return and see that my unit is properly rescued."

"They ran away," I shouted. "They left you. Besides that, you'll be blamed for those deaths. They'll need a sacrificial lamb and that will be you! You must know all too well how people like you get taken care of in your country."

"Not if you help me by being my cover-up guy. I'll say you assaulted me and escaped."

"Assault you? How will that work?"

"You will hit me and knock me out coldly as you leave here. When I regain life, I will go for help. That will take hours and you will have the chance to escape. I believe you call that a heads up."

"Head start," I said. "*Heads up* means something else."

I paused and thought about this for a moment.

"All right, we'll do it your way because I don't have time to argue. You are sure you don't want to go with us?"

He nodded and I turned to the group, who seemed to be getting restive.

"I think we're ready to move out. Ben, you and Alan take the point. Don't forget the weapons and the ammo."

"Jane and Susan will come next."

"What about him?" asked Jane, pointing at Kirov.

"I'll fill you in later," I said.

"Who elected you God?" said Susan.

"Shut up, Susan!" said Jane. "This is hard enough for Tom to do without your constant second guessing."

"Danny and I will bring up the rear."

They walked out the door and began walking to the east, retracing our route of the day before toward the bay. They had chosen not to notice that I had not answered Jane's question about Kirov's place in the scheme of things. When they had all left, I walked up to him and we shook hands.

"I won't forget you," I said.

"Nor I you," he replied. "Did I have that sentence constructed correctly?"

"Like the finest building," I laughed. "How will you get them to believe you? And how will you get out of here?"

"I have not survived the rigorous training of the *Spesnatz* service not to know how to think creatively and talk my way out of difficult situations, Professor Martindale. I also have an emergency frequency for my radio." He patted one of his pockets.

"Please. Call me Tom. We *are* friends after all. I'm sorry to say I don't remember your first name."

"It's Gregor."

"I've got to get going."

I turned to leave. He grabbed my arm.

"You will hit me about the face and then knock me out."

"I can't do that," I protested.

He began to slap himself so hard that his eyes began to water.

"You need to finish the job now, Tom. I'll sit on the bed, then you hit me until my mouth bleeds and I black out. I'll fall on the bed, but then you pull me off on the floor. I want to be found that way, in a crumple."

"A heap," I corrected him. "You'll be in a *heap*."

I did what he said and after two punches, blood began to trickle from the corners of his mouth.

"Now, finish me off!"

It took only one additional haymaker to complete the job.

I overtook the others in 10 minutes. It was good that it didn't take longer because the wind began to blow and the temperature to drop by that time. It crossed my mind that the Russians might be the least of our worries.

By the time we reached the bay, Aniak had run ahead and was trying to dislodge the Zodiaks from the ice. Although he was having some success, the effort might be futile, given the prevalence of the ice as far as the eye could see. I mean, it wasn't like we were going to be able to jump in the boats and speed away.

"Getting them loose?" I asked as I reached his side slightly out of breath.

"Almost," he said. "The sun's been melting the ice around the edges. I'm gradually working them free."

"Yeah, like that's going to do a whole lot of good," snapped Susan, who was becoming increasingly difficult. She was right, but it wouldn't hurt to think positively.

"That's true here, Sue," I said somewhat condescendingly, as if I was speaking to an errant child, "but the inlet will be free of ice when we get out to it. I'm thinking of that. We can use the boats there, as I'm sure you realize."

"We're going to drag those boats?" she said, unmollified by what I said. "And where's the good major? I suppose you let him go? How stupid you are, Tom. He'll send someone for us as soon as he can. Then it's Siberia here we come."

"Put a cork in your blabbing mouth," said Jane. "If you can do any better than Tom, by all means take over!"

"Ladies, please," said Hopkins. "This is bad enough without you two getting into an argument over the things you can't change."

Finally a voice of reason, I thought.

"Got it!" shouted Ben, who proudly pulled the second Zodiak free of the grasping ice and lifted it up on the solid shore. It bounced like a ball, then skidded to a stop.

"How's this for a plan?" I said. "Let's leave the third one where it is. We can't really manage more than two. We'll head east along the shore where the ground is not totally iced over. Alan and I and Ben and Danny will take turns dragging the boats along. We'll watch for open water and when we find it, we'll head for Tuk. I don't think we should go out to sea this late in the day. We'll look for a likely place to camp for tonight."

"Wonderful. I've always wanted to camp with people I love!"

"Shut up, Susan!" I shouted. "For once, think of someone other than yourself! Could you do that for me?"

Her eyes flashed, and filled with tears. Given her various outbursts, I was definitely not going to give her any sign of comfort. I doubted anyone else would either. Some time, long ago, I think she lost her soul to Scott Szabo.

When I hoisted my pack onto my back, the others did the same. I checked the nylon rope on one of the Zodiaks, made sure the outboard motor was swung out of the way, and started dragging it. Alan did the same with the other one.

"Gas. What about gas?" I said to Aniak.

"Extra amounts of it in those large rubber bladders inside." he replied.

"How's the mileage on those engines?" I laughed. "How far will we get?"

Ben shrugged and held his hands palms up. "Beats the hell out of me!"

The others formed a line, Aniak in the lead because he had a map and some experience with the island. Jane came next, followed by a downcast Susan. Salcido walked behind her, with Hopkins next, and yours truly bringing up the rear.

The wind started to blow and I quickly discovered how diabolical it was. It sought out the path of least resistance in my protective armor—a tear in my pants and a small hole in one boot—and soon found its way into the inner sanctums of my body. I put on my eyeglasses, but the condensation on the lenses soon made it impossible to see anything and I couldn't wipe it off. When I took them off, however, I soon had trouble blinking my eyes because the frost on my eyelashes made them stick together. I assumed everybody else was having the same kind of trouble.

The sun was starting to descend, although its rays warmed my skin every time they touched it amid the lengthening shadows. I was really playing it by ear here, improvising as I went because I wasn't sure what the next hour would hold, let alone the next day. I was going to do my best to get us out of this mess—how, I really wasn't sure.

Despite these physical worries, we made progress the first hour. As we walked, I kept looking at the ice along the shoreline. It was still solid and bound to stay that way in the waning hours of today and through the night. I decided we would stand a better chance of making open, ice-free water the next morning. We would be better off finding a place to camp and push on tomorrow.

As we waited, I scanned the area constantly for any sign of movement. I doubted the Russians had had time to regroup. The bears were long gone too, so I was somewhat relaxed. But, hell, you never know.

At one point, I thought I saw a flash of white to my left, but when I stopped and focused on the low brush of the tundra, I decided I had been wrong. I didn't want to alarm the others, so I kept my worries to myself.

In another hour, it was 4:30 p.m. and getting colder by the minute, although the wind had stopped. Up ahead, I saw a dark object that on closer inspection, turned out to be a low structure.

"Ben! What's that?" I shouted.

The entourage stopped in its tracks and people began taking their backpacks off.

"Probably an old hunter's cabin," he replied, "or what's left of a cabin."

I left the trail and walked up to the ruin: two walls intersected, forming a barrier to the waterside, but no roof. If we put tarps over the top of the walls and built a fire near the opening, we would be safe and reasonably warm for the night.

"Let's hole up here for the night," I shouted. "We can eat and sleep and push on tomorrow. We've got protection too, after a fashion."

The others looked relieved and trudged over to the ruin. Soon, Hopkins and Salcido had stretched nylon tarps over the walls on one side and extended them to a tent pole and an upturned Zodiak on the other. We had our roof.

Jane and Aniak gathered driftwood and started a fire just out from under the covering lest we all suffocate from smoke during the night. I pulled out what few cooking utensils and food I had scavenged and tried to figure out what to fix. Only Susan remained uninvolved. She sat as far away from the rest of us as she could and still be in the encampment. She kept looking at me with a glance that would have killed me if that was possible.

The ever-resourceful Jane Baugh fashioned a supper out of beans and rice and even made some tortillas out of the cornmeal I found in our cache. It was good and filling. If we died tonight, it wouldn't be from starvation.

When we settled down for sleep at about 10 p.m., I was feeling more optimistic than I had all day.

"I'll take the first watch," said Hopkins.

I chewed the last bite of food and wiped my mouth with my sleeve.

"That's not necessary. Let me do it."

"I want to. I don't feel all that sleepy. I promise I'll call you at 1 a.m."

"Okay. I'll relieve you then. Don't forget to wake me."

"Don't worry, Tom," he said as he walked outside to take his post. "Things are looking up. Tomorrow's another day."

"Says you and Scarlett O'Hara," I laughed.

✧ ✧ ✧

Seventeen

3:45 a.m.

The time glimmered back at me from the luminous dial of my watch. I sighed and tried to get my bearings. I didn't feel cold. I didn't particularly feel frightened. So far, we had managed our survival fairly well. The others must have been equally calm because I could hear their soft and steady breathing around me.

3:47 a.m.

I sat up as if I had been shot. I was supposed to relieve Alan at 1 a.m. Why hadn't he called me?

I got up as quietly as I could and ducked around the makeshift door that was really an inflatable boat. I pulled my parka up around my face to deflect the cold. The wind had stopped. I looked up to enjoy for a moment the beauty of the clear night. Here, at the roof of the world, the stars did seem closer because there was nothing around to distract your eyes from looking at them. No artificial light, no buildings, nothing.

Hopkins was not asleep by the fire as I had expected him to be. In fact, the fire had burned down to the glowing ember stage. We had all agreed on the importance of keeping it going. I threw a log on it quickly, hoping it would reignite. After a lot of smoking and steaming, it did just that, throwing out a few sparks in the process.

I pulled a flashlight out of my pocket and shone it around in search of Hopkins. My heart started beating faster when I failed to see any sign of him. When I got up the courage to move away from the fire, the lump in my throat restricted my breathing. My lips were dry and my head was throbbing as I walked in the direction of some footprints I saw in the icy crust of the ground.

Fifty yards away, the footprints ended at a point where the ground looked as though it had been raked clean of ice. There had obviously been a struggle between Hopkins and someone, or something. At the outer edge of this patch of earth, more indentations picked up. I breathed easier because Alan had been able to walk away.

When I got closer, however, I realized that these prints were bigger than that of a man, even a big man like Hopkins. They were probably a foot across and made a deep impression.

I shined my light ahead and saw a print in the distance where the tundra was no longer flat. I suppose that this was one of the shallow crevices that laced this island.

I pushed ahead and found myself on the edge of a natural trench that extended away from me in both directions. It was bordered on either side by the low growing brush that passed for vegetation here. I stepped down into the ditch itself, now eye level with the sides. For no special reason, I headed north, aiming the flashlight at the ground as I walked.

Twenty-five yards or so later, the trench ended abruptly so I turned around and reversed my steps in the other direction. Every so often, I stopped to listen for any sound of life.

Nothing.

I probably should have called for Hopkins, or for help, but my vocal cords failed to work. Even when I cleared my throat, no sound emerged. My head and my chest were throbbing at the anxiety I felt. I pushed on, stumbling over clumps of permafrost now and again. After another 20 yards or so, the beam from my flashlight skittered by something yellow up ahead.

"Alan," I shouted. "Is that you?"

He was leaning against the side of the ditch in a sitting position. At first I thought he was resting.

"Alan, thank God."

I bent over him ready to help him to his feet. He moaned softly.

"Alan. What happened? Why'd you come out here?"

Then, I saw it: a gaping hole in his chest several inches wide. In fact, his chest had been torn open so badly that he had to hold the skin over his internal organs, as if he hoped it would reattach and become whole again. There was less blood than I would have imagined, given the severity of his injuries. The rising sun enabled me to see him more clearly at least.

"The bear?" I whispered to him as I took off my parka to put it over him in a futile attempt to ward off the state of shock he was undoubtedly already in.

He moaned again but did not speak.

I put my arm around him in a futile attempt at comforting him. What to do? He was probably near death, but could even elemental first aid save him?

Danny Salcido was a good medic, but he wasn't *that* good.

Hopkins' pulse was faint but at least he still had one. "Hang on, buddy," I said.

"Tom? Is that you?"

He coughed and a small trickle of blood ran out of the corner of his mouth.

"Did that polar bear come back?"

He coughed again and a small blob of blood flew out of his mouth onto my sweater.

"Sorry," he said, reaching over to try to rub it off.

"Forget about that," I consoled him.

He raised his head and looked directly into my eyes.

"That . . . bear . . . surprised me . . . the fire . . . didn't see . . . chased after . . . knocked . . ."

The coughing totally overwhelmed him this time and he stopped talking as his body shook violently.

"Save yourself . . . he's . . ."

Before Hopkins could finish this sentence, a huge shadow loomed over his cowering form and me.

I stood as still as I could, trying to decide if I should follow the old advice about never trying to outrun a bear. Hell, I didn't want to outrun it, I just wanted to become as invisible as possible.

I could smell the bear, not an altogether unpleasant scent, like wet wool. Then the unmistakable odor of blood wafted into my nostrils, probably Hopkins'.

The poor guy had lost consciousness again, but he was still breathing—how I could not fathom. What he had been through would have killed almost anyone else.

Behind me, the bear grunted and its shadow moved. It was no longer covering Hopkins' slumped body or my back. The bear was definitely not standing where it had been.

Why was it moving away with so tempting a morsel within his grasp? I couldn't be sure. Perhaps a full stomach, poor eyesight, and the direction of the wind contributed to his lack of interest. I wasn't complaining.

How to tell for certain that it was leaving? I decided to risk a slow, careful turn of my whole body. Inch by inch, I maneuvered around to find out where he was. A centimeter at a time, I moved. It took only seconds, but it seemed much longer. Just keep calm and do this nice and easy, I thought. Don't panic and you'll get through this. By this time, I had decided that I would live through this, although I wasn't exactly sure how.

When the bear came into view, I decided immediately that she was the one who had killed the Arab and whose cub had been killed. She was the same general size and had a large dark splotch under one eye, just like that one.

Had she hunted us down for revenge? Are bears capable of vengeance? Or were we targets of opportunity for a mammal always in search of her next meal?

She was paying no attention to me at the moment, but sniffing the tundra, perhaps for an appetizer of a rabbit or a vole before he returned to me as a main course?

I was more scared than I had ever been in my life. It was all I could do to keep my knees from buckling under me and my teeth from chattering. But I was in awe of this magnificent creature. I didn't think her a monster. We had, after all, invaded her territory.

Then I heard a tiny squeal off to one side. In a moment, another roly-poly cub scampered into view. I didn't wish them harm and only hoped they would move along and leave us alone.

Suddenly, the bear stopped grazing and sniffed the air. Her low-pitched growl served as a signal for the cub and the two of them quickly retreated away from where I was standing.

I looked to my right to see Salcido and Aniak advancing on the bears with rifles to their shoulders.

I ran toward them as fast as I could to try to stop more needless slaughter. "Nooooo!" I shouted, before I tripped. As I fell, I heard loud explosions from both weapons.

From my vantage point on the ground, I couldn't tell what had happened. All I could see was soggy ground and gnarled brush. I was afraid for the bear, but also afraid for myself if she decided to charge me. For the time being, I kept quiet and just listened.

"More than 20,000 bears in the Arctic, why did we have to attract the attention of this one?"

Salcido talking to Aniak.

But where was the bear?

I got up slowly to find out.

"There he is!" shouted Aniak, pointing in my direction. They waved and started walking toward me. If they were so casual, I assumed the bear was dead and no longer a threat. I stood up and brushed myself off. My pants were wet and muddy and my boots covered with a dark, slimy substance that looked like it would eat through the leather.

I looked back at Hopkins and he didn't seem to be moving. I wanted to run to his side, but my legs weren't functioning. I was, quite literally, paralyzed by the bitter cold.

"Are you okay?" asked Salcido, looking me up and down. "Did the bear get you?"

"No. I'm fine, just embarrassed that I fell down. Alan's pretty bad. I'm not sure he's still with us."

Salcido ran over to Hopkins and checked his pulse. He shook his head.

"God," I said. "We're dropping like flies! Who'll be next?"

Aniak and I walked over to Salcido and Hopkins' lifeless body.

"He looks like he's sleeping," said Salcido.

"Lift up the parka," I said. "You'll see what happened."

Aniak did that and gasped at what he saw. The bloody skin had become stuck to the cloth. Pulling the parka away created a large three-cornered tear in the skin covering his chest.

"Shit!" he shouted, jumping back.

I checked Hopkins' neck but found no pulse so I covered his body with the parka, then began to shake. Salcido took off his parka and draped it over my shoulders.

"You're in shock, man. We've got to take you back to camp."

I shook my head.

"We can't leave Alan."

I wiped tears from my eyes.

"We won't leave Alan."

I kept shaking my head.

"Where's the bear? In all the excitement over Alan, you didn't tell me."

"That sucker ran when he heard the guns go off. She'd heard that sound plenty of times before and knew what it meant. He didn't wait around to find out, at any rate," said Salcido.

"I don't get it. Did you both miss? You guys are good shots. You told me so yourselves. Did you miss on purpose?"

The two men looked at the ground before looking at me.

"We saw her and the cub," said Danny.

"We both fired over her head," added Aniak. "Close enough to get her attention, but not so close that we'd kill her. She ran like hell."

"We were going to shoot her if she came back at you," said Salcido. "I've read the polar bear has a big enough mouth that he can fit an entire human head inside."

"Now *that* is a really useful piece of information," I said, bursting into loud laughter for the first time in a long time. Once I started to giggle, I couldn't stop. All the pent-up terrors and stress of the past few weeks caught up with me and I suddenly was unable to control myself.

"I guess I do look like a seal sometimes," I added. "That's why I'm irresistible to bears. Or maybe it's my after shave."

The two of them joined in the hilarity over my dumb joke and we were all soon engaged in that side-slapping, laughed-so-hard-I-cried convulsion that sometimes strikes when you least expect it.

"All right. I guess we broke the tension," I said after a minute or so more of merriment. "We've got to get back to the ladies and do something about Alan. Any ideas?"

"I'll look for some driftwood over on the beach and we can wrap him in your parka and suspend it between the poles until we get him back to camp," said Ben.

"Then what?" asked Salcido. "Can we bury him in this mucky stuff?" He pointed to the ground.

"Once we get him back there, we'll regroup and figure out what to do. We can't leave him here. That much I know."

While Aniak went to look for suitable wood, Salcido and I wrapped Hopkins' body in the parka and tied it with some rope he had in his pocket. That took about 10 minutes, after which Aniak reappeared dragging two long pieces of driftwood.

The three of us went about the grim task of making a sling out of Ben's parka and tying it to the pole with some strips of rope.

"Rawhide?" I asked.

"Yeah, from caribou hide," he said. "I always keep some. It's good to chew on if you're out of food."

"Fills you up, not out," laughed Salcido. "You know, like that old diet ad."

We hoisted the body up and carried it back to camp. The sun had vanished when we got there and it started to snow.

Jane saw us coming and stopped stoking the fire. From the look on her face, she seemed to have guessed what the shroud dangling between us concealed. Tears rolled down her cheeks as she walked out to meet us.

The ground was so hard that we couldn't put Alan Hopkins *in* it. Instead, we buried him *on* it, under a pile of the biggest stones we could find. I didn't want to think about the animals that would undoubtedly dig him up.

There was nothing I could do about that, so I dismissed it from my mind.

After Aniak, Salcido, and I completed our work, I called everyone together to discuss our options.

"I don't need to tell you that we are in one hell of a mess," I began. "Wild animals, the cold, probably more Russians. It doesn't seem that we have much choice but to go on."

"We can't go back," said Salcido. "That's for sure."

"I simply can't go one step further," said Susan. "I'm cold, I'm tired, I'm hungry. Someone who I loved is dead. I'm at the end of my sanity."

"Come off your high horse, Susan," said Jane. "Your grand diva act won't do you any good here. This is life and death, not a bad hair day or a broken fingernail."

"At least I care about my appearance," Susan replied. "I haven't let myself become some overweight frump who is more at home in front of a microscope than in . . . "

"In what?" exploded Jane. "The bed of a man who used me, the bed of a man who preferred to have sex with other men than the woman—I'm talking about you, Susan—who taught him everything she knew about science and got her career handed to her on a plate for her trouble."

"Eeeeeh!" screamed Susan, leaping on Jane and grabbing her by the throat. "Shut up, you fat bitch! Shut up! Shut up! Shut up!"

It took both Aniak and Salcido to pull the two apart. They rolled around on the ground for several minutes before they could disentangle them. Jane got in a well- placed slap or two and Susan pulled a handful of Jane's hair out in the process.

"Enough!" I shouted. "This isn't helping us get out of the mess we're in. I'm not leaving anyone else behind on Herschel Island. Save your energy for our real enemies. Get out your maps, Danny. Let's plot our route."

For the next hour or so, we forgot all our past differences and figured out what we were going to do. With the weather alternately snowing and blowing, we decided to wait until the next day to resume our trek. We would spend the day resting and organizing our remaining supplies. We discarded anything we would not need. I hoped the going would be easier now that we were down to one Zodiak to carry along. The bear had dragged off, and undoubtedly shredded, the other one so it was foolish to try to find it. I was confident that the five of us would fit into the one we had, when we reached open water.

Part of me wondered if *when* was really *if*, but I had to keep believing that we would get out of here. Several times that day, I checked the ice. It was as firm as if it were midwinter instead of mid-September. Although highly unusual, it was not unprecedented. It had happened in 1897, the year of the catastrophe I had signed on this voyage to research. That night, before it got dark, I dug out of my pack the diaries of that year to look for parallels. I soon saw in explorer Charles Brower's words the sad fact that this had happened all before, in only slightly different ways.

> *I had seen the insidious creeping action of ice too often not to call Captain Whiteside's attention to the danger. But instead of steaming south of the Shoals again he seemed to think it safe to tie up to a large floe, apparently grounded. So here we stayed, while drifting ice gradually packed in solid on all sides. More concerned with keeping two quarreling women apart than with the safety of his ship, he never woke up to our peril until the large floe to which we were anchored broke loose without warning and drifted out, carrying the Monarch with it.*
>
> *This seemed to paralyze the man's ability to act. Vital hours passed during which he might still have smashed his way out of*

the gathering trap. When he did try to work loose, there wasn't a chance.

Forced farther and farther into the offshore pack, the Monarch finally reached a point from which ice stretched in every direction—miles of it. The whole world had turned into drifting ice.

I went to sleep that night vowing not to be caught off guard by the marauding ice. I wasn't about to have history repeat itself in any kind of similar disaster. We had already had enough travail to last a lifetime.

✧ ✧ ✧

Eighteen

I rousted everyone out at first light the next morning at about 5 a.m. Ben Aniak stoked the fire and made coffee and biscuits. We ate pretty much in silence. The arguments of the night before, Alan's death, and thoughts of what we were facing put a damper on any small talk.

An hour later and we were on our way. Aniak was in the lead, the two women in the middle and Salcido and me bringing up the rear. We took turns pulling the remaining Zodiak.

The day smelled wonderful—a musky odor from the boggy ground mixed with the whole panoply of ocean scents from kelp to sea creatures. The snow flurries of the day before had been replaced by a weak sun. Unless it got a whole lot stronger, it wouldn't be melting the ice cap anytime soon.

I thought about the ice as I walked along. Here in the Arctic, it was as much a part of life as whales and polar bears. It was a factor to be reckoned with, as you would deal with a mercurial co-worker or an irascible relative you didn't much care for. You exist in the Arctic if the ice allows you to do so. If we were lucky and courageous, the ice would let us survive.

I hated to think about bravery and survival because I didn't want to imagine that our plight had worsened to the extent that we might not make it out of here alive. Normally, it is not my nature to be all that brave. I try to deal with things as they come. But, like most people, I do have a strong instinct to survive. I did not sign onto this expedition to have my courage tested or my survival placed in doubt. And I certainly didn't sign on to be the leader of four other people. Whatever the odds against it, however, I would bring us through this.

I wondered if anyone else was as philosophical this morning. Susan and Jane had come to blows the day before and looked grim now, but at least they weren't hurling verbal threats. That was something.

Ben Aniak and Danny Salcido were diamonds in the rough. I could count on them for anything. I would never have to fear that either one would double-cross me in any way. I would trust them with my life. We had forged a bond that would outlast our current ordeal. If we survived.

By 10 a.m., we had gone 5 miles and the terrain was unvarying: mushy tundra, covered in places with snow and ice. During the entire trek, I saw nothing that moved under its own power. I knew the hole in my boot was getting bigger because I could feel my foot getting wet in more places. And with the wet came more freezing and numbness.

Up ahead, I saw Aniak stop and slip his pack off his back. The others did the same. I caught up with Salcido and the two of us maneuvered the Zodiak on the ground so that its engine would not be damaged.

"What's up?" I shouted to Aniak, walking toward him as I spoke.

"We are at the easternmost point on the island," he said. "It's hard to tell but that's the Beaufort Sea out there."

"The solid ice?" I asked. "That can't be right. The ice pack stays well away from 70 degrees north latitude until Halloween at least. It's only early September for God's sake!"

"I know, Tom. I've never seen it get this bad this early, and I've lived here my whole life."

"God, is that fog?" I said, looking up at the sky, its blue gradually disappearing under a shroud of swirling moisture. "That's all we need. So where are we really?"

Aniak unfolded a map as the others crowded around. He kept tapping his compass whose needle was moving around wildly.

"Damn thing! What's going on? It worked up till now."

"Sometimes a magnetic field radiates out from the North Pole and puts compasses out of business," said Jane.

"Miss Science strikes again!" muttered Susan.

"Bitch!" answered Jane with a sweet smile.

"I know we are going in the right direction, Tom," said Ben. "I've lived here too long not to know where I'm at."

"So we bear right and we're headed for Tuk and the Mackenzie River Delta?"

"Exactly!" he said. "No other way is possible."

"So we move slowly, with you testing the ice and then what?" asked Salcido.

"We get to open water soon, jump into the Zodiak and we're gone. We'll be in Tuk by dinner time."

He held a long pole out for my inspection.

"Made this yesterday out of some driftwood I found. It'll do well for what I want."

He turned to the others.

"Stay well back of me, then walk where I walk."

Because of the circumstances of our meeting in the Edmonton Airport, I had dismissed Ben Aniak at first as one more drunken Eskimo. I had really underestimated him. We would have faltered days ago without him, I was very certain of that.

We continued to walk carefully across the ice, following Aniak in a fairly straight line. I kept thinking we'd reach the open water that would allow us to put the boat in the water and speed to safety in Tuktoyaktuk.

The cold was more penetrating than it had been up until now, which seemed odd given the fact that we were heading toward land and not out to sea. My feet were beyond feeling uncomfortable. With each step, I began to worry about the consequences of frozen toes. I hoped the others weren't having similar problems, but I didn't have the strength to ask them. My responsibilities as accidental leader had their limits.

The sky was gray and impenetrable, showing no signs of opening up to the sun that so recently had been there. As we walked, fog continued to waft around us to the extent that I couldn't always see Salcido walking in front of me, let alone Aniak.

The whole situation made me nervous. I felt as if I was walking around with a paper bag over my head with only tiny slits cut out for sight. If we couldn't see, we were vulnerable to all the terrors the Arctic held.

In another 15 minutes, Salcido stopped walking. I put down the towrope for the Zodiak and caught up with him.

"What is it?"

"Don't know. I can't see a damn thing!"

I stepped carefully around Salcido and was soon behind Susan on the narrow trail.

"What is it?" she said, her eyes showing fear for the first time.

"I'll see what I can find out. Wait here."

Jane was next in line and she had dropped her pack to make a place to sit. She plopped down immediately.

"Not a good idea to get your pack wet, Jane," I said, ever the supercilious tour guide.

She glared at me.

"I'm sorry. You've got more experience in the Arctic than I'll ever have. That was the first thing I thought of."

"That's okay, Tom. You're right and I know you're right. I'm just pooped out. I used to do all this derring-do stuff and not feel it. My fifty-year-old bones are telling me to go back to a campus in a warm climate and stay there."

When I got to Aniak he was looking into the murk and listening intently.

"Ben. What the hell are you doing?"

"I'm listening, Tom."

"For what? Boats, bears, people?"

For a time he ignored me, then turned slowly in my direction. "The ice is coming."

Before I could fathom the meaning of his strange remark, I heard a cracking sound so loud that I stepped back. As I blinked in disbelief, a ridge of ice 20 feet tall rose from the sea in front of us and gobbled up Ben. He didn't even scream as his body was completely obscured by an avalanche of ice that moaned and groaned like the monster it had become.

As I blinked in disbelief, Susan's screams broke my paralysis.

"Tom, save me! Oh God, please save me!"

She disappeared in the swirling cauldron that remained after the ice ridge hit the water and stirred it up. I looked in vain for something to grab—an arm, a leg, a parka—but nothing remained. I scrambled back, trying not to fall over the newly formed edge. Salcido stepped forward and took hold of my arm.

"Tom! Hang on!"

And that I did as he easily pulled me away from danger.

"Ice ridge," said Jane. "But I've never seen one form this close to land. They're usually out to sea. They come from the North."

She paused.

"Oh God! This means we've been going in the wrong direction. We've been heading toward the North Pole, toward the Beaufort Sea."

"Ben's compass was off," said Salcido. "I knew it. I just thought he knew what he was doing. I mean, *he* was the Eskimo!"

I heard their conversation but I couldn't seem to form the words to reply in any intelligent way. I dropped to my knees and felt woozy.

"He's going into shock," said Jane. "We've got to get him warm and get some liquids into him. We've got to go back a ways and set up a camp."

"Yeah, yeah," Salcido answered. "We are headed out to sea anyway, in the wrong direction. I saw some boulders a quarter mile back. Maybe we can fix up some shelter in them."

Jane nodded in her no-nonsense way and we turned around.

"Boat," I mumbled. "We still might need it."

"I'll pull it," said Salcido.

"Can you walk, Tom?" asked Jane.

I nodded that I could, but my legs felt like icicles about to break off when I tried to stand on them.

"Use me as a crutch, Tom," said Jane.

"I'll go up ahead and find those rocks," said Salcido.

As we staggered along, my mind raced back and forth to what was happening to us—and happening so fast. We had started out with the best intentions weeks before on a scientific expedition that was well-planned, well-funded, and well-equipped. Through a variety of often bizarre circumstances, most of our party was dead, the promising science long forgotten. We were in a battle for survival that I was not certain we would win.

We reached the boulders quickly. Danny Salcido had been right: they would form an ideal place to rest and recover. The two sides of the rocks faced the north and would shield us from the wind I felt certain would start blowing at any time.

Salcido lashed two tarps to the rocks for cover and placed the upturned Zodiak in position as a third wall. As the three of us sat down in the rear, he found driftwood and lighted a fire near the opening. Before long, I began to feel warm for the first time in several hours. Then, the reality of what had happened washed over me like waves from the sea we were trying to avoid.

"Susan and Ben," I moaned, rocking back and forth and holding myself. "I lost them. Some leader I am. I lost them."

Jane poked around in her duffel bag for a pan and bottled water and was soon dropping tea bags into the boiling result. She threw me some high protein biscuits.

"Eat, whether you're hungry or not," she said with a smile as she poured water into a tin cup and swirled the tea bag around. "You can't do anything about what happened. It wasn't your fault. Now drink this. It's herbal and should soothe your ravaged nerves."

I did what she said and began to feel better as soon as the warm liquid hit my stomach. My head was feeling clearer and I didn't feel feverish anymore.

"I'm going to live," I said after 15 minutes in my stupor.

"That's good to hear," smiled Jane.

"Where's Danny?"

"Gone to get wood."

She wrapped her arms around her body.

"You're getting too cold, Jane. Quit worrying about me. Take one of these blankets."

"No. I'm okay."

At this point, Salcido returned, his arms full of driftwood.

"Whew! I'm sweating even in this cold."

He dropped the wood and looked at me.

"You've returned from the dead, I see."

"Yeah. I'm better and feeling pretty guilty that I'm not helping you."

He shook his head.

"Don't be dumb, man. You need to get your strength back so you can figure out how to get us out of this."

"I don't think I've got enough brainpower left to come up with a miracle. We are definitely going in the wrong direction—that much I know. Ben's trusty compass was not so trusty. The nearness to the North Pole messed it up somehow."

"Yeah, you can say that again," said Salcido. "It didn't work for shit."

"What are we going to do?" asked Jane. "You got any bright ideas, Tom?"

"Only one, but I'm not sure it'll work." I pulled out the Russian cell phone.

"I almost forgot I had this thing. It's the one Kirov gave me. Its batteries were dead but I found some in Ben's stuff. I guess I grabbed his duffel in all the confusion. These might work."

I held up the batteries as if they were gold. In our present dire circumstances, I guess they were the equivalent. "Does 9-1-1 work in the Arctic?" I said, as I snapped the batteries into place and pushed the ON button. "Did Cliff give you phone numbers for the ship?"

"Yeah, he gave them to me," said Salcido. "I was the communications guy, you know. I've got them here." He pulled a 3 x 5 card out of his shirt pocket. "But there's not a phone number in the bunch. Just radio codes."

"The *Polar Sea* is thousands of miles from us," I said. "The captain said they were heading towards the Bering Strait. Our hope is contacting Search and Rescue in Tuk, or the Canadian Coast Guard. I guess we're still in Canadian waters."

"Beats the hell out of me," said Jane, casting a quick glance at Salcido as if to reassure him that she, too, liked to swear once in a while.

"I'm going to try something else that may work faster," I said, as I started dialing a number in Oregon from memory.

"Angela Pride, Oregon State Police," said a familiar voice at the other end of the line as clear as if she was 5 miles away.

"Hello, Angela. It's Tom. How are you doing?"

"Tom. Hello. I thought you were in the Arctic for the summer."

Angela Pride, a lieutenant in the Oregon State Police, had been a longtime friend—and sometime lover—for several years. We had had our ups and downs, mostly over her anger at my constant tendency to play detective and put myself in what she considered unnecessary danger.

We had been in a definite rocky stage since before I left on this trip. We had agreed on a break and decided to reassess things when I got back in the fall.

But that kind of thing was not important now. I had other, more vital concerns on my mind as I filled her in on what had happened and our current predicament.

"Let me get this straight, Tom," she interrupted. "You're in the middle of the Arctic. Ice is all around. You aren't sure where you are. Russians are after you. Polar bears are lurking."

"Yeah. I know it's hard to believe, Angela. That's exactly how I'd sum it up. I guess I've outdone myself this time."

"You must be putting me on, Tom. You're trying out a plot for a novel."

She laughed but said nothing else.

"Angela, are you still there?"

"I'm waiting for the punch line."

"There is no punch line. This is happening to me. I'm telling the truth, believe me."

"You know I care about you, Tom. You know I'd do anything to help you, but this is the most outlandish predicament you've even been in, or tried to suck me into. God, what do you expect me to do for you from here?"

"I expect you to use your canny instincts for working miracles and contact someone up here who can help us. Maybe the Coast Guard will launch a search. Maybe they can put choppers in the air or send an icebreaker. I'm fresh out of Rollodexes right now."

"This is only mid-September, Tom," she said. "You're sure you've got ice that thick already?"

"Oh yeah," I said, looking out the opening of our makeshift shelter at the frozen expanse around us. "We are in a big-time freeze up!"

At this point, the line got very staticky and Angela's voice started breaking up.

"Angela, can you still hear me?"

"Tom . . . you . . . break . . . don't think . . . hopeless . . ."

I looked at the dead cell phone in my hand as if my penetrating gaze could somehow bring it back to life. My efforts at restoring it did not work. Danny and Jane stared at me and the phone in equal dismay.

"I lost her!" I said, throwing the cell phone on the hard ground.

It was then that we heard something that sounded like a freight train hitting a brick wall. First came a loud crash, then a grinding noise. We rushed to the opening of our shelter in time to see the formation of a fissure in the ice several hundred yards in front of us. Soon, we felt movement in the area immediately around us. I realized that our small island of safety had broken apart and, quite literally, set sail in the open ocean, like a tiny twig in a rushing river.

❖ ❖ ❖

Nineteen

When people faced death, I had heard their whole lives passed before their eyes. I had never been sure precisely how that happened. Was it in small snippets like clips in a movie preview? Or did scenes play out at greater length?

As our piece of tundra sped away from the larger landmass, nothing like this happened to me. Instead, the three of us looked at one another with a mixture of both terror and awe.

"Holy shit!" shouted Salcido, as always the person able to cut to the essence of things. He grabbed Jane and held her tightly.

"Hang on," I yelled lamely, for want of anything better to say, although the noise of the grinding ice made it impossible to hear much of anything else.

Our natural raft started drifting northwest, headed for the Beaufort Sea. This was both good and bad for us: good in that we'd be out of solid ice; bad in that we were heading toward a colder region.

Our speed increased because of a wind that picked up and pushed us away from land. Damn Ben's faulty compass. If his readings hadn't been off, we'd be resting comfortably in Tuktoyaktuk, thinking about our flights home.

We passed other floating ice traveling in the same direction. We would head for one of these bobbing cakes of ice, almost smack against it, then suddenly veer off and pass it several yards away. I began to suspect that the powerful current carrying us along was unstoppable.

After several minutes, I stood up with difficulty and staggered to the opening of our makeshift enclosure. Oddly, the fire pit near the door was still intact, its embers smoldering and sparks flying in every direction as gusts of wind touched them.

On we plunged, with the other ice floes dwindling in number and our tiny natural craft taking the lead in this bizarre regatta from Hell. I could smell the open sea as I stood shakily in front of our hut.

"Sit down, Tom," shouted Jane. "We can't lose you too."

I stepped back and sat down near the others. The noise was lessening and we could actually hear one another for the first time since our adventure had begun a half hour before. Our raft slowed.

"For the first time in a long time, I'm speechless," I said to them. "I honestly don't know what to do. I've never felt so helpless in my life."

"What about your friend?" asked Salcido. "That chick you called."

"Yeah. Angela. I know she'll do everything she can and call everyone she can think of to help us, but she's thousands of miles away in Oregon and we're here . . ." I looked around. ". . . wherever *here* is."

"Look there," said Jane, standing up and pointing. "What is that?"

We turned and I got up and staggered again to the opening. At first, I saw nothing but dark choppy water, its surface dotted now and again with pieces of ice. We had almost stopped moving. Then I picked out a small patch of red right in our path.

My first thought was that we had encountered in animal—a seal, a walrus, a bear. But red? It must be something bloodied and dead. If so, it wouldn't do us any good, however, even though we needed food—or would need it soon enough.

All of these unconnected and aimless thoughts filled my head as the red object came closer. I quickly realized that it was not an animal at all but a parka. Ben's parka.

"Is that . . .?" Salcido stopped talking.

Jane screamed and I bent down for a closer look.

Ben Aniak's head bobbed into view, the rest of his body soon visible. He looked peaceful as if he was enjoying a pleasant dip in a swimming pool.

We pulled Ben out of the water fairly easily, by grabbing onto his parka and tugging him up. Salcido and I carried him to a spot near our rock enclosure and laid him out on his back.

"It's too cold for him to smell real bad," said Salcido matter-of-factly. "If we wrap him in a sleeping bag, we can keep him intact for now."

"And out of sight," I said.

Jane was crying as she stood to one side watching us deal with Ben's remains. "He looks like he's sleeping," she said. "No sign of the violent death he suffered. Poor kid. I liked him. He overcame a lot in his short life. Fetal alcohol syndrome. Alcoholism common to his people. He fought to go to college so he could better himself. You know Cliff helped him a lot."

She glanced at me.

"I know you didn't like Cliff, Tom, but he *was* capable of doing good from time to time. He just hid it from the world. He thought it would diminish his authority if he looked like a softy."

"He succeeded at that," I said. "A softy he wasn't."

I decided not to mention that Ben had hinted at something he was holding over Jameson's head. With both of them dead, what that was did not matter.

"That's for damn sure," said Salcido.

I suddenly remembered the computer disk and walked over to Ben's body to get it.

"What are you doing, Tom?" said Jane sharply. "Leave him alone! He's suffered enough!"

I went through the outer pockets of his parka. Empty.

"Tom, stop it!" Jane was getting more agitated. I ignored her and reached inside to find a zipper. Sliding it open I found what I was looking for: a flat object encased in a heavy plastic bag. I yanked it open and held the disk aloft in triumph.

"What the hell is that?" asked Salcido.

"A few days ago, Ben took a disk from Cliff's computer with the ice data on it. Then, he and I exchanged disks and relabeled them. The ice results were on the one marked 'Public Relations Background Material,' which I hid during the search. Ben kept the one marked 'Ice Research Results.' But it really had the PR stuff. That's the one Belinsky found on him but he never took the time to read it, just felt he had gotten what he wanted. Yesterday, I discovered that my inside pocket had a hole in it so I gave Ben the valuable disk for safekeeping. This is it."

"Yippee!" shouted Jane, "the good guys won for a change!"

"I'm not so sure," said Salcido. "Listen."

A loud pinging noise was coming from the cell phone I had thrown on the ground.

"It's probably got a locator device built into it," he said, picking it up. "When you threw it down, you activated something. Kirov's been tracking us."

At this point, we stopped what we were doing and listened to the distinct *thump, thump* sound of a helicopter approaching from the north.

Two huge helicopter gunships appeared first as black dots in the clearing sky. Even before I saw the double eagle emblems on their sides, I knew they were Russian.

The glimpse of that insignia clarified everything for me: why Kirov hadn't defected and joined us, why he would turn against his country and allow us to escape as harmless nobodies he hated to kill. But when he discovered Ben had given Belinsky the wrong disk, he needed to find us. He probably remembered the cell phone and used it to track us.

It was all part of a plan to regain possession of the computer disk containing the ice research results. I guess I had underestimated the value the Russians placed on the data. I had allowed my personal animosity toward Clifford Jameson—and his role in jeopardizing our welfare—to cloud my judgment about the importance of his work. In my mind, if he had anything to do with the research, it couldn't be all that vital. How wrong I had been and how sad a lesson I was about to learn.

Our floating ice island had come to rest against a larger landmass that wasn't moving. That would allow the helicopters to set down with ease and whisk us away. Where would we wind up? Did Russians still hold prisoners in Siberia? Would anyone miss us if they did? As I watched the dots grow into distinctive shapes, I thought of that line from *Dr. Zhivago* about Lara, the love of the doctor's life. She had, said another character, "vanished without a trace . . . forgotten as a nameless number on a list that afterwards got mislaid." Would that happen to Jane, Danny, and me?

Just then a machine gun rattled bullets from above, missing us by a long way, but no doubt fired to keep us in line. The helicopters landed on the landmass adjacent to where we were stuck.

I yelled for Jane and Danny to step behind me. My voice was drowned out by the whine of the engines. With the propellers still turning, the doors on both units opened and men in white uniforms jumped out and ran toward us. They would not, apparently, be spending much time on the ground.

Kirov emerged at the head of these fully armed commandos smiling and waving as if we would still consider him in his nice guy role.

As we advanced toward him, I motioned for Jane and Danny to stay close behind. It was fruitless to run and I wanted us to be together, no matter what.

Kirov easily stepped onto our little island and walked over to us.

"Professor Martindale," he said. "You, no doubt, wondering why I call you together again on this day."

Then he laughed as he always had when he tried out his fractured English on me. The tone of my reply lacked the rage I really felt. Instead I joined him in his laughter.

"You took the words right out of my mouth, major. How very right you are!"

Kirov smiled and seemed to accept my words as praise for a language lesson well done.

"I will be wanting the proper disk now," he said to me. "Never have so many persons of all types sought after such a tiny product of the computer age. I will have the disk at this time."

I pulled the disk from my pocket and held it up for the major to see.

"Can we make a trade," I said. "Our lives for the disk?"

"Tom, don't do it!" shouted Jane.

"Don't be a fuckin' traitor," added Salcido.

I held up my hand.

"Shut up! I'm in charge of this!" I yelled, not believing what I said for a minute.

"I did not suspect you for a foolish man," answered Kirov. "I can order my men to shoot you down like bears on a hunt.

Then, I will happily avail myself of the disk and be on my merriest of ways."

"Yeah, yeah. All right, all right. I guess you've got me. Tell me, major, are you getting back into the good graces of your government by turning over the ice data? Or are you going to sell it?

Kirov said nothing. He was concentrating so hard on me that he was paying no attention to the low hum I was beginning to hear in the distance. I kept talking to distract his attention.

"But you forgot one small problem. I can throw the disk in the water faster than you can shoot me. I will be dead but the disk will be plunging to the bottom of the Beaufort Sea by then. We'll both be out of luck if that happens."

Kirov relaxed a bit and smiled.

"I did not take you for an American patriot, professor," Kirov said. "We can make deal. You go with me and I can guarantee a spot for you as writer in the new Russia. Everything you write will be published. You can teach eager Russian minds. No more of that terrible worry of publishing before you perish that I read about your American universities. We reward our favored writers very deliciously."

He signaled to his men to move in on me from both flanks. He held out his arms as if he wanted to embrace me.

"Stop," I shouted. "Don't come any closer! I'll toss this in a minute."

"I will now be calling your bluff," he said, and he kept walking.

As I threw the disk as hard and as far as I could, I dropped down to the ground, hoping Jane and Danny would do the same. Just then, a deafening splitting sound filled the air, as if a hundred axes were tearing through a plywood wall. The Russians were so startled they didn't fire a round.

Instead, they turned toward the sound and we all saw the gleaming bow of the *Polar Sea* crash through the ice wall to our south.

"THIS IS THE UNITED STATES COAST GUARD!" said the unmistakable voice of Captain Alexander Healy. "YOU WILL LAY DOWN YOUR WEAPONS AND PUT YOUR HANDS ON YOUR HEADS! YOU ARE UNDER ARREST!"

✧ ✧ ✧

Twenty

When I woke up, I wasn't sure where I was or what day. I was in a bed with clean sheets and blankets, a great improvement over my life for the past week. As I took stock of my body, everything seemed intact, except for the toes of my left foot which burned a little.

As I lay there moving my toes, the door opened and bright light from the hall splayed across me and my bed.

"Mr. Martindale?" said someone in a low voice.

"Yes?"

I sat up in bed as the whole ceiling was illuminated by fluorescent light. A man in white stepped over to the bed.

"Craig Corey," he said, shaking my hand.

"Is it morning, commander?"

He looked at his watch.

"Eighteen twenty hours, sir."

He leaned over and listened to my heart through his stethoscope.

"Lean forward, please."

He did the same thing on my back, then looked in my ears with another device.

"Open your mouth, please. Say *aaaah*."

"How am I, doctor?" I laughed.

"In remarkably good shape, considering what you've been through. You do have a touch of frostbite on three of your toes. Not all that serious."

"Where are my friends? I . . . can't . . . seem . . . to remember . . ."

"You blacked out on the ice, I'm told. Collapsed, really. You were a real mess when they brought you in here."

"So everyone is dead but, but me?"

I turned my face away from him and tried to keep from crying, but the thought of Jane and Danny dead so close to rescue overwhelmed me.

"Why did I make it? I let them down. Some leader I turned out to be. Why did . . ."

"If there's anything I hate, it's a blubbering professor," said a voice from the door.

Danny Salcido stepped into the room, hobbling on crutches.

"Danny? God, it's great to see you. Where's Jane? Is she . . ."

"Down here," said a tiny voice. A medic wheeled a smiling Jane into the room.

"Jane, thank God. I thought you guys were . . . Aren't we a trio?" I laughed, drying my eyes.

"Yeah, we can call ourselves the three gimps," said Salcido.

"All three of us combined might make a whole person," said Jane, as she reached up to squeeze my hand.

"I'll leave you three to talk," said Dr. Corey, as he walked out trailed by the Coast Guard medic.

"Where to start?" I asked. "How are you guys?"

I looked at the two of them. "An infected foot they thought they'd have to amputate," said Jane. "But it's healing."

"A broken ankle," said Salcido. "On the mend."

"Good news," I said. "I'm relieved. What about everybody else?"

"Kirov and his men were in the brig last time I heard anything," said Salcido.

"How did we get here?" I asked.

"The icebreaker lived up to its name and came crashing through the last ice barrier to the sea," said Jane. "We had almost made it to the open water and maybe freedom."

"What did the Russians do?" I asked. "I can't remember a thing beyond the sound of breaking ice and seeing the bow."

"Gave up without firing a shot," said Salcido.

"The Coast Guard guys were wonderful," said Jane. "They were over the side and onto the ice so fast, the Russians gave up without a fight of any kind."

"But how did they find us?" I asked.

A loud voice answered my question from the door.

"We got a call from your friend, the policewoman. She told us about hearing from you and we started back this way."

Captain Healy stepped into the room with the regal authority he always conveyed.

"We owe you a great deal, captain," I said. "Thank you very much. I really can't find the words."

"Your gratitude is accepted," he said briskly.

"How long did it take you to find out where we were?" asked Jane.

"As we commenced our eastward course, we picked up the movement of the Russian fleet on our sonar and then heard the pinging of a GPS unit imbedded in the cell phone. We actually saw them launch the helicopters so it was easy to follow them to you."

"But how did they miss you?" I asked. "I mean the *Polar Sea* isn't exactly invisible. You got a stealth shield of some kind?"

I was laughing, but the captain was serious.

"I'm not at liberty to comment any further. We got to you in time, that's the important thing."

"Were they going to take us with them back to Russia?" asked Jane. "To Siberia or some prison somewhere?"

The captain frowned. "We can't be certain. They were flying two of their best helicopters, the Mi-8, Hip-E. They can get in and out of tight places, but don't have a lot of room for passengers. I'm not sure of their range either. The Russians aren't saying and I didn't press them."

"The bodies? I asked. "Did you get everyone?"

"Ben Aniak you know about. Miss Baugh and Mr. Salcido gave us an account of who was dead and where they were. Mr. Aniak was with you. I sent a retrieval team to Herschel Island. We never found the Eskimo woman." He looked down at the floor.

"I'm afraid we were not able to find Miss Foster. I understood that the two of you were close."

"At one time, yes, we were. Not lately. We had grown apart, but I'm sorry for what happened to her, of course."

Thoughts of Susan Foster as I knew her flooded into my head—a Susan Foster I once loved and cared deeply about, a Susan Foster who was once a respected marine biologist. All of that was before she became, quite literally, addicted to a man who ruined her life.

"What about the Russians?" I asked the captain.

"We haven't sorted it all out yet," he said. "Kirov is pleasant enough, but he isn't giving up much either. I think he's a double agent sent to infiltrate Belinsky's operation. And then there is the matter of his Chechen mother."

"Yeah, he told me about that," I said.

"There is no question that his government wants that ice data, either by taking over Belinsky's group or having Kirov get the disk from you by whatever means necessary. This has had one major benefit. We know what the Russians are up to now in terms of trying to gain control of the ice-free passages across the Arctic. Even though they are more friend than enemy these days, we can't let them succeed with a plan like that."

He paused and looked at all three of us.

"We're trying to keep this as quiet as possible. With that country's help in the war on terrorism so important, the United States government has no wish to create any incident that would sabotage future cooperation. The Russians are being returned to their country as we speak. It is too complicated to sort out who shot who and where it happened. And, adding to the dilemma is the fact that Herschel Island is Canadian territory. You were picked up in U.S. territorial waters, however. It's so complicated it has been decided by an authority higher than my own to let it end here. We hope—for the good of the country—that the three of you will be quiet about what you experienced up here."

I said nothing. Thoughts of this great story flashed through my mind, but I didn't say anything. Could I keep from writing about it?

"What about the Arab?" I asked.

"Well, for one thing, we never found a trace of him—only bits of a white robe. We think he came to the Arctic to get out of Chechnya where he was a wanted man. His injuries made him less effective as a commander of rebels. He might also have brought funds to Belinsky. We found half a million dollars hidden in several duffle bags on Herschel Island. It is hard to say how he got this far north, or who helped him get there. I'm not sure we will ever know the whole story."

"What about Paul Bickford?" I asked. "We got to know one another a bit and he was always a big help at various times. I never could figure out his story. He wasn't one of your guys, so why did you defer to him? I mean, with all due respect to you, he seemed to be calling the shots."

Healy didn't react to my jab as I thought he might.

"I am not at liberty to say anything other than he left the ship a few days ago and is on another assignment. He is some kind of international consultant."

"He's a spook, if I ever saw one," said Salcido.

The captain smiled and changed the subject.

"Oh, by the way, we think Belinsky or Zukov killed Nadia Chernoff. Some kind of lover's quarrel. I can't be sure. Then they tried to pin it on you. When you insulted Belinsky's honor that day on the ship, you really made a lasting enemy—someone very keen on revenge. I have some photos I think you may want to destroy."

I blushed as he handed the photos to me. He didn't seem to want an explanation and I didn't really want to give him one. I quickly changed the subject.

"I have to say, captain, that I admire Gregor Kirov a lot. He didn't kill us when he could. He was a gentleman at all times, acting in the best interest of the country he serves."

"He feels the same about you, Martindale. Ensign!"

The young officer guarding the doors stepped aside and Kirov stepped into the tiny room. He was smiling despite a black eye and having his wrists in handcuffs.

"It is my distinct honor to encounter you face-to-face yet again, once more," said the young Russian in his usual fractured English.

"Major Kirov. Good to see you again. I hear you are going home."

"Yes, professor. It appears that our actions may be feared to bring about an incident with international happenstances."

"Your English lessons?" I asked. "Have they been suspended?"

He laughed heartily. "I only need tutor as beneficial to me as you always were. For that, I am filled with much gratefulness."

We shook hands.

"I am only saddened that we did not achieve our mission in totality. You threw a lot of valuable research away when you let fly through the air that computer disk."

"Creating a shortcut through the Arctic ice is a laudable goal."

He smiled. "I cannot reveal the purpose of my mission."

"You are a patriot and I would expect you to do no less," I answered in my best Fourth of July voice.

"At best we can all start over from baseline—from, how do you put it?" Kirov asked.

"From scratch." I said.

"Yes, yes, of course."

He clicked his heels together and saluted me as the ensign led him away. Healy paused a moment, I suppose to make sure Kirov was out of earshot of what he was going to say. Then, he pulled a disk from his pocket and held it up for all of us to see.

"Better for him to report to his government that the research data was lost," said the captain.

"But how? I thought . . ."

I was sputtering.

"Clifford Jameson was very thorough. In the last day you all functioned as a working scientific expedition, he sent me the ice research data as an attachment to an e-mail. It's been safe on this backup disk and on the hard drive of the ship's computer system for several weeks. What you did—to throw the other disk away added years to our lead-time on the ice research. You saved the day without knowing it."

✧ ✧ ✧

That night, I felt well enough to hobble up on deck for a breath of fresh air. It was cold and clear, one of those nights when you realized you had forgotten there were so many stars in the heavens. The ship must have been going at maximum speed because the broken ice careened off its sides like it was being shaved by a bartender mixing drinks. As I stood there I thought of this remarkable region, where beauty and treachery, both natural and man-made, are always so close. I thought of yet another brush with death and vowed to stay out of similar circumstances in the future. I needed to stick to what I knew best: my writing and teaching.

I patted my pocket and touched the small book that had sent me here in the first place. In a series of odd coincidences, so many of Charles Brower's remarkable experiences had now happened to me. He had guided and counseled me with words written over 100 years before.

I had been reading the ending to his book earlier in the day. It now seemed very appropriate to the end of my own Arctic Odyssey:

> *It's the long winter nights that bring the past to life. Nights when the North Pole sends a gale howling around Barrow and I sit working on my specimens, or writing, or carving a bit of ivory. Or perhaps saying to myself, as we used to in the old days, "But just wait 'til next spring!"*
>
> *For on such a night, familiar echoes come easily to the ear of memory; ghostly sounds which, nevertheless, will always typify the Arctic to me. I hear them plainly as I work—the rhythmic beat of the devil-driver's drum, windswept shouts of a triumphant crew, or, mingling with the boom of ice, the dying swis-s-sh of a Bowhead whale.*

❖ ❖ ❖